*As Juliana watched, unseen,
Rafael reached out and touched
the statue's face.*

As gently as if with a lover's caress, he ran the tips of his fingers over the mouth, the delicate throat, then stroked down over the breasts, as if by his touch he could make them warm and soft, flesh and blood.

This was more than a mortal man touching inanimate clay; this was a man giving life and love to a woman. It was all Juliana could do not to cry out, for somehow it was as though Rafael were caressing *her* breasts.

As though drawn by an invisible force, she moved closer, until she could see the figure clearly....

The breath stopped in her throat. She couldn't breathe or move, she could only stand there, staring at *her* face, *her* body. This was a statue of *her*....

Dear Reader,

Another month of eerily romantic reading has arrived, and you won't want to miss either of our spooky selections.

Reader favorite Barbara Faith is back with *Dark, Dark My Lover's Eyes*, a cautionary tale about marriage to a man with a mysterious past. In this case there's a first wife who died amid strange circumstances and who just might be jealous of the woman she thinks has taken her place.

Sandra Dark is a new author to the line, but you'll be eagerly awaiting more books from her after you read *Sleeping Tigers*, a story about a woman whose newest assignment lands her right in the den of a man who's as dangerous as any jungle beast.

You'll also want to keep an eye out for *Lovers Dark and Dangerous*, the third of our annual Shadows short story collections. This year's volume brings together stories by Lindsay McKenna, Rachel Lee and Lee Karr, and I promise you this—every one will haunt you.

So enjoy your time in the shadows—Silhouette Shadows.

Yours,

Leslie Wainger
Senior Editor and Editorial Coordinator

Please address questions and book requests to:
Silhouette Reader Service
U.S.: 3010 Walden Ave., P.O. Box 1325, Buffalo, NY 14269
Canadian: P.O. Box 609, Fort Erie, Ont. L2A 5X3

Barbara Faith

Dark, Dark
My Lover's Eyes

V SILHOUETTE® *Shadows*™

Published by Silhouette Books
America's Publisher of Contemporary Romance

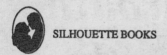 SILHOUETTE BOOKS

ISBN 0-373-27043-7

DARK, DARK MY LOVER'S EYES

Printed in U.S.A.

BARBARA FAITH

is a true romantic who believes that love is a rare and precious gift. She has an endless fascination with the attraction a man and a woman from different cultures and backgrounds have for each other. She considers herself a good example of such an attraction, because she has been happily married for over twenty years to an ex-matador she met when she lived in Mexico.

Now is the witching time of night
When churchyards yawn and hell itself breathes out....
—William Shakespeare
Hamlet

CHAPTER ONE

Because she missed the first-class bus leaving Guadalajara, Juliana Fleming had to take a second-class one. It stopped at every small Mexican village, and the journey to Patzcuaro, in the state of Michoacán, had turned into a scenic but too-warm nine-hour trip. By the time she arrived at the small downtown bus station her summer suit was wrinkled and her hair looked as though it had been through the fluff-dry cycle.

Taking this summer job had seemed like the right thing to do when Professor Melendez, the head of the language school in Guadalajara, offered it to her, but the bus ride had dampened Julie's spirits. She wasn't sure that committing herself to three months here had been such a good idea.

"The pay is exceptional," the professor had said when he'd told her about the job. "But of course Rafael Vega is a very rich man. He plans to send his seven-year-old son to school in the United States in the fall and he wants the boy to be proficient in English. I'm offering the job to you because you're one of my best teachers. You'll live at the family home on Janitzio."

"Janitzio?" she'd asked.

"A small island in the middle of Lake Patzcuaro. Actually I should think it would be an interesting way to spend the summer. You've heard of Vega, haven't you?"

"No," Julie said, shaking her head.

"He's a well-known sculptor, famous in Mexico as well as most of Latin America. Two years ago he had a show in New York, the year before that in Paris and Madrid. Unfortunately the art world has heard little of him since his wife's death a year ago. He became something of a recluse after she died and I've heard that he rarely leaves the island."

The professor took out a thin Havana cigar and lit it. When it began to glow, he went on. "Margarita Villareal was an actress when she and Vega met. I saw two of her movies. They weren't very good and neither was she, but she was so beautiful no one really cared. Everyone said Vega worshiped her and that he was devastated when she died. There've been rumors..." He hesitated, as though reluctant to go on.

"Rumors?" Julie prodded.

"That he hasn't been the same since her death. Art critics say he's lost his talent. He gets into brawls. The one with Felipe Gonzáles, the same Gonzáles who was his agent at the time, made all the Mexico City newspapers."

"Sounds like a real charmer."

"*Perdón?*"

"He doesn't sound like a very nice man."

Melendez waved his cigar. "But he's an artist, my dear. Or at least he was. All artists are entitled to be a little crazy."

How crazy was a little crazy? Julie wondered as she gathered her luggage and looked for a taxi. Maybe this hadn't been such a good idea, maybe she should have gone back to Florida for the summer. But it was too late to turn back; she'd signed a three-month contract so she'd have stick it out. Unless, of course, Rafael

Vega turned out to be as crazy as Melendez had suggested.

The taxi took her to the pier and as soon as she stepped out onto the boardwalk her spirits lifted. The waterfront teemed with vendors selling small souvenir fishnets and straw hats, postcards, clay ashtrays and flowerpots, glass lamps, snakeskin belts and wallets and leather jackets. From the *fondas,* the small restaurants that lined the pier, came the smell of fried fish, dried shrimp, frijoles and beer, and the jumbled cacophony of a dozen radios all tuned to different music stations.

A boy hurried toward her. "Take your bags?" he asked. When Julie nodded, he said, "You need a ticket, yes? I take you. *Ven conmigo.*"

She followed him through the press of people to the ticket office. After she purchased her ticket they went down a few steps to one of the already half-filled launches. The boy helped her aboard and she gave him ten pesos.

The boat was perhaps thirty feet long. A long bench lined each side and another narrow bench ran down the middle. It held, Julie estimated, between sixty and seventy passengers. She was the only North American.

There were a lot of young people aboard. Girls in T-shirts and tight jeans, middle-aged ladies in summer dresses and straw hats, *novios*—couples in love—who held hands and smiled at each other, husbands and wives and small children.

Four musicians came aboard just as the launch was about to cast off. As soon as it did they began to play two guitars, a violin and a battered horn.

The sky was a deep cerulean blue. Clouds drifted low over the mountains. White herons perched on shallow sandbars, and the lake was calm and clear.

The musicians played old rancher songs and a little girl sitting on her mother's lap began to clap her hands in time to the music.

Julie leaned out the open side of the boat, glad now that she had come. She loved being near the water. This would be a new experience for her. She'd be making good money, three times what she made teaching in Guadalajara, and the money would go into her six-months-in-Spain fund.

She looked around at the passengers sitting near her, and when a small boy scooted off his seat and tottered against her legs to get by, she said, *"Cuidado, niño,"* and steadied him.

"Ah, you speak Spanish?" The child's mother smiled. She came from Morelia, she said. She and her husband and son had come to Patzcuaro to spend the day. Where was Julie from?

"I live in Guadalajara now," Julie told her. "But I'm from Florida."

The little boy squirmed up onto the seat between his mother and Julie, and Julie squeezed over to make more room for him. She turned to look out at the water and when she did felt the first splat of rain against her hand. Clouds that only a few moments before had been full and white had turned an ominous gray. Thunder cracked and lightning split the darkening sky in a streak of jagged orange. Suddenly the rain came down hard and a wind as fierce as a small-size tornado swept in on the passengers.

Men and women scrambled to let down the canvas sides. The little girl who had been clapping her hands began to cry. The boat pitched and a fat woman farther down in the center slid off the narrow bench. Another woman cried, "*Dios mío,* this is terrible! We have to turn back."

"No, no," the man next to her said. "It is too late. We're halfway there now. We have to go on."

Julie braced her feet. Part of the canvas near her broke loose, and when she turned to fasten it she saw the fishermen in their dugouts struggling to pull in their nets. Swiveling around on her knees, she managed to fasten the canvas, but by the time it was in place she was drenched and shivering with cold.

The musicians stopped trying to play. In the near darkness of the boat, passengers looked at one another. Husbands and wives held hands and mothers clasped their children tighter. Twenty minutes went by. Thirty. At last a man near Julie lifted a corner of canvas and said, "We're almost there. I can see the island."

Julie lifted her own edge of canvas and looked out through the rain and past the roiling waves. In the distance she could see Janitzio like a huge dark rock in the middle of the lake. A few lights glimmered on the hillside, but as she watched they went out and the island seemed shrouded in a frightening darkness.

Okay, she told herself. Boats like this one have been making this trip day after day for years. So it's raining and a little rough. And overcrowded. If anything happens... The boat lurched. A woman screamed. Julie slid out of her seat and down to her knees. A man on the bench in front of her grasped her arm and pulled her back up.

"*Gracias,*" she managed to say. "*Muchas gracias.*"

Another fifteen minutes crept by. The boat pitched and rolled. Rain slashed under the canvas and waves crashed against the sides. Children clung to their parents. The woman across from Julie fingered her rosary. Finally someone called out, "We're here!" and with a sickening jolt the boat smacked into the dock.

Passengers, eager to get off, jostled against one another as they made their way to the front. Julie picked up her suitcase and travel bag, staggering with the roll of the boat, as anxious to get off as everybody else.

"Let me help you," a young man said. He took the suitcase, and when she went to step onto the dock, a man there reached down and took her arm.

The rain pelted down and the wind almost knocked her off her feet. She took the suitcase from the young man, murmuring her thanks, and started down the pier.

Professor Melendez had written Señor Vega that she'd be arriving today. Would he be waiting for her? Maybe, even though she'd taken a later bus, he'd be at the dock.

But when Julie got to the end of the dock there was no one there who looked as though they might be waiting for someone. She splashed her way through the puddles and the rain to an open-air restaurant. As she approached the lights came back on. She put her suitcase down and said to the woman behind the counter, "Is there a taxi? I need to go to the house of Señor Rafael Vega."

"There are no taxis on Janitzio," the woman answered. "No cars, señorita. It is a small island. Here everyone walks."

Julie looked out at the steady downpour and wondered what in the world she was going to do now.

"Is there no one to meet you?" the woman asked.

Julie shook her head. "Do you know where Señor Vega lives?"

"Everyone knows, *señorita*." The woman came from behind the counter to the edge of the awning and pointed upward. "There," she said. "Up there. Almost to the top of the hill."

Julie peered through the pouring rain, then down at her high-heeled pumps, and wondered how in the world she was supposed to get all the way up there with two pieces of luggage. With a resigned sigh, she asked, "Which path do I take?"

"The one down at the end, past the other restaurants, to the right. But you cannot carry your bags up the hill. No, no, my son will help you." Before Julie could object, she called out, "Ignacio! *Ven.* There is a lady here who needs help."

He came in from the back, a skinny young man of sixteen or seventeen. He looked sullen, angry at having been disturbed.

"The lady must go to the house of Señor Vega. You will show her the way and help her with her bags."

"Up the hill? But it's raining."

"I'll pay you." Julie summoned a smile. "Twenty-five pesos."

"Twenty-five?" He nodded, then with a shrug said in English, "Hokay. For twenty-five I take you."

Julie thanked the woman. The young man took her bags and she followed him out into the rain. He walked ahead, not waiting for her, head down, splashing his way through the puddles to the end of the row of restaurants and curio shops. There he turned right and started up slanting concrete steps. Julie followed a few paces behind. The steps ended at another level of small *fondas* and closed stalls. He turned and started up a second flight of steps that were no more than a foot and a half wide.

The wind had lessened but the rain still came down in blinding sheets. Julie was drenched and cold and her wet feet squished in her muddy shoes. It was difficult to see. Once she stopped to catch her breath, and when she did she looked up through the rain and saw the flicker of lights through the approaching darkness.

The young man looked back. *"Ven,"* he shouted. "Come!" And without waiting for her, he left the narrow steps and started up a path—what had been a path but was now a river of mud. Her shoes sank into the oozing wetness. She took a swipe at her hair and with a muttered curse followed the boy up to the top of the hill.

"Ya estamos aquí," he said at last. "We are here."

The lightning cracked and in the brief light she saw the high stone wall with the shards of broken glass all along the top, the black iron gate and, beyond it, the house, almost hidden by thick-trunked trees whose heavy branches bent with the force of the rain.

The young man opened the gate, put her bags down on the wet ground, and held out his hand.

Julie glared at him. "No," she said firmly. "Take me all the way to the house."

He muttered an expression in Spanish she'd never heard before, but she held her ground. *"A la casa,"* she repeated.

He looked through the trees and an expression somewhere between bluff and fear crossed his face. With a muttered curse he picked up her luggage and started down the path that led to the house.

They splashed their way across a patio toward a sliding French door and when they reached it he threw her bags down and holding out his hand again, demanded, "Money."

Julie reached in her purse, took out the twenty-five pesos and handed it to him. He snatched it up and without a *gracias*, turned and ran back toward the gate, leaving her alone, puzzled by his apparent fear of the Vega house. She picked up her bags, and that's when she saw the little boy standing just inside the door.

He stood looking up at her with big dark eyes. He was small and slight, with dark hair that curled in a silky fringe over his forehead. Before Julie could say anything, he said, "What do you want?"

"I'd like to come in out of the rain."

"Who are you?"

"My name is Juliana. Is this the house of Señor Vega?"

"*Quizás,* perhaps."

"I've come a long way. I'm tired and I'm wet and I'm not in a very good mood. Either open the door or call somebody who will."

The boy stepped back a pace. "You're the schoolteacher, aren't you? Why did you come? School's out. I don't need a teacher—"

"Get away from the door, Enrique." A woman peered out at Julie. "You are the *profesora?*" she asked.

"Yes."

The woman slid open the door. "Don't stand there," she snapped. "Come in."

She was as tall and as spare as a whooping crane. Her hair, skinned back tight off her face, was black except for an inch-wide patch of white along her nar-

row brow. She wore a black dress that came to mid-
calf, black stockings and sensible shoes. Julia guessed
her to be in her early fifties. With her hand clasped on
the little boy's shoulder, she looked Julie up and down.
"You're dripping all over the floor," she said.

Julie stared at the growing puddle at her feet and the
mud-caked shoes that would never be the same again.
She'd had one hell of a day. Nine hours on a too-hot
bus, a dangerous crossing in a storm-tossed boat and a
climb up a muddy hill. She was cold and she was wet,
and too upset to apologize because she was getting the
floor wet.

"My name is Juliana Fleming," she said. "I've come
from the American Language School in Guadalajara.
Is Señor Vega here? If he is I'd like to speak to him."

"Señorita Fleming?" A man spoke from the dark
shadows of the room. "You were expected earlier. I
sent someone to meet the bus from Guadalajara, but
you weren't on it. Why not?"

"I had to take a second-class bus. It took longer."

There was very little light in the room, but she had
an impression of someone very tall and very dark.

He stepped out of the shadows. She'd been right
about his height and his darkness. It was not so much
that *he* was dark, rather that he gave the overall impression of darkness, dressed as he was in black jeans
that hugged his narrow waist and hips and a black tur-
tleneck sweater. His short-cropped hair was black and
so were his eyes. He had at least a three-day growth of
black whiskers and he was barefoot.

He didn't smile, he didn't offer his hand.

"I'm Vega." He gestured toward the boy. "This is
Enrique. We call him Kico. And Alicia Fernández, my
housekeeper."

He paused to look Julie up and down. "We eat at seven," he said. "Alicia will show you to your room."

With that he turned away and faded back into the shadows. "Follow me," Alicia Fernández said.

There were no flowering plants in the outside corridors of the hacienda as there were in other Mexican homes Julie had seen. And when they turned into an inside corridor there was nothing to soften the monastic somberness of the gloomy halls. The low, arched ceiling seemed tomblike, dank and damp. Candles flickered from wall sconces, reflecting ghostly light on the paintings of long-faced, sad-eyed saints who looked as though they were in the last throes of unbearable agony.

The Fernández woman stopped at the end of the corridor and opened a door. "This will be your room," she said. "The boy's room is two doors down." She looked down at Juliana's sodden shoes. "I suggest you take those off before you go in." With that she turned and went back down the corridor.

The room was as large as Julie's whole apartment in Guadalajara, but she would have traded the bright cheerfulness of her tiny bedroom for the somber coldness of this room. The high wood-beamed ceiling, the marble-tiled floor, partially covered by a brown-and-gray Mexican Indian carpet, and the dark, heavy furniture gave her the shivers.

A massive bed stood at one end of the room, with nightstands on either side. There was a double dresser against one wall and two large chairs on either side of the fireplace.

A chill that had nothing to do with the temperature permeated the room. Wet shoes in hand, Julie crossed to the fireplace. Logs had been laid but no fire had been lit. She found a book of matches on the mantel, struck one and knelt down to light the fire. Five matches later the fire caught.

She put her suitcase on the luggage rack in the closet and crossed to the bathroom. It, too, was large, with both a tub and a shower. She turned on the hot-water faucet of the big claw-footed bathtub, then went back into the bedroom and, opening her travel case, took out a bottle of bubble bath and shampoo. By the time she stripped out of her wet clothes, the water, hot and scented, was ready. She got in and sank in it up to her chin.

Lord, how she needed this. Leaning against the back of the tub, she closed her eyes and wondered how she'd survive the next three months. The boy Enrique was unpleasant and the housekeeper was a witch. As for Señor Rafael Vega . . . Julie shook her head. Melendez had said he was an artist, a sculptor turned recluse and brawler. He'd even suggested that all artists were a little mad.

Was Vega?

With a sigh she ducked her head under the water. Just as she lifted it out the lights went off. She paused, shampoo in hand, wet hair dripping.

"Damn!" she cried.

And wondered what in the hell she was doing in this godforsaken place.

CHAPTER TWO

He'd made a mistake. He should have specified that he wanted a *profesor,* not a *profesora.* This young bedraggled *gringa* most certainly was not his idea of what a teacher should look like.

With a muttered curse, Rafael went into his studio and slammed the door behind him. In the dim light of the fading afternoon he saw the half-finished bust of Cervantes. The vacant eyes seemed to be looking directly at him accusingly.

He slammed a fist into his hand, cursing both the bust and himself for having accepted the commission almost a year ago. He wasn't satisfied with what he'd done, nor did he have any desire to finish it.

Another half-finished bust of the boy stood on a work pedestal. He went to it, stood in front of it, hands on his hips, frowned and turned away. He did not even glance toward the work in the far corner of the room, which was covered by a cloth and hidden from his view.

He looked out of the window at the slanting rain and thought about the young *profesora.* He didn't want her here. Not her or any other woman. Tonight at dinner he'd tell her she wouldn't do. He'd explain that perhaps Professor Melendez hadn't understood he wanted a male teacher. He'd give her a month's pay and send her packing. That would be the end of her.

* * *

The dining hall, because surely no one could call this massive Spanish medieval room a dining *room*, was as depressing as the other rooms she'd seen in the hacienda so far.

From the high-beamed ceiling hung a huge copper chandelier, whose light cast an unpleasant dull glow over a table that looked large enough to seat thirty. A fireplace filled with big burning logs did little to relieve the chill of the room. Neither did the heavy drapes that covered the windows.

Vega, attired in a black shirt, tie and trousers, sat at the head of the table. The boy, Kico, at his right, looked very small in a too-big chair.

Vega rose when Julie entered and motioned for her to take the chair to his left. "You're late, *señorita,*" he said in Spanish. "Dinner is at seven, not 7:10."

"I'm sorry." Julie pulled out the heavy chair. "I'm afraid I got lost."

"You got lost?" Kico's dark eyes widened. "How could somebody get lost in a house?"

"It's not easy." Julie smiled. "I guess I took a couple of wrong turns. Up one corridor and down the next. I was about to light a campfire in the outside corridor and send up a smoke signal."

"A smoke signal? Like the Indians used to do just before they attacked a wagon train?" He grinned a little-boy grin. "I know all about them from television." He put his elbow on the table and leaned toward her. "When I go to Texas, will I see some Indians?"

Julie pretended to think about it. "Probably not," she said. "Cowboys and Indians are farther west, in states like Montana and New Mexico, Idaho and

Wyoming. But we can read about them tomorrow if you'd like to."

"Have you ever seen an Indian?"

"Take your elbows off the table," Rafael said before Julie could answer. "And sit up straight." He frowned, first at the boy, then at Julie. "We're not in the habit of talking at mealtime," he said.

"Oh?" One delicate eyebrow rose, then, as though she hadn't understood, Julie said to Kico, "I have three brothers and two sisters, so every meal at our house was noisy. Every one of us had something to say, about school or the books we'd read and about everything that had happened that day."

She looked up as a serving maid entered with a tureen of soup, said *"Buenas noches"* to the girl and kept on talking, telling Kico about her brothers and sisters, about the two dogs she'd had. "Funny fluffy-looking dogs," she said. "I called them Ike and Mike because they looked alike."

Por Dios, she was a talker! She hadn't paid any attention at all to his telling her they weren't in the habit of talking at dinner.

At least she looked better tonight than she had earlier when she'd stood dripping like a bedraggled cat in his doorway. Her pale blond hair curled about her face in a tousled flyaway style. Though he preferred women's hair in a more classic style, hers wasn't altogether unattractive. Her cheeks were flushed, from good health rather than makeup, he thought. Her eyes were green. She had a wide smile and good teeth.

She was a small woman, no more than five foot three or four, good bone structure, slim white neck, a small waist. But she was wearing pants and he didn't like that. Margarita had always dressed for dinner.

"Are there Indians where you come from?" Kico asked, cutting in on Rafael's thoughts.

"Seminole Indians," Julie answered. She helped herself to a roll and after she buttered it said, "I'm from Florida and the Seminole Indians there live mostly in or near the Everglades. My mother and dad and my younger sister live in Key Largo. That's where I was raised. In a big white house right on the water."

She passed the bread and with a smile said, "I bet you love the water, too."

The little boy's face went still. He looked down at his soup and shook his head.

The soup dishes were taken away. A different maid served an artichoke and hearts-of-palm salad, broiled whitefish and baked potatoes. The little boy stared at his plate and barely touched his food.

She'd said something wrong. But what? Kico looked unhappy and Vega looked as though he'd like to smite her with the back of his hand.

He had an interesting face, as somber, as aesthetically cruel as the tortured faces of the martyred saints whose portraits hung on the corridor walls. His forehead was wide, his cheekbones high and sharp. Dark eyebrows accented his dark eyes, which at first glance seemed almost without expression. Only when she looked deeper did she see the bitterness there, the pain and the unforgiving hardness.

But if his eyes were hard, his hands were not. They were an artist's hands, a sculptor's hands. The fingers were long, broad and smooth and beautifully tapered. The nails were clean and clipped.

"Have you finished, *señorita?*" The maid waited beside Julie's plate.

Julie took a deep breath. It was an effort to look away from his hands, to smile at the woman standing over her and say, "Yes, thank you."

"Would you care for coffee?"

"Please."

"Is there a *postre*, a dessert?" Kico asked.

"Bread pudding," the maid said.

"I hate bread pudding! Why can't we ever have cake?"

"Señorita Alicia knows what's good for you." Rafael turned to Julie. "Alicia supervises the kitchen and selects the menus," he explained. "She's also in charge of running the household and looking after Kico."

"Now that I'm here, perhaps I could relieve her of that," Julie said. "Since Kico and I will be spending so much time together, I mean. I thought we'd have a few hours of lessons in the morning, then lunch and playtime, and perhaps another hour of lessons in the afternoon."

"I prefer that the lessons continue on through the day." Rafael folded the white linen napkin and placed it alongside his coffee cup, forgetting for a moment that, after all, this young *gringa* would not be teaching the boy. "I want Kico to be fluent in English by the time he goes away to school. He won't be if the lessons and study sessions aren't intense."

"But surely..." Julie did her best to keep her voice friendly and reasonable. "Kico is only seven, Señor Vega. I'm sure he's a bright little boy, but it's hard for a youngster his age to concentrate on one subject over a long period of time. If he's with me and we're doing things together and I speak to him in English, he'll learn just as much as he will in a classroom."

Vega frowned, and without commenting turned to the boy and said, "If you don't want your dessert you may be excused." With that he picked up the small silver bell next to his plate and rang it. "Say good-night to Señorita Fleming."

Head down, Kico slid out of the chair. *"Buenas noches, señorita,"* he whispered.

"Buenas noches, Kico."

Alicia Fernández opened the kitchen door. "You rang, *señor?"* she asked.

"Yes, Alicia. Kico wants to be excused. Take him to his room, please."

"Very well." She nodded sharply to the boy. "Come along," she said. "Be quick about it."

He swallowed hard and his Adam's apple bobbed. For a moment he hung back, but when Alicia put a hand on his shoulder and gave him a little shove, he did as he was told.

That was it? No good-night kiss from his father? No hug? Julie shoved her chair back from the table and stood. "Good night, *muchacho,"* she said. "Sweet dreams. I'll see you in the morning. Maybe you can show me around outside if it isn't raining. Okay?"

A small smile trembled on his lips. *"Sí,"* he said. "Yes, I would like that."

"Good." She blew him a kiss. *"Hasta mañana."*

"Hasta mañana, Señorita Fleming."

When she sat back down she said, "He's a nice little boy."

"At least he's well behaved."

She stared at Vega, surprised by the harshness in his voice. Before she could comment, he said, "Kico isn't a baby, Miss Fleming. He's a boy and he is to be treated like a boy, not coddled and petted like a little girl."

"But he's only seven years old."

Rafael shook his head. "I'm afraid you don't understand boys. I'm not sure women do." He tapped his long fingers against the white tablecloth and decided now was the time to tell her that she simply wouldn't do. "I'd really expected Professor Melendez to send a male teacher," he said. "I don't mean this as a reflection on your teaching skills, but I doubt you've had sufficient experience to tutor a boy like Kico. Since his mother's death a year ago he's been difficult to deal with. Because of my work I'm not able to spend a lot of time with him. My housekeeper takes care of him."

"I've seen how she does that," Julie said.

He frowned and shot her a look that had had grown men quaking in their boots. But Julie wasn't quaking. She thrust her shoulders back in a defiant gesture. Her breasts pressed against the silken fabric of her blouse. He caught a glimpse of two small hardened nipples, felt heat rise and couldn't look away.

"I've been teaching since I was twenty-two, for the last two years at the American school in Guadalajara," she said. "I've taught first-, second- and third-grade students and I've tutored children with special needs. However, if you feel that you'd prefer someone else—" the green eyes sent him a scathing look "—a *man*, then of course I won't force you to stand by your commitment."

Julie pushed her chair back from the table and stood facing him, small, defiant, angry.

He stood, towering over her. "Sit down," he ordered.

She looked at him, startled, but did what he said.

From the advantage of his height he stared down at her. "We'll try it for a couple of weeks," he said. "If it doesn't work out I'll get in touch with Melendez."

He picked up the napkin, slapped it against the table, frowned again and said, "You will teach from nine until twelve and break for lunch, after which you'll return to the schoolroom until three in the afternoon. The classroom is in the east wing, my studio is in the west wing. I'm never to be disturbed. That is an absolute, a definite order that is not to be broken. If there's something you need, Alicia Fernández will attend to it. But you must never, under any circumstances, interrupt me or my work."

"I won't."

He headed for the door.

"Will I see you at breakfast?" she asked. "In case I have any questions."

"Probably not. I keep erratic hours. Good night, Miss Fleming."

"Good night, Señor Vega."

She watched him stride across the room, a tall dark figure of a man, broad of shoulder, slim of waist and hip. Impossibly long legs. So incredibly male he scared the hell out of her.

Let him get somebody else if he wanted to. A man. She didn't have to take his rudeness. She'd go back to Florida. Spend the summer sitting on her parents' porch counting mosquitoes.

Her chin firmed. No, dammit, she wouldn't leave. She'd do whatever she had to and she'd stay, not because of Rafael Vega but because of his son. The little boy needed her and neither Vega nor his witch of a housekeeper was going to scare her away. She was here until the end of summer.

* * *

Though the rain had stopped during the night there was a mist in the air and the clouds hung so low over the island that Julie couldn't even see the lake.

"Maybe the weather will clear later," she told Kico when she saw him at breakfast. "As soon as you're finished we'll start our lessons."

They went into the schoolroom together. There was a small desk for Kico, a large teacher's desk for her and a worktable, where she decided she would sit so she could be closer to her pupil. This wasn't an ordinary classroom, there was only this one little boy. They would do better in a one-on-one relationship, if she could get him to relax and realize that learning could be fun.

Though he knew a few words in English, he was reluctant to use them and she didn't press him. There would be time enough for lessons once he'd gotten to know her a little better.

She knew from his conversation in Spanish that he was a bright little boy with a rather amazing vocabulary for one so young. When he asked her about Florida and the Seminoles, she told him about the alligators and the kind of snakes there were and suggested they look Florida up in his encyclopedia.

He responded with eagerness and excitement, pointing to the pictures and asking questions. But when, after half an hour, she opened her English book and suggested he open his, the small chin firmed and his frown was almost as ferocious as his father's had been the night before.

She'd thought about Rafael Vega last night after she left the dining room. During the two years she had lived in Mexico she had dated several Mexican men.

They had been gallant, considerate, usually charming and above all courteous. Rafael Vega, from what little she'd seen of him, wasn't any of those things.

There was an aura of darkness about him. It was as though he were closed into his own private world, bedeviled by a weariness of soul that left no room for softness, not even toward his own son.

She was appalled at the idea that he was going to send Kico to a country where he knew no one, where he would live in a boarding school among other little boys whose families were too busy with their own interests to make time for their children.

She had been hired to teach English to Kico, and she would. But first she had to gain his confidence, to give him time to know and trust her. She decided to begin with a game of finding how many English words were almost the same as Spanish words. Nation, *nación,* vacation, *vacación,* education, *educación.*

"See how easy it is," she told him with a smile. "By the time you get to the United States you'll be speaking English like everyone else."

"I don't want to go to the United States," he said in Spanish. "I don't want to speak English."

"But your father wants you to learn. Don't you want to please him?"

He bowed his head and, in a voice so low she could barely hear, said, "He doesn't like me."

"Doesn't like you?" Julie put a finger under his chin to raise his face. "He's your father, Kico. He loves you."

But did he? Last night at dinner Rafael Vega had displayed little or no interest in his son, other than to tell him to take his elbows off the table and sit up straight. Obviously he was still suffering from the loss of his wife and trying to lose himself in his work. And perhaps, as Professor Melendez had said, Vega was upset and angry because things were going badly in his artistic career. That would be frustrating for an artist, but still, why would he take it out on his son?

She tried to talk to Kico that morning, but when she realized the boy had closed in upon himself, Julie said, "Why don't you draw me a picture?"

"A picture?"

Julie nodded. "I don't really know anything about Janitzio. It was raining when I arrived yesterday so I hardly saw anything of the island. You could draw me a picture of it or of the lake. Or anything else you'd like to draw. Okay?"

"Okay."

She smiled and said, "See, you're already speaking English."

But he didn't smile back.

She gave him several pieces of heavy white paper and a box of crayons, and when he bent to his work she went to stand by the window.

Through the mist the trees and lawn looked fresh and green. But except for a spray of scarlet bougainvillea over a distant wall, there were no flowers. Nor was there a view of the lake from here.

The schoolroom, though efficient, was spartan. The bookcase displayed a set of encyclopedias and history books. But there was no fiction, no stories that would hold a small boy's interest or encourage him to read.

There were no pictures on the walls, only a large round clock over her desk that ticked the time.

As soon as she could, she decided, she'd go down to the village or to Patzcuaro and find something cheerful to hang up. Perhaps Kico could go with her and together they could choose some things to brighten the appearance of the room.

His head was bent over one of the papers she had given him. He chewed his lower lip and his brow wrinkled in concentration. He was a handsome boy, a needy boy. And she was glad now that she had come.

"All done," he said.

"Let me see." Julie pulled a chair up beside him and he handed her the drawing.

She had given him crayons in a rainbow of colors, but he had used only the black, the brown and the gray. Though he showed a surprising talent, what struck her was the terrible somberness of his drawing.

Heavy black clouds hung over the lake, which was dark and dangerous, much as it had been yesterday when she had crossed. There was an empty boat out on the water, caught on the roiling crest of a wave as though it were about to be swamped. On the shore there was another boat and beside it stood a boy. A boy with no hands.

Julie stared at the drawing. "Well," she said. "Well, this is very good, Kico. But my goodness, what a terrible storm." She gave a mock shiver. "It's like the one I was in yesterday when I crossed on the boat. Really scary."

He nodded but he didn't say anything.

She pulled her chair closer and put her arm around him. He stiffened, but he didn't pull away. "Who's the little boy?" she asked. "Is that you?"

"*Sí.*" He leaned against her.

"And you're watching the storm?"

"Uh-huh."

She pretended to study the drawing more closely. "I think you forgot to draw the hands."

He pulled away from her. "I'm hungry," he said. "When can we have lunch?"

She looked at the clock on the wall. It was a little before twelve. "Pretty soon. Why don't you go wash up and I'll meet you in the dining room in a few minutes." She ruffled his hair. "Okay?"

" 'Kay."

She waited until he was out of the room, then took the drawing and carried it to the window. It was, as she had first thought, remarkably good for a seven-year-old. But it was also disturbing. Why was the boat on the lake empty? Why did the little boy have no hands?

A worried frown crossed Julie's face. She took an envelope out of the desk drawer and slid the drawing in. Rafael Vega had said he didn't want to be disturbed, but this was important. She had to see him alone, and if that meant going to his studio and disturbing him, then she would, whether he liked it or not.

The little boy had a problem; she had to do something about it.

CHAPTER THREE

She stood in the doorway of the dining room wearing a summery dress in a shade of green that matched her eyes. She was only five minutes late this time, and as they had been last night, he and Kico were already seated. She came toward the table. He watched her under lowered eyes. And noted that her legs were as well formed as a prize mare he'd once owned.

The thought crossed his mind that he might like to do a sculpture of her, not just a bust, but a full figure. A nude, with her head high and her shoulders back, the same stance she had taken last night when she faced him. He brushed the thought away as nonsense. He still had the unfinished bust of Cervantes he'd been commissioned to do, as well as the one of the boy that he'd started. He had neither the time nor the inclination to ask her to pose for him.

"Don't just stand there," he said more harshly than he had intended. "Sit down."

He stood and went around the table to hold her chair. She had a brown manila envelope in her hand. When he seated her she murmured a thank-you, and he caught the scent of her perfume, of musk and old roses. Heady, he thought, and frowned.

She wasn't a beauty in the classic sense of the word. Rather she had a gaminelike quality and a certain litheness of motion and movement, similar to the dancers Degas had both painted and sculpted and which, as an artist, intrigued him. She was not, of course, the type of woman who would appeal to him in the physical sense, but slightly interesting in a purely artistic way.

Wanting to draw her out, he asked, "Did you and Kico have a good lesson today?"

"Very good," she said enthusiastically. "We found a lot of words that are alike in both Spanish and English." She smiled across the table at the boy. "Didn't we, Kico?"

"Uh-huh."

"*Uh-huh?* When Señorita Fleming speaks to you, you say 'Yes, ma'am,' or 'Yes, Señorita Fleming.' Do you understand?"

Kico hung his head. "Yes, Father."

Julie saw the hurt and embarrassment in his big dark eyes and quickly said, "How about Señorita Julie, Kico? That's what my students in Guadalajara called me. Okay?"

"Okay."

God, how he disapproved of that bastardized word, but before he could say anything, she looked at him and said, in what seemed to him a sweetly deceptive voice, "*Okay* is such an international word, isn't it? No matter what the language or nationality, everyone understands. It's the one word in all the world, along with a smile, that helps people communicate."

Damn the woman! She'd known he was going to object and she'd stopped him before he could. He kept silent then, hoping that would discourage any further conversation, but it didn't. She talked to Kico, drawing him out, asking what he liked to do.

At first the boy was unresponsive, but little by little he warmed to her.

"I like to play with my cars," he said. "And dinosaurs. I have a big green one that a friend of Papa's brought me when he visited last month."

"What kind of stories do you like to read?"

He looked puzzled. "I don't know."

She took a sip of water and to Rafael said, "I noticed today there weren't any storybooks in the classroom, Señor Vega. Are they in Kico's bedroom? If they are I'd like one or two so that I could send for the same books in English and read them in class."

"There are textbooks and encyclopedias he can read in class."

Julie paused, fork halfway to her lips. "But surely you want him to read fiction, as well—books for youngsters by Mexican and Latin American writers, and things like Dr. Seuss in English. They're wonderful for children."

"Kico will go to the United States at the end of August. I'm sure literature will be included in his studies."

"I'm sure it will be," Julie agreed. "But if we began reading now, he'd be that much further along. Very likely the boys that will be in his class will have read many of the classic children's stories and—"

"I don't care what other boys have done." As though with great patience, Rafael put his fork across his plate. "Life isn't made up of fairy tales or storybooks, Miss Fleming. I want Kico to be prepared for the realities of life."

"The realities of life?" She stared at him. The little boy had lost his mother a year ago. He lived here on this island with a father who had no time for him, and under the supervision of a dour-faced housekeeper. Apparently there weren't any children for him to play with. He was alone, isolated. Was Rafael Vega so blind, so preoccupied with his own life that he couldn't understand how difficult life was for his son?

Julie said nothing for the rest of the meal, but when at last coffee had been served, she said, "If you can spare a few minutes this evening, Señor Vega, I'd like to have a private word with you."

"I work in my studio at night."

"This won't take long. It's important."

"Can't it wait?"

"No, it can't."

"Very well." He rose. "We can talk in the study." To the boy, he said, "You may be excused."

Kico looked from his father to Julie, but obediently he slid off his chair and said, "*Buenas noches,* Papa. *Buenas noches,* Señorita Julie."

"How about a good-night hug?" When he hesitated, Julie said, "C'mon. Even if you don't need one, I do."

Small white teeth nibbled his bottom lip, then, head lowered, he went to her. She put her arms around him. His body stiffened and he looked over his shoulder at his father. Julie gave him a squeeze and said, "Mmm, that's nice," then brushed his hair back and kissed his forehead. "Sleep well," she said. "I'll see you in the morning."

Dark eyes, so serious, so questioning, looked up at her. A sigh trembled through his small body. For the barest moment he leaned against her, then without a word he turned and hurried away.

Rafael's mouth tightened with disapproval. He threw down his napkin. "Very well," he said, "let's go into the study."

He didn't approve of her take-charge attitude. Most Mexican women weren't like that. They knew their place—in the kitchen as well as in the bedroom—and didn't interfere when their husbands made a decision on how things were to be done.

This little *gringa* had a lot to learn about Mexican men, he thought grimly. And by God, he'd like to be the one to bring her in line, to teach her how a proper woman behaved.

But that was nonsense, of course. If, and it was still a very big if, he decided to let her stay, she'd be gone in three months and neither he nor Kico would ever have to see her again.

He opened the door of his study and stood aside for her to enter. "All right," he said. "What is it?"

"It's Kico. I'm disturbed about him."

He bristled. "Has he misbehaved?"

"No, of course not. But he's a troubled little boy, Señor Vega. I'm sure he misses his mother. He needs a lot of attention. He needs to know how much you care about him."

"Do you have any children, Miss Fleming?"

She shook her head. "I've never been married."

"Then I really don't think you should tell me how to deal with my son."

"Deal with him?" Julie shook her head. "What happened to the word *love*, Señor Vega?"

His expression darkened. "How dare you speak to me that way? I know what's best for the boy."

"Is that why you're sending him away?"

He took a step toward her and she thought for a moment he meant to strike her. "That's it," he said. "End of discussion."

"Not quite." She handed him the brown manila envelope.

"What's this?"

"A drawing Kico did this morning."

He took it, slapped it against his thigh and said, "I'll look at it later."

"I'd like you to look at it now."

He wanted to tell her to go to hell, but her eyes held his. She didn't back down and he had a feeling that if he left the room she'd come after him. He opened the envelope and took out the drawing. He studied it, surprised because for a seven-year-old it was very good.

"Well?" he asked.

"I gave Kico a box of crayons with all sorts of colors, yet he used only the dark ones."

"He drew a storm, Miss Fleming. Of course he would use dark colors."

"But the empty boat," she pointed out. "The high waves and the clouds."

His nostrils pinched. He didn't answer.

"The little boy on the shore is Kico," she said. "He... He has no hands."

Julie heard the rasp of breath in Vega's throat. For a moment he didn't speak. Then he said, "Leave me."

His face was without expression, his eyes were dark. She started to speak but stopped. And quietly left the room.

He stared down at the drawing. "My God," he whispered. His hands tightened, wrinkling the paper. What have I done? he asked himself. What horror have I perpetrated?

A sound of pure grief came from his throat and he flung the paper away from him onto the floor and started for the door. But halfway there he hesitated, and swinging around he went back and picked the drawing up. He smoothed the edges he had wrinkled, then folded it and put it in his pocket.

"Pobre muchacho," he muttered under his breath. "Poor boy."

In the days that followed, Rafael did not appear at breakfast or at lunch, and most evenings she and Kico had dinner alone.

Little by little the boy warmed to her. He still resented having to learn English, but he did his lessons and almost in spite of himself began learning more than he realized.

When the weather was nice they took long walks around the island, but each time she suggested they go down to the waterfront he said, "No, I'm tired. I want to go back."

A maid by the name of Eloisa served their breakfast and lunch. She was a pleasant young woman, close to Julie's age, and though at first she was shy, little by little she loosened up and chatted while she served them.

The cook, the few times Julie had seen her, was friendly, too. One evening, just as she and Kico had started their dinner, the cook came out of the kitchen to ask if everything was all right and if there was anything special Julie would like to have her fix.

Julie, with a smile at Kico, said, "How about cheeseburgers for lunch tomorrow?" Before the cook could answer, Alicia sailed in from the kitchen like a battleship armed and ready to fire.

"I've already ordered a chicken pie with peas for tomorrow's lunch," she announced in a voice that brooked no argument.

"But surely that can be changed," Julie said. And trying to be reasonable, she added, "We could have the chicken pie for dinner."

The older woman glared down at her. "I'm in charge of selecting the menus," she said. "Not you. Not the cook." She frowned at the hapless woman. "As for you, Juanita, your place is in the kitchen. Remember that."

Juanita's eyes flashed, but she retreated without a word. Kico, uncomfortable because of the angry words, squirmed in his chair and reached across the table for a roll.

"Don't do that." Alicia picked up a wooden serving spoon, and before Julie could stop her, she hit the boy across his knuckles. He drew his hand back, but she grabbed it, hit him again and raised her arm as though to strike a third time.

Julie grabbed the woman's wrist. "Stop that!" she cried.

"Take your hands off me. Kico is my responsibility, not yours. I'm in charge."

"Not anymore." Rafael strode into the room. Dark eyes flashing, he said, "I've told you before that you are not to strike the boy." He saw the red mark across the back of Kico's hand. "Never do that again, Alicia," he said in a low and angry voice. "Never. Do you understand?"

"How do you expect him to learn good table manners if I'm not able to correct him?"

Rafael took the spoon away. "He will learn, but not this way."

Two bright spots of color appeared in Alicia's cheeks. She seemed about to speak, then clamped her thin lips shut and marched out of the dining room.

Rafael sat down. For a moment no one spoke. Then Kico leaned forward and in a conspiratorial whisper said, "I don't like Señorita Alicia."

"Understandable," Julie said in English.

"She's been with me for six years," Rafael said, also in English. "She knows her job and she runs the household efficiently."

"She got mad at Juanita because Señorita Julie asked Juanita to let us have cheeseburgers for lunch tomorrow," Kico explained.

"Cheeseburgers?" Rafael actually smiled, and with a shake of his head said, "I can see what an influence you've already had on the boy, Señorita Fleming. Next thing we know the two of you will want hot dogs and french fries."

"Maybe we'll really go wild and have chocolate ice cream." Julie folded the white napkin across her lap. "If it would be all right with you, Señor Vega, I'd like to go into Patzcuaro in a day or two and see if I can find a few books in English for the schoolroom. I've been thinking that perhaps Kico could come with me." She smiled at the boy. "I bet if we look hard enough we could find a restaurant that serves cheeseburgers."

"Books in English?" Rafael asked, ignoring her remark about the cheeseburgers. "I doubt you'll find what you want in Patzcuaro."

"If I don't I'll send away for them. But I'd still like to go to Patzcuaro and pick up a few things to brighten the classroom up a bit. Is it all right with you if Kico comes with me?" She turned to the little boy. "Would you like to?" she asked. "If it's all right with your father?"

His eyes widened. "Yes!" he said with so much enthusiasm that she laughed.

"There's only one condition," she said. "From now on we speak only English at mealtime.

"Only English?"

"That's right."

"What if I don't know a word?"

"Then you'll say..." And in English Julie said, "I don't know that word." She went on in Spanish. "I'll tell you what it is and we'll practice saying it."

He looked pained. "And if I do, can we go to Patzcuaro?"

"If it's all right with your father."

Rafael frowned. "I'll think about it," he said.

Kico's lower lip trembled. "I want to go," he said, and looked down at his plate.

"And I want to think about it. Now we will have our dinner and there will be no more talk of the trip until I've thought about it." He picked up the platter of potatoes Eloisa had brought in. "What is this?" he asked in English.

"Potato," Kico said.

They began speaking English then. Rafael's was surprisingly good and Julie learned, after a bit of prodding, that he had graduated from Notre Dame.

At first Kico was hesitant to speak, but with a little gentle prodding he began with simple sentences. "May I have the bread? *Un vaso*... I mean, a glass of milk."

"Very good," Julie said, praising him.

And even Rafael said, "Yes, that's fine."

When they had finished dinner and the table had been cleared, Rafael said, "I'd like to speak to you later, Miss Fleming. I'll take Kico to his room, but that will only take a few minutes. Will you wait for me in the *sala*, please?''

"Yes, of course."

As she had the previous evenings, Julie gave Kico a hug and told him she'd see him in the morning. But she made no more mention of the proposed outing to Patzcuaro. If Rafael objected there was nothing she could do. She was sorry now she'd brought it up.

She went into the living room to wait for him and when, in less then ten minutes, he appeared, she said, "I hope you're not upset that I suggested I take Kico into Patzcuaro with me."

"But I am," he said. "It isn't a good idea." He motioned her to a chair. "The boy's afraid of the water. He hasn't been out on the lake in over a year."

"Why? I've only crossed it once and that was during a storm, but I should imagine that in good weather the trip would take no more than half an hour and would be quite pleasant."

Rafael walked over to the fireplace. He wasn't sure how much he wanted to tell her, but sooner or later she was bound to find out what had happened.

"His mother drowned in the lake," he said at last. "Kico had just turned six when it happened, but he remembers and he's been terrified of the water ever since. I'm surprised that he agreed to go with you."

So that was it. She'd had no idea how Rafael's wife had died. She'd simply assumed there had been an accident of some kind.

"We were in our speedboat," Rafael said. "Margarita wanted to go to Patzcuaro and I didn't want her to because...." He hesitated. "Because the weather was bad," he said. "There was a storm that day, a bad one.

The wind was up, the waves were high. It was raining and difficult to see."

He turned away from her and leaned both hands against the side of the fireplace. "We hit a wave and she...Margarita went over the side. I dived in after her. I tried to find her, but the water was too dark, too stirred up with sand and mud from the bottom. I couldn't see. I couldn't..." He looked back at Julie. "It took the police and divers three days to find her body."

"How terrible that must have been for you. I'm so sorry, Señor Vega."

"It was traumatic for Kico. For months any mention of the lake upset him. The last time I took him in to Patzcuaro he panicked halfway there. That's why I don't want him going out on the lake."

"But he can't stay on the island forever," Julie said. "He has to get over his phobia of the water, of the lake, sooner or later."

Rafael ran a hand through his hair. "Even if he says he'll go with you, once he gets down to the dock he'll change his mind."

"If he does I won't insist. But I honestly don't believe he will. I think the promise of an outing will help him get over his fear."

"For someone who's never had children you seem to know a lot about them."

"Not a lot," Julie said. "But I'm willing to learn." She hesitated. "I haven't known Kico long, Señor Vega, but I sense that he's feeling terribly lost and lonely. I know you care about him, that you love him, but he needs..." Without thinking, Julie put her hand on his arm. "He needs to be assured of your love, Se-

ñor Vega. He needs to know how much you care about
him."

He looked at the hand that rested on his arm. A
small hand, pale and delicate. He took a deep breath
and his expression hardened. He didn't need this young
gringa telling him what he should or should not do
where the boy was concerned. She had no right . . .

Julie took her hand from his arm and stepped back.

"All right," he said abruptly. "You can take him to
Patzcuaro with you, if he'll go. I don't approve, I don't
think you should, but I won't stop you."

She drew her breath in. "Thank you," she said. "I'll
take good care of him."

"I hope so." He nodded. "That's all, Señorita
Fleming," he said, dismissing her. "You may go now."

She didn't say anything, she only looked at him.
Then turned and left the room.

He touched the arm that she had touched and imagined that he felt the warmth of her hand still there.

He had told himself after Margarita's death that he
had no need for a woman's tenderness in his life. He
had his work, that was enough. But now he wondered,
was it?

Her scent lingered in the room. Musk and old roses.

He leaned his head against the rough stone of the
fireplace. In three months she would be gone, both she
and the boy. Perhaps when he was alone it would be
easier to work, and, yes, easier to bear the unbearable.

CHAPTER FOUR

Julie sat by the fireplace in her room for a long time that night, as chilled by the cold and dampness as she was by her conversation with Rafael Vega. All too well she remembered the violence of the storm when she had crossed from Patzcuaro to the island, the roiled water and the waves that had threatened to swamp the boat. Rafael's wife had drowned in that dark water. He had dived down after her, risking his own life in a vain attempt to save hers.

How grief-stricken he must have been, how the memory of that day must linger. Was that why there were no pictures of his wife in any of the rooms or along the corridors? Was his grief so deep that even now he could not bear to be reminded of the woman he had loved and lost?

He was a difficult and taciturn man, but she understood him a bit better now and she would try to be more understanding, more compassionate, both with Señor Vega and with his son. She would even try to be civil to the housekeeper. Alicia Fernández didn't like her, she didn't like Alicia. Nevertheless, because the woman was Señor Vega's housekeeper she must learn to accept her.

When the hour grew late and the fire had died to smoldering embers, Julie went to bed. She slept fitfully and when she awoke felt tired and out of sorts.

She showered and dressed, and, gathering up her purse, opened the door of her room.

There on the threshold, facedown, lay a small, crudely made doll, no more than six inches tall, with short blond hair and a pale green dress. For a moment Julie couldn't move, so frozen was she by the doll who, in a macabre way, resembled her. She leaned down to pick it up. When she did she gasped. "No!" she cried. "Oh, no!"

The doll was wet, the hair soaked, the dress dripping. Scarcely daring to breathe, Julie turned it over. The scarlet mouth was agape, round sightless eyes stared up at her. The doll, with hair like hers and a dress the color she often wore, was supposed to have drowned. Like Rafael's wife.

Horrified, sickened, holding the doll by the wet blond hair, Julie rubbed her wet fingers up and down on her jeans. Who had put the doll here? What kind of sick joke was this? She looked around, the corridor was empty. But somebody had put the doll here, not last night because it was dripping with water, but this morning. Somebody wanted to spook her, but who? Alicia? Rafael?

Last night Rafael had told her about his wife's death by drowning. Was he now trying to frighten her away? Or could it be someone, something else? Had the ghost of his dead wife returned to frighten her?

"Oh come *on!*" The sound of her own voice in the quiet of the corridor startled her. This was a joke, a disgusting joke, and she was damned if she was going to let it spook her. She marched back into her room and flung the doll into the wastebasket. Then with a muttered curse, she picked up her shoulder bag and marched out of the door.

At the breakfast table Julie found an envelope beside her plate. In it was several hundred pesos, with a note that read, "Buy whatever you need." A scrawled "R" was the only signature.

She hadn't asked him for money, but it was a nice gesture and it surprised her. When Kico looked curious, she said, "Your dad has given us some pesos to buy whatever we need."

She told herself to forget about the doll, told herself it was a sick prank, meant to rattle her. But when she tried to eat she couldn't. The eggs made her stomach queasy, the toast tasted dry as sawdust.

Still, she made herself smile at Kico and say, "We're going to have fun today. As soon as you finish your breakfast we'll be on our way."

He had dressed for the outing in a pair of short khaki pants, a white shirt that looked as though it had too much starch, white socks and sturdy shoes. His face was scrubbed and he'd slicked his hair down with water.

He cleaned his plate, took a last sip of his milk, and when he announced that he was ready they left the house and started down the path to town.

In the ten days that Julie had been here, she'd left the hacienda only to take short walks with Kico. Now she was anxious to have a look at Janitzio as well as Patzcuaro.

As they descended the last of the stone steps, she saw that several launches were waiting at the dock and said, "We'd better hurry."

But Kico hung back. He didn't say anything, didn't say that he didn't want to go, but his small face looked pinched with concern.

Julie kept talking as they drew closer to the boats. "Look how calm the lake is," she said. "Isn't this going to be fun? We'll have a real outing, a day away from your English lessons. Let's get a seat on the side so we can see everything, and when the boat leaves you can show me where your house is."

She took his hand. It was cold as ice and for a moment she thought about turning back. But they'd come this far. If, as his father had said, Kico had a fear of the water because of his mother's death, he had to, sooner or later, get over it. He couldn't stay on the island forever.

He sat close to her, eyes lowered, looking neither right nor left. He flinched when the motor started. The boat left the dock and the musicians began to play. Julie looked back. On the shore of the island women were doing their laundry. The clothes already washed were strewn over the rocks to dry in a a brilliant array of colors, red and green and orange and blue and purple.

Farther out on the lake they passed small dugouts. She said, "Look at the fishermen, Kico," and turned to watch as the men in the hand-hewn boats cast their yellow butterfly nets into the water.

"Isn't this fun?" she said. "Isn't this just the most perfect day?"

His small face pinched with worry, he only nodded.

The musicians started a lively rancher song and a boy of about Kico's age looked at him and said, "I can play a guitar. Can you?"

Kico shook his head but he didn't answer. Not to be put off, the boy went on, "My father says I'm as good as anybody and that someday I'm going to be a big star."

Kico's chin jutted out. "Can you speak English?"

The boy looked startled.

"I can," Kico said. With that, ignoring the boy and turning to Julie, he said in perfect English, "The water is calm today, is it not? I hope we will find a good restaurant for our lunch. I myself will have a Coca Cola."

She looked at him, amazed. In the ten days she'd been teaching him he'd barely spoken a word of English except at mealtime in front of his father. The little bandit! Here all along he'd been learning, absorbing everything she'd taught him, but too stubborn to say more than a word at a time. She wanted to shake him. Instead she said, "I, too, will have a Coca Cola."

He grinned, and after that actually seemed to enjoy the trip.

They walked into town from the dock. He knew where the open market was and, taking Julie's hand, led her past the fruit and vegetable stands to where other things were sold. She found an *Ojo de Dios,* a colorful Huichol Indian Eye of God cross decorated in pink and orange and green and blue yarn. Next, because Kico thought it *"estupendo,"* she bought a ferocious looking carved mask with painted eyes, a bulbous nose, and tufts of hair sticking up from its head.

Then a piñata made of brightly colored papier mâché, with a clay pot inside that would be filled with candy and small toys. On the occasion of a birthday or a Christmas party, the piñata would be broken and the candy and toys scattered for the children. This piñata had been made in the figure of a bull with short, bowed legs, a stout body and curved horns.

"We can hang him at one end of the school room," Julie said. "And when your birthday comes we'll have a party."

"I won't be here for my birthday."

"Oh?" Julie hesitated. "When is it?"

"In October. I'll be gone by then."

She didn't know what to say. More and more the thought of the little boy being all alone in a strange country bothered her. He didn't want to go; she couldn't understand why Rafael wanted to send him away. The Mexican families she had met loved to have their children with them. They took them wherever they went, to church on Sunday morning, to midnight mass at Christmas. Sometimes the little ones slept in their parents' arms. Occasionally an older child broke away to run up and down the church aisle, and if he did there were only indulgent smiles and a whispered "*Niño,* come back."

Children went with their parents to see late-night fireworks displays, to neighborhood fiestas and family celebrations. If things lasted until one in the morning they dozed beside their parents, or roused to drink *un chocolate* or have a sip of *atole.*

Most Mexican families would have been appalled at the idea of sending a child as young as Kico away. It was bad enough when a son or daughter went off to a university. And certainly, if one or all of the daughters remained unmarried, they lived at home until they were. For they were all family, loved and cherished forever.

Why was Rafael so different? Didn't he love his son? The thought chilled her and she said, "We'll have our own special birthday celebration. We'll fill the piñata with toys and candy and we'll invite some of the local children. Juanita will bake a cake, we'll have lemonade, and I'll buy you a very special present."

For a moment his face brightened, then it sobered and he said, "I don't know anybody."

"Of course you do, boys and girls you went to school with last year." She tugged on his hand and in English said, "We'll round 'em up and head 'em out and we'll have an absolutely wonderful party." She pointed to a small papier mâché clown. "How do you like him? Let's buy him for my desk. Okay?"

When finally they left the market they went to a restaurant on the square and sat outside. They ordered cheeseburgers and french fries. And Julie said, "Remember what we said about speaking English at meal time?" She smiled encouragingly. "Will you pass me the salt, please?"

Kico hesitated only a moment before he picked up the salt shaker and handed it to her.

"Thank you."

"You are welcome." He took a bite of his cheeseburger. "This is very good, is it not?"

"Yes, it's very good." She gave him a smile. "And so is your English, Kico. I don't understand why you don't want to speak it."

He picked up a french fry and held it while he thought. "I like to speak it with you," he said. "If you lived here all the time, if I didn't have to go away to that place, I would speak it with you." He took a bite of the potato, and said in Spanish, "Maybe you could ask Father not to send me away. Maybe if you told him I don't want to go, he'd let me stay." He smiled at her. "You could stay, too, Señorita Julie."

He leaned closer, looked around as though afraid someone would overhear, and said. "I don't like the Señorita Alicia. And you know what?"

"What?" Julie asked.

"She's an *hechicera.*"

"*Hechicera?* I don't know that word, Kico. What does it mean?"

"*Bruja.* She is a *bruja.*"

"A witch?" Julie smiled a little uncertainly. Was it Alicia who had put the doll at her door? Had she only meant to frighten her or had it been an omen, an object to call up evil spirits?

Julie picked up her cola, but when she saw that her hands were shaking, she set it back down. In a careful voice she said, "I don't like her very much either, Kico. But I don't think she's a witch."

"Yes, she is," he insisted. "I know she is." He took a bite of his cheeseburger. "So will you talk to Father?" he asked, still speaking Spanish. "Will you tell him I should stay at home?"

Though Julie had insisted they speak English at mealtime, she didn't interrupt him now. Polite table conversation in a foreign language was one thing, speaking about something that was so important, so close to your heart, was another.

She didn't agree with Rafael's decision to send Kico to the States to school, but she doubted there was anything she could say or do to dissuade him. He was the parent; she was only the teacher. And a temporary one at that. Still . . .

"All right," she said. "I'll have a talk with your father. Maybe I can convince him to wait a year or two."

Kico grinned. "Then after that you could talk to him again."

She reached across the table and covered his hand with hers. "I'm only going to be here for a couple of months, honey. I have a job I have to go back to in Guadalajara."

"I don't want you to go." He frowned and his small chin stuck out. "How come you can't stay here? I don't like the Señorita Alicia. I don't like my—"

"No." She stopped him before he could say the word. "Finish your cheeseburger," she said. "There are a few more things I want to buy. If we don't want to be too late getting back we'd better get busy."

They didn't speak until they had finished eating. When they did, she signaled for the check. "I thought we'd buy a couple of pictures for the walls," she said. "Let's go see what we can find."

They only found one—a colorful drawing of a matador. "To go with the bull piñata," Kico said.

Next door there was a bookstore and she led Kico inside. They browsed for a little while and she told him they would each choose a book. He chose one about spacemen, she selected a Dr. Seuss.

By then it was after four and time to start back. Dark clouds had gathered while they were in the bookstore and it worried her that it might storm. She wasn't sure how Kico would react if a storm struck while they were out on the lake.

They took a taxi back to the dock. Thunderclouds threatened and she hurried him aboard an already half-filled launch. Fifteen minutes went by before it was filled and they left the dock. By then rain had begun to spatter.

"We'll be home soon," Julie said.

He didn't answer. He turned away from her to look out at the water. Waves splashed hard against the side of the boat and the water that had been blue-green when they left that morning looked a malevolent gray.

Kico's face was pale, his lips quivered. On his knees he leaned over the side, looking down. Down into the dark, dark water.

"Kico?" With one hand on his arm, Julie drew him back beside her. "Sit down," she said.

He turned from the water and sat beside her, staring at his shoes, his small body close to hers, rigid, frightened.

The spatter of rain stopped, but the sky was ominous. It was almost dark by the time they reached the island and made their way up to the hacienda.

As soon as they entered, Alicia Fernández appeared. "Where have you been?" she asked. "It's almost dinnertime." She frowned at Kico. "Your father won't like your being so late. You've got a smudge on your pants and your shirt is wrinkled. Go and change at once."

"I want to help Julie with the packages."

"*Señorita* Julie." Alicia loomed over him. Dressed all in black, with her white-winged streak of hair, she looked like a huge hawk about to swoop down on its hapless prey.

Kico took a step backward.

"*Inmediatamente!*" the woman repeated.

"Kico's going to help me put these things in the playroom first," Julie said pleasantly but firmly. "Then both of us will change for dinner."

"Are you countermanding my order?" Alicia, her face tight with anger, glared at Julie.

"An order?" Julie cocked her head to one side. "Maybe that's your problem, Señorita Fernández. Maybe you'd get further if you asked nicely instead of ordering." She put her arm around Kico's shoulders. "Come along," she said. "We'll just leave the things in the schoolroom for now. Tomorrow you can help me arrange them."

He shot a worried look over his shoulder and moved closer to Julie. She knew she'd made an enemy. Actually she'd known from the first moment she'd set foot in this house. That didn't bother her, but she didn't want the Fernández woman taking it out on Kico. She planned to make darn sure she didn't.

Rafael didn't appear for dinner that night. His absence upset Julie almost as much as Alicia Fernández's unpleasantness earlier. Had the man no interest at all in his son? Didn't he want to know what kind of a day Kico had had? Whether or not the boy had been frightened out on the lake?

As soon as they finished dinner, Julie said, "I guess your father's working. Would it be all right if I tucked you in tonight?"

"If you want to," he said.

"I want to."

She took his hand when they started down the dimly lit corridors that led to the bedrooms. She didn't like the corridors at night; what must it be like for Kico to come down them alone?

And it wasn't just the corridors; the whole hacienda was dark and cheerless. Maybe after all it would be better for Kico if he went to school in the States. At least there he'd be with boys his own age.

She'd never seen his bedroom. It, too, was dark and cheerless. The walls were tan, the bedspread and curtains brown. A heavy wooden cross over the bed was the only ornament. No little-boy things softened the room, no airplanes or toy cars, no pennants or posters. It was as stark as a monk's cell.

She told him to undress while she ran his bath, and when he was in the tub she sat on the one straight-backed chair and thought, Yes, the school will be better than this is. At least it won't be worse.

When he came out of the bathroom in his brown pajamas she pulled the sheet and blanket back and said, "All set? Hop in."

He got into bed and looked shyly up at her. "I had a nice time," he said. "Maybe we can go again next week."

She smoothed the hair back from his forehead. "Maybe. We'll see what your father says." Then, because there were no storybooks in his room, she said, "Would you like me to tell you a story about the Seminoles?"

"Uh-huh."

"Scoot over." She sat on the bed beside him and put her arm around him as she began to make up a story about a Seminole boy. "Who's just your age," she said.

Five minutes later his eyes drifted closed. She slid off the bed, kissed his forehead and turned off the bedside lamp. "Good night, sweetie," she said softly. "Sleep well."

At the doorway she turned back. In the dim hall light he looked so little, so vulnerable. How could his father ignore him the way he did? Didn't he know how much Kico needed him?

With a sigh Julie closed the door and went to her own room. But it was a long time that night before she went to sleep.

* * *

The storm that had threatened earlier hit in the middle of the night. The crack of thunder woke Julie. And something else. A scream?

She reached to turn on her bedside lamp, but nothing happened. The electricity had gone off again. She lay still for a moment, waiting, listening. She heard the cry again, a high, keening wail. And knew it was Kico.

She reached for her robe but couldn't find it in the dark. On the nightstand she found a candle and matches. She lit the candle and ran barefoot out of her room into the dark-as-a-tomb hallway. Thunder crashed and she gasped in fear.

The voice came again, thin, piping, frightened. She quickened her steps, but it was dark, so dark with only the tiny flare of light from her candle. Then through the darkness she saw a thin beam of light and suddenly a dark figure loomed up at her.

Hand to her throat, she stopped, waiting, scarcely breathing.

"Señorita Fleming? Juliana?" His voice was rough, accusing. "Is that you?"

She let out her breath. "Señ—Señor Vega?"

He came closer, tall, menacing. Dark robe. Black hair tousled. Dark, dark eyes.

He raised his candle.

"I heard Kico," she said.

Thunder crashed again and a flash of lightning split the darkness. In the orange glow they looked at each other. She wore only a short white nightgown. Her face was pale, her eyes were big, frightened.

"Go back to your room," he said.

"But Kico. I . . ."

He opened the bedroom door. She heard the little boy moaning, thrashing in his bed. "She's down there!" he cried. "In the lake... Deep, deep..."

"Dear God," Julie whispered.

"It's your fault," Rafael said. "I didn't want you to take him out on the lake, but you insisted." He started into Kico's room. "Leave us," he said. "I'll take care of him."

He left her standing there in the hall. She heard him murmuring to the boy, heard Kico's startled gasp, then the sobs. Tears sprang to her eyes because she wanted to go to him, to hold him and tell him that everything was all right, that it was only a dream. But she couldn't. He wasn't her child.

Back in her room, Julie sat on the edge of her bed while the storm, like a wild beast let loose, raged all around her. Ten minutes went by, fifteen. Someone knocked. She stood, nervous, hands clasped, and said, "Come... come in."

Rafael stood in the doorway. "He's gone back to sleep," he said. "I left his door open. I'll hear him if he stirs again." He hesitated. "I'm sorry I said what I did about it being your fault. It wasn't."

She moved away from the bed, the soft glow of the candlelight behind her. The simple white gown had a round, lace-edged neckline and short sleeves. It came just to her knees. In the back light of the candle he could see the outline of her body, the fullness of her breasts, the sweet curve of waist and hip, her white thighs, only partially concealed by the thinness of her gown.

An almost forgotten flame stirred deep in his belly and ran through his body as bright and hot as the lightning outside. He stirred, hardened. And took a step toward her.

The lightning came again, slashing like a demon across the room, lighting her pale face. Her mouth trembled. Her eyes were wide with something akin to fear. And something else. Something . . .

Heat drummed through him, suffocating, terrible heat that begged to be appeased. He took another step forward.

"Señor Vega," she said in a voice so low he could barely hear. "Señor Vega."

He stopped. "I . . . I just wanted to tell you. About Kico, I mean. He's all right now. Go back to bed."

But still he stood where he was, looking at her, wanting to touch her, to feel the warmth of that slender body close to his. Wanting . . .

He reached out his hand to her, hesitated, then with a muttered oath turned and left the room. And Julie was alone in the candle-lit darkness.

She blew out the candle and lay down. But he was there in her mind, there behind her closed eyelids. And no matter how she tried to stop it, his dark, dark eyes seemed to be burning into her, raking her body with his hot, sensual gaze.

In the darkness of the night she whispered his name. "Rafael. Rafael."

CHAPTER FIVE

In the dim light of dawn the shadowy figure beckoned to her. Though afraid, she took a tentative step forward. Then another.

"Come to me," he whispered.

"I can't see you. I don't know who you are."

"You know. You know."

She reached out to him. He took her hand and brought her closer. Strong arms held her and would not let her go. She looked into eyes as dark as the night had been. She felt the heat of his body, and of her own.

"Oh, please," she whispered, and did not know what she pleaded for. But still her voice, "Oh, please. Oh, please."

His eyes were hot with desire. As though afraid she might move away, he held her. His face was close, so close... His cruel mouth almost touching hers. Almost...

Julie awoke with a start, heated, trembling, unsure for a moment where she was. A sigh quivered through her. The shadows of the night disappeared. She was alone. And she remembered.

Last night when thunder crashed and lightning snaked like a bolt of electricity through the room, Rafael, his dark eyes burning with strange and frightening desire, had held out his hand to her. What would he have done if she had taken it?

She drew the white linen sheet up to her chin, wondering, wondering.

In the clear, clean light of day it seemed as though those moments alone with Rafael Vega had been a dream she had awakened from. Yet he had been here. He'd looked at her with his dark and brooding eyes. He'd held his hand out to her. He—

Someone knocked, and before she could say "Who is it?" Alicia Fernández opened the door and came in.

Julie sat up and reached for her robe. With a frown she said, "Do you usually enter a room without being asked, Señorita Fernández? What do you want?"

Alicia closed the door and stood with her back against it. "You didn't bother putting your robe on last night," she said. "I saw you out in the hall with him, half-dressed, shameless."

"I ran out because I heard Kico. The lights were out, I couldn't find my robe and I . . ." She stopped. What was she doing? She didn't have to defend herself to Alicia.

"He came into your room. I saw him. I know what happened." Black eyes narrowed to angry slits. "I know what you're up to, *gringa*. I knew the first minute I saw you what you had up your sleeve."

Julie pulled the robe closer around her and stood facing the woman. "I'd like you to leave," she said.

"It won't do you any good, you know," Alicia went on as though she hadn't heard. "He has a dark soul, a devil in him that clamors to get out. If you're not careful . . ." She let the words hang in the silence of the room, and a small, sly smile thinned her lips. "His wife drowned, did you know that?"

"Yes, I know."

She moved closer, a fearful, threatening presence. Though a moment ago the room had been warm with the morning sun, now it grew damp and chilled.

As she sensed Julie's fear, Alicia's terrible smile widened, stretching the skin across her face like the death mask of a very old mummy. "Be careful," she whispered, "or you'll wind up at the bottom of the lake just the way she did."

Julie stared at her, so startled by the venom in the other woman's voice that for a minute she was too frozen to speak. She clutched the robe tight around her throat and took a deep breath. "Get out of my room," she said. "You're not welcome here."

"But he is, isn't he?" Alicia reached behind her and opened the door. "Stay away from him," she warned. "Because if you don't—"

Julie picked up the brass candlestick. "Get out," she said again. "Now."

"*Puta,*" Alicia snarled, and slithered out of the room.

Julie closed and locked the door behind her, breathing hard, gripping the candlestick so tightly her fingers hurt. The woman was a raving maniac. She'd as much as accused Rafael of murdering his wife. She . . .

"Down, down," Kico had cried out in the night. "Down in the bottom of the lake."

A wave of dizziness unsteadied Julie. She swayed and clung to the bedpost. She thought of the cruel mouth, the dark, dark eyes that only last night had drawn her to him like an irresistible magnet. Had he been responsible for the death of his wife? Was there a grain of truth in the housekeeper's words?

No, she wouldn't believe that. A little boy, badly traumatized by his mother's death, had had a nightmare. It meant nothing.

She ran a tub of hot water and soaked in it for a very long time. But the chill of fear did not go away.

The storm that had swept through Janitzio the night before presaged the hurricane gathering force off the Pacific coast of Mexico. Jezebel, aptly named because of the destruction she had already caused in Baja California, hovered over the Pacific trying to make up her mind which direction to take. Storm warnings went out, but so far there was no indication that Jezebel would head inland.

Because it was so oppressively warm, and because she and Kico were usually alone at breakfast, Julie slipped into a pair of shorts and a T-shirt that morning. She wondered how Kico would be after last night's nightmare, or if he even remembered it. She wouldn't mention it if he didn't, she decided as she left her room and started toward the dining room. But if he did remember, and if he wanted to talk about it, she would let him.

She wondered if there had been other nightmares, for although a year had gone by since his mother's death, it obviously still preyed on his mind.

Kico was already at the table. As always, even though Rafael rarely appeared, three places had been set.

She said, "Good morning," and going to Kico, she kissed the top of his head. "Everything all right?"

"Uh-huh," he said, but did not look at her.

She helped herself to a slice of papaya and smiled when Eloisa came through the kitchen door with a pot of coffee.

"I'll have a cup of that," Rafael said as he strode into the room. "Good morning, Señorita Juliana. Good morning, Kico."

"Good morning, Papa."

Julie watched him under lowered lashes. He had barely glanced at her. It was as though the night before had never happened, as though there had been no nightmare. As though he had not entered her room. Had she only imagined that moment of heated desire she'd seen in his eyes?

"I'm going to Mexico City today," he said. "I'm not sure how long I'll be gone."

"Do you have a number where I can reach you in case I need to?" she asked, keeping her voice as coolly impersonal as his.

"I'll be at the Sheraton." He poured himself a cup of coffee and to Kico said, "How do you feel this morning? Are you all right?"

"Yes, Papa."

"It was only a bad dream, you know. All children have them. Sometimes adults do, too. While I'm gone perhaps you'd like to leave your bedroom door open. That way if you have another bad dream, Señorita Julie will hear you." He took a sip of coffee, glanced at his watch and said, "I'm taking the ten o'clock plane from Morelia. I have to leave now."

He'd started to push back his chair when Julie said, "I'm sure your father would like a goodbye hug, Kico."

The boy looked at her in surprise, then shyly at his father. He slid off his chair and came hesitantly forward.

Rafael sat very still.

"*Adiós*, Papa." Kico raised his arms.

He embraced the boy, stiffly, awkwardly. "Be a good boy," he said.

"Yes, sir."

Rafael stood and, reaching in his pocket, handed Julie a sheaf of bills. "For anything you need."

She shook her head and tried to hand it back to him. "You gave me money for the trip to Patzcuaro yesterday."

"Take it," he insisted. "There might be something you or the boy will need."

He wanted to tell her that he was glad she was here in his home and what having her here meant to him. Last night she had been as concerned about Kico as he had been. Without thinking, she had responded to the child's cry, something Margarita would never have done. Margarita would simply have summoned one of the maids and told her to see what on earth was wrong with the boy.

Juliana wasn't like that. Her concern for Kico had been real. She had a womanly softness that pleased him, and though he had seen little of her during the time she had been in his home, he was very aware of her presence. More aware than he wanted to be. He had to be careful about that.

Last night he had almost made a mistake, but when he'd seen her like that, with the softness of her body shadowed by candlelight, he'd been overwhelmed by a desire unlike anything he'd known before. He'd wanted to hold her, to feel the warmth of her body against his, to kiss those sweetly curved lips. It had taken every bit of his will not to lay her down on her bed, to feel her beneath him, to bury himself in her softness so that he could forget all of the terrible things that had happened before.

Por Dios, he must have been mad. The idea of another woman in his life was impossible.

He clenched his fists and a look of unutterable pain crossed his face. Because he knew he wanted the *gringa.* And because he also knew how dangerous that wanting could be for her.

The hacienda seemed strangely empty without him. Julie worked with Kico on his lessons. They took walks together and every night Julie tucked Kico in and together they read either the space book in Spanish or a Dr. Seuss story in English.

The days were too hot, too humid. A stillness in the air made everyone uneasy. Julie suggested they move the classroom outside under the trees, but even there the heat and mugginess made it difficult to work.

"Let's skip classes for the rest of the day," she said on Friday morning. "I'm sure your father won't mind if we take a break."

She needed one, needed to get away from the island for a little while. She wanted to talk to her mother and dad, and though she could have done that from the hacienda by reversing the charges, she preferred doing it from the office of *larga distancia* in Patzcuaro, where she knew no one might listen in.

Though Alicia Fernández had stayed out of her way these past few days, Julie had a feeling the woman lurked somewhere in the shadows, watching her every move.

As she gathered up the books to take them inside, she said to Kico, "I think I'll take the boat into Patzcuaro today. Would you like to come with me?"

He shook his head and she wondered if the terror of the nightmare he'd had a few days ago still lingered.

"I'll be back before dark so we can have dinner together. And I'll bring you a surprise. All right?"

"I guess so."

She hesitated, reluctant to leave now that she'd made up her mind to go. But except for the afternoon she and Kico had gone to Patzcuaro, she hadn't had a day off since she'd been here. She needed a few hours away.

She found Eloisa in the kitchen with Juanita and told her she wanted her to keep an eye on Kico while she was gone. She handed Eloisa some money. "Take Kico down to the village for lunch if he'd like to go. Let him order whatever he wants and if there's something special he'd like to have buy it for him. I'll be back before dinner, but till then I want you to be with Kico."

The young woman nodded. "I will stay with him, Señorita Julie. You can depend on me."

"*La bruja,* the witch, won't like it," Juanita said. She lowered her voice. "She is a bad one, Señorita Julie. They say in the village that her mother was a witch before her. They say she could bring back the dead and that Alicia, too, has that power." Juanita lowered her voice and looked around to make sure the three of them were alone. "It is said she brings forth the ghosts of those who have passed to the spirit world, that she speaks with them and walks with them."

Julie stared at the older woman. Bring back the dead? Talk to ghosts? What utter nonsense. Yet the thought of it, of the dead Margarita prowling the dark corridors of the hacienda at night made the small hairs at the back of her neck rise. Someone or something had placed an effigy at her door. Had it been Alicia, or...?

Julie stared at the older woman. A sudden wave of dizziness made her cling to the back of a chair. Stop it! she told herself. And in a voice that was sharper than she had intended said, "I hope you don't talk about those kinds of things around Kico."

"Of course I don't. But what I say is true. And what is more, Señorita Julie, Alicia doesn't like you. You must be careful of her." Juanita measured flour and sifted it into a bowl. "She won't like it that you've asked Eloisa to take care of the boy."

"If she says anything to either you or Eloisa, tell her those are my instructions." Julie patted Eloisa's shoulder. "Have fun today," she said. "I'm counting on you to take care of Kico until I return this afternoon."

She liked both Eloisa and Juanita, and she was sure Eloisa would do as she asked. Still, when she boarded the launch an hour later, Julie felt uneasy.

Her spirits lifted as soon as the boat pulled away from the island. Though the sky was a flat gray and the air felt like a solid damp mass, it was a bit cooler on the lake. She relaxed, elbow on the wooden side of the boat as she leaned out to watch the fishermen with their butterfly nets and the graceful swoop of birds against the leaden sky.

When the boat reached Patzcuaro, she walked into town, and when she found a long-distance booth she placed a call to her parents' home in Florida.

Her mother answered. Julie said, "Hi, Mom," and smiled into the phone with the sheer pleasure of hearing her mother's voice again.

"Are you all right?" her mother asked. "Is anything wrong? How's the job?"

"Just fine," Julie said. "Everything's just fine."

"What about the hurricane?"

"What hurricane?"

"Jezebel. I heard on the news this morning that it had turned toward land and headed to... Wait, let me think. A place called Mansan-something."

"Manzanillo?" Julie asked. "You know more than I do. I didn't have the radio on either last night or this morning."

"How far are you away from ... whatever the name of that place is?"

"About three hundred miles, I think."

"Oh dear."

She heard the worry in her mother's voice and quickly said, "I doubt it will hit here, Mom. But don't worry. Even if it does I'll be all right. The hacienda is solid as a rock."

Her father wasn't home, her mother said, but her sister Susie was. So Julie talked to Susie, too. She didn't care how much this cost, she needed to speak to her family.

But finally, because her mother insisted that this was costing her a fortune, she said goodbye, after sending hugs and kisses to her father.

The call had cheered her while she was making it, but once she hung up she felt more depressed, more alone, than she had before.

She strolled around the square, then went to the Museum of Popular Arts and Crafts, which was housed in a beautiful old building where a Bishop Quiroga had originally founded a college. The small museum was charming. In the gift shop she found a carved wooden top and bought it for Kico.

After that she wandered into one of the old churches. It was a quiet place, and cool. She slipped into one of the pews and, though she was not Catholic, found herself kneeling. She said a prayer for her mother and father, her sisters and her brothers, and for Kico. And because it didn't seem right not to, for Kico's father.

The minutes passed, and still she knelt there in the peacefulness of the church. The faint scent of incense hung in the air, faded flowers ringed the altar. The Virgin of Guadalupe, the patron of Mexico, looked down at her.

"Help Kico," Julie whispered. "Keep him safe."

When she left the church she made her way across the square to the restaurant where she and Kico had eaten. She sat outside as they had done, but just as she'd given the waiter her order, the wind started to blow and suddenly the skies opened up. Wind swept the tablecloths away and sent the waiters scurrying after them. The customers ducked inside and the headwaiter said, "Ay, ay, ay. It is the hurricane. A little while ago it came on the news that it was hitting Manzanillo with winds of over a hundred and thirty miles an hour."

"But it won't hit here," another waiter said. "Surely it will move farther down the coast toward Acapulco."

"How do you know that?" someone else said. "It could just as well turn inland."

A waiter brought Julie's club sandwich. "And the check," she said. "I want to get a taxi to go down to the docks."

The man shook his head. "I doubt you will find a taxi, *señorita*. It will be better to wait until this deluge passes. Then perhaps it will be possible."

"No," she said. "I can't wait."

She shouldn't have left Kico alone. Eloisa seemed like a responsible young woman, but with his father gone, she should be with him, especially in a storm like this one.

She ate quickly and paid her bill, and when she stepped out under the arcade she saw that the rain and wind had increased. She looked up and down the flooded street for a taxi. Fifteen minutes went by. Twenty. At last she saw one approaching around the side of the square. She waved, and when he didn't see her, she dashed out into the rain. He stopped and threw open the back door.

"I want to go to the docks," Julie said.

"To get a launch to the island?" The taxi driver shook his head. "I doubt they will be running, *señorita*. The storm has veered in our direction. No more boats will go out today."

Julie insisted. She had to get back to Janitzio.

But the taxi driver had been right; there would be no more boats leaving Patzcuaro until this was over. He waited for her when she came running back from the pier. "You will want a hotel, yes?" he asked when she came inside.

"Yes. All right. Take me to a hotel."

"The Posada de Don Vasco is the best," he said. "I will take you there."

It was away from the downtown area. When they arrived, Julie paid the driver, then splashed into the small lobby and asked if they had a room for the night.

"You have no luggage?" the young woman behind the reception desk asked.

"I'm staying in Janitzio," Julie said. "I got caught in the storm. Do you have a shop with something in it I can buy so that I can get out of these wet clothes?"

"The shop is closed," the woman said. "But I will see that it is opened for you."

"And I have to use a telephone. I have to call Janitzio."

"There is a phone in the room. While you're making your call I'll have someone open the shop." She handed Julie a key. "Your room is upstairs. I will see that you have extra towels."

Julie thanked the young woman. "Has there been any news of the hurricane?"

"*Sí, señorita.* It appears that it is headed our way. But do not have fear, the Posada is a sturdy hotel. We will be all right."

But will Kico? Julie asked herself as she hurried up the steps and down the long rain-swept corridor to her room. Once inside she went straight to the phone. "I want to call Janitzio," she told the woman at the switchboard, and gave the the number.

Juanita answered. *"Bueno? Bueno?"*

"It's Julie, Juanita. I'm in Patzcuaro. I can't get back because the boats aren't running. Is Kico all right?"

"He's here in the kitchen with Eloisa and me right now. Would you like to speak to him?"

"Yes, please."

He came on the line. "Señorita Julie?" he said. "Where are you?"

"I'm in Patzcuaro, Kico. I'm so sorry, honey, but I can't come back tonight. Are you all right?"

"Eloisa and I made cookies. Pretty soon they're going to be ready and then we'll have cookies and hot chocolate. I wish you were here."

"So do I. But you'll save me a cookie, won't you? I'll be back just as soon as I can, Kico. Now let me talk to Eloisa."

"Bueno!" the young woman shouted into the phone. "Señorita Julie? You must not worry. Everything is all right here."

"I want you to keep Kico with you, Eloisa. Do you understand?"

"Sí, señorita. ¡Cómo no!"

"Very likely the lights will go out tonight. I want you to sleep in his room with him."

"I will do it, *señorita.*"

"Let me speak to him again, please."

He came on the line. "The cookies smell real good. I wish you were here," he said once more.

"So do I, Kico. But Eloisa will stay with you tonight, and I'll be back tomorrow."

"Did you buy me a surprise?"

"Of course I did."

"What is it?"

"If I told you it wouldn't be a surprise." She forced a laugh that brought a giggle in response and said, "Bye-bye, Kico. I'll see you tomorrow."

If the boats were running. If the storm didn't blow them all away.

The small shop had only a few things to offer, souvenir items mostly, some skirts and blouses. Julie bought an ankle-length Tarascan Indian skirt and an off-the-shoulder white blouse and paid for them with her credit card.

When she went back to her room she showered and washed her hair. Both the wind and the rain had grown in intensity. The shutters on her window rattled, and when she fastened them the room was darker, closed in.

The lights flickered, and though they didn't go off, Julie knew they would, and soon. She checked to make sure there were candles and matches in the room, then dressed and hurried into the wide outside corridor and down the stairs to the dining room.

It was an attractive room with beamed ceilings, copper chandeliers and hanging plants. Old-fashioned *trasteros* displayed pretty blue china. The tablecloths were colorful and candles glowed from each table.

A waiter with a red jacket said, "Table for one, *señorita?*" and when Julie nodded, he led her to one side of the room. Before he could pull the chair out for her, a man's voice said, "Juliana?"

She turned. Rafael Vega stared at her from the next table.

He pushed his chair back and stood. "What in the hell are you doing here?" he asked.

CHAPTER SIX

Julie stared at him, too startled for a moment to speak. "I—I just came over for the afternoon. The storm hit. The launches stopped running. I couldn't get back."

"You didn't know the hurricane had veered and headed this way?"

"Not until I called my mother in Florida this afternoon."

Rafael indicated the chair opposite him. "Sit down," he said.

It sounded more like an order than an invitation and for a moment Julie hesitated. Then the waiter held out the chair and she really had no choice.

Rafael indicated the bottle of wine in front of him. "Would you care for some?"

"Yes, thank you."

The waiter set another place. Rafael filled her wineglass.

"I called the hacienda as soon as I got here," she said. "I spoke with Kico. He and Eloisa were in the kitchen baking cookies. She'll sleep in his room tonight."

"I spoke to Alicia earlier. She didn't appreciate the idea that a serving girl had taken over her duties."

"Her duties?" Julie's hackles rose. "I'm sure Señorita Fernández is efficient," she said. "I don't doubt that she knows how to keep a house clean, how to order food and supervise the kitchen. But she doesn't know a damn thing about little boys. She'd be as much comfort during a storm as an open window.''

Her eyes intent on his, she went on. "Kico is still a little boy. He's suffered a terrible trauma and I'm amazed that he's handled it as well as he has. He needs patience and understanding. He—"

"Are you saying I don't understand the boy?"

Julie shook her head. "We're talking about Señorita Fernandez," she said with some asperity. "There's not a drop of human kindness in the woman's body. If Kico were my child I certainly wouldn't want her taking care of him."

"But he's not your child."

Her gaze met his. "No," she said quietly. "He's not."

When she bent her head, candlelight turned the pale blond hair to gold. She must have just washed it, he thought, because it had a tousled look and curled in soft ringlets around her face.

"How old are you?" he asked abruptly.

Surprised at the switch in conversation, she said, "Twenty-seven."

"You look younger."

"How old are you, Señor Vega?"

"Thirty-five."

Her lips twitched. "You look older."

He started to frown. Then he laughed and said, "Touché, Señorita Fleming."

It was easier after that. The waiter brought the menus, they ordered, and Rafael poured more wine into her glass.

From outside he could hear the roar of the wind. It was picking up; they were going to get at least part of the hurricane. But because he didn't want to alarm her, he didn't say anything.

She looked very pretty tonight. Although in his opinion the off-the-shoulder blouse was too revealing, he had to admit it looked good on her. Her shoulders were smooth and creamy white, and though a ruffle partially hid the fullness of her breasts, he didn't think she was wearing a bra.

"I haven't seen the outfit you're wearing before," he said.

"I was soaked to the skin when I got here." Julie took a bite of her roll. "I bought the blouse and skirt in the hotel shop."

Soaked to the skin. That meant she wasn't wearing underwear. Something stirred. A not unpleasant warmth snaked its way down from his belly.

She leaned forward to take a sip of water and just for a moment he caught a glimpse of décolletage, smooth white skin, suggested roundness of breast.

The warmth turned to heat.

"I'm sorry I left Kico alone," she said. "I only meant to be away for a few hours. I wanted to call my parents."

"You could have called from the house."

"I didn't want to reverse the charges."

"You wouldn't have had to," he said impatiently. "*Por Dios,* call anybody you want. I don't mind."

She nodded her thanks. "I asked Eloisa to spend the day with Kico. She's a nice young woman, Señor Vega. I like her."

"Rafael," he said. "My name is Rafael."

She blushed, and when she did she looked younger than her twenty-seven years, and innocent. He liked that.

Margarita, as well as the women he'd known before her, had all been fairly sophisticated women of the world. When, in his mid-twenties, he'd lived in France, he'd had an affair with an older French actress. After her there had been a model, then the ex-wife of a general.

By the time he returned to Mexico he had already gained some fame as a sculptor and was welcomed into the society of Mexico City. He'd dated politicians' daughters, a well-known Argentine writer and several actresses before he married Margarita.

Of all the women he had known, none of them was anything like Juliana Fleming. She piqued his interest. He liked her spirit, the way she stood up to him when they disagreed. He was grateful for her kindness toward the boy and he was glad he'd decided to keep her on—for the boy's sake.

They ordered *sopa Tarasco,* the regional soup, which proved to be an appetizing blend of tomatoes, beans, chipotle chili and cream. It was spicy hot but delicious, and Julie loved it.

"It was wonderful," she said when the waiter took their plates away. "Almost as good as Florida conch chowder. Have you ever had that? It..." Suddenly a terrible gust of wind hit the hotel. The lights went out. The building shook.

In the flickering light of the candle, Julie's eyes looked wide and frightened.

"The storm's getting worse," Rafael said. "I'm afraid we're in for it." And because he knew she was afraid, he said, "This is my first hurricane, but I imagine you've been through them before."

"Hurricane Andrew," she said. "My parents lost our patio room and the laundry room. My mother's clothes dryer shot out through the wall, never to be seen again."

She took a fairly big sip of her wine. "But it was worse in Homestead. That's where it hit the hardest. It flattened everything in its path. I had friends living there. When the storm hit and the house started to go, they barricaded themselves and their three children in the bathroom. The house came down. It just . . . blew away. I saw the place where it had been and I can't imagine how they survived." She looked at him and shook her head. "I know what a hurricane can do. I've seen the destruction it can cause."

He wanted to reach across the table and take her hand, but he didn't. He only said, "We'll be all right and so will Kico. Believe me, Juliana, the hacienda is sturdy enough to withstand a storm much stronger than this one."

"He'll be frightened. I shouldn't have left him."

"You didn't know the storm would hit. Eloisa will be with him. He'll be all right and so will . . ."

A terrible force of wind hit the building. With a screeching wrench, a shutter tore loose. A window shattered and the candles on the tables close to the window went out. Tablecloths, along with the china and glasses that had been set there, were swept to the floor.

Two of the waiters grabbed a table and held it against the window while another ran into the kitchen. He came back with a hammer and a handful of nails. The men struggled to hold the table in place, pushing hard against the wind, which blew like an evil force determined to get into the room and destroy everything in its path.

One of them held a flashlight while the others nailed the table over the window and piled chairs up tight against it.

"That will hold it," one of them said. Another waiter forced a smile. *"No problema,"* he assured the few customers that were still in the room.

Their waiter served the fish. Julie barely touched it, or the dessert of *ate* and cheese. She knew what a hurricane could do and she was afraid, not for herself as much as for Kico. She wanted to be with him, not here in the hotel with his father.

Rafael signed for their supper. "I'll see you to your room," he said. "I brought a flashlight in from the car earlier. We'll need it."

He rose and went around to pull her chair out. What few patrons there had been in the dining room had already left. The waiters were huddled together near the kitchen. Rafael took Julie's arm and led her out into the reception room. The front door had been locked and bolted. The door that led to the patio was closed. In spite of the several candles at the desk, where a lone man sat listening to a battery-powered radio, the room seemed shrouded in darkness.

"Es un ciclón terrible," the man said. "In Morelia, less than an hour's drive from here, *señor,* the winds have reached one hundred and thirty miles an hour. The lights have gone, now the telephones are out." And though it was not cold, he pulled the serape close about his shoulders as though to protect himself.

He offered a candle, then said, "No, no, it will do you no good in this wind. I am sorry. Perhaps it would be better for you and your wife to stay in the dining room tonight.''

Rafael looked at Julie. "No," she said in English. "I'd rather be in my room." She hesitated. "It's upstairs."

"Very well." Rafael took her arm. "We have to go outside to get to the stairs. Stay close to me."

"It is unwise to go out in this," the man behind the reception desk warned. "The storm is dangerous, *señor*. Only God himself knows how long it will last."

"Are you sure you wouldn't rather stay down here?" Rafael asked.

She thought of how the shutter had been blown away, how the window had crashed in, and shook her head. "I think it will be safer upstairs."

"You're probably right." He tightened his hand on her arm. "Let's go."

The clerk came to help Rafael unfasten the door to the patio. "Go!" he shouted above the howl of the wind. "I will close it."

They stepped out into the storm. The wind hit them with a terrible force, taking their breath, and the rain drenched them before they'd taken more than two steps.

Rafael put his arm around Julie's waist and brought her closer. "Hang on to me," he shouted above the roar of the wind.

Heads down, struggling against the force of the wind, they made their way toward the shelter of the stairs. Even there the rain swept in, but they were out of the worst of the wind, at least until they reached the open corridor that led to her room.

Rafael had his arm around her waist, but still the wind almost tore her away from him. He knew now they shouldn't have left the dining room, but it was too late to turn back; they had to go on.

He thrust Julie to the side of the corridor wall and they leaned into the wind, bent over, struggling hard against it.

By the beam of Rafael's flashlight they saw the broken branches and debris that had blown into the wide open corridor. The wind grew in intensity, vicious, dangerous.

"What's the number of your room?" he shouted close to her ear.

"Thirty."

He beamed the flashlight on the sides of the doors they passed. Twenty-seven, twenty-eight. A heavy branch blew past, almost striking them. He pushed Julie against the wall and covered her body with his, while all around them plants and branches, pieces of wood torn off a building and half a shutter whirled and flew by.

Holding Julie close, Rafael struggled on toward her room. He took her key, opened the door and shoved her inside.

It took every bit of his strength to slam the door shut. He leaned his back against it. "Are you all right?" he gasped.

Except for the thin beam of his flashlight they were in total darkness. "Yes," she said. "Yes, I'm all right. I...I didn't think it would be this bad." She panted with the effort to get her breath. "We should have stayed in the dining room."

"It's too late now." He shone the flashlight around the room. When he saw the two small candlesticks and the matches beside them, he went to light the candles.

Then he turned off the flashlight. "We might need it later," he said. "We'd better save the batteries."

We? Of course. He couldn't go out into the storm again. He had to stay here. She found the thought disturbing. On the other hand... A gust of wind rattled the shutters and shook the building and she was glad he was here. She remembered what Hurricane Andrew had done to her friends Dottie and Hal and the incredible devastation she had seen. She thought of Hurricane Donna in 1960, of Camille and other storms that had swept away everything in their path. The 1935 storm that hit the Keys and killed more than two hundred men. She gripped her arms and shivered.

"We'll be all right here." Rafael took off his suit jacket, hung it over the chair and loosened his tie. When he looked at her again he saw that she was trembling, partly from cold, partly from fear.

He said, "Miss Fleming? Juliana? Are you all right?"

Her bare shoulders were wet from the rain. Before he realized what he was doing, he had laid his hands upon them. They were cold to his touch, but smooth. So smooth.

The white blouse clung to her skin and he saw the rise of her breasts pressed against the wet material. And the nipples, like small pebbles, hard because of the cold. He tightened his hands on her shoulders. He knew she wore nothing under the blouse and the desire to touch her breasts was so overwhelming it took his breath. He should let her go, step back, turn away. But he didn't.

He cupped a hand around the back of her so slender neck and drew her closer.

"Señor Vega, please."

"Please what?"

"Let me go."

"Say my name and perhaps I will."

She looked up at him. His face was shadowed by the flickering glow of the candles. His eyes were dark. So dark.

"Say my name," he whispered.

"Rafael."

He sighed, and before she could move away, he cradled her head between his hands and held her so that she could not move at all. He took her cool lips. Her mouth was honey sweet.

She tried to turn her head, but he held her there. He licked the corners of her mouth and ran his tongue across her lower lip. He kissed her again and again. His mouth was warm, his lips were firm.

"Part your lips for me," he murmured. "Let me taste you." And when she wouldn't, he pressed his mouth against hers and took what he wanted.

The hands that had reached to push him away faltered. His mouth was so hot, his tongue so persistent.

She trembled and her mouth softened under his. And when it did he began to kiss her with great tenderness. He explored the warmth of her mouth and a bright hot flame shot through him and he knew he didn't ever want to stop kissing her.

He nibbled at the corners of her lips, he sucked at her tongue, and when his mouth left hers, he rained kisses across her closed eyes, her nose, her cheeks.

He couldn't get enough of her. He wanted more, so much more.

His hands slid down to her shoulders. He eased her blouse down, and all the while he kissed her mouth.

She felt weak in his arms, powerless to move away. Her body was on fire, and when he urged her closer, she pressed against him and felt a thrill of excitement when he gasped with pleasure.

The raging wind that threatened to topple the building didn't matter. Nothing mattered. Only Rafael. She was lost in him, in the feel of his mouth on hers, in the strength of the arms that held her. Only when his hot hands cupped her breasts did she realize that he had pulled her blouse down to her waist. She tried to move away from him then, but he wouldn't let her go.

"No," he murmured against her lips. "I have to do this. You're so soft, Juliana. So sweet."

He ran his hands over the rounded flesh. He squeezed a nipple between his fingers, and when she cried aloud he took her cry into his mouth.

"This is madness."

"I know." She clung to him. "I know."

He ran his thumb across her other nipple, and when she moaned and moved against him, he went wild with need. Without taking his mouth from hers, he backed toward the bed. He sat on the edge of it and with his hands around her waist drew her close and buried his face against her breasts.

Outside the storm raged. He heard the scream of the wind, the slash of the rain. He didn't care if the whole hotel blew away. All that mattered was the feel of Juliana in his arms.

He rubbed his face back and forth against the fullness of her breasts, and though she tried to get away, he wouldn't let her go. He took a nipple in his mouth, scraped it with his teeth and lapped it with his tongue.

Though only a moment ago she had tried to push him away, now she held him there, her hands in the thick dampness of his hair. He sucked hard at her nipple, all the while caressing her other breast with his fingers.

Her whispered sighs and moans added fuel to his passion. He drew her closer, breathing fast because he knew he had to have her. She'd told him at dinner that all her clothes had been wet. She was naked to the waist; he knew she wore nothing beneath the long Indian skirt.

He pulled her onto his lap. He covered her mouth with his and began to caress her bare leg.

"We have to stop," Julie whispered. "We can't do this." Then he kissed her and she clung to him, holding him as he held her, melting against him, lost in his kisses, in his warmth. His touch was so strong, so sure. Never before had she felt this kind of heat, this all-consuming desire. It would be so easy to surrender to the sweet urgings of her body. So easy.

He cupped her bare breast, and when he did she began to struggle with the buttons of his shirt. A button popped, the fabric tore. She touched his bare skin and now it was he who moaned into her mouth. "Juliana. Juliana."

Her fingers clutched around the mat of his chest hair and encircled his nipples with her fingertips. He strained against her and the hand on her thigh crept upward.

She was lost. It was too late to retreat, too late...

Something crashed against the bedroom window. The shutters flew open. The window shattered and glass sprayed into the room. Rafael let her go and ran to close the shutters. More glass cracked. A shard of it sliced the palm of his hand. He swore but managed to get the shutters closed again. Broken glass crunched under his feet.

"Your hand," Julie cried. "It's bleeding." She ran into the bathroom for two facecloths. He held his hand up. The blood ran down his arm. She pressed one cloth tight against the cut to try to stop the bleeding.

"It's nothing," he said. "I'm all right."

She wrapped the other cloth around his hand and tied it.

They didn't look at each other.

"You'd better get into some dry clothes," he said.

"I . . . I don't have any. My other clothes aren't dry yet."

He pulled the blue cotton bedspread from one of the twin beds and handed it to her. "Take your clothes off and wrap this around you." She hesitated and he said, "It's going to be a long night, Juliana. You can't sit here in wet clothes."

Neither can you, she almost said. But didn't. She knew the danger they were in, not from the storm, but from each other. If the window hadn't broken, if the glass hadn't shattered . . .

She took the spread from him and one of the candles and went into the bathroom. She slipped off the blouse, which she'd quickly pulled back up over her breasts, and the skirt and got into the shower. It was barely warm. She pressed her hands against the side of the stall and took deep, shaking breaths. What had she almost done? Dear God, what had she almost done?

When she came out of the shower she dried herself, then wrapped the cotton bedspread sarong-fashion around her body.

Rafael was sitting on the edge of one of the beds when she came out. He'd taken off his shirt, his wet socks and his shoes. He looked at her, then quickly away.

"Will the candles last?" she asked.

"We'll only use one." He blew the other out and now there was only a small corner of light. He lay back on one of the beds, hands clasped over his chest. "It's late, Juliana," he said without looking at her. "You'd better try to get some sleep."

She came across the room, holding the spread around her body, and sat on the other bed. "What time is it?" she asked.

He glanced at his watch. "One-fifteen." He looked over at her. "How long do these things usually last?"

"It depends. It will probably go on until morning."

"I tied the shutter with my tie. I think it will hold. We'll be all right."

His voice sounded matter-of-fact, impersonal. It was as though what had passed between them a little while ago had never happened.

Julie looked at the hands that rested across his bare chest. Beautiful hands. Strong hands with long, well-shaped fingers. She thought of the way they had felt on her skin, stroking her breasts, her thigh.

She had thought him a cold man, devoid of emotion. But oh, he wasn't cold. There was a fire in him, and a tenderness that surprised her.

The rain beat hard against the roof. The wind howled. Something slammed against the door and she cried out, remembering Hurricane Andrew, her friends Dottie and Hal and how they had barely survived.

The storm was at its worst now. This was the peak, the most dangerous time, with the wind shrieking like a woman in pain and the rain pounding hard against the shutter.

She sat up, her eyes wide, frightened.

"Juliana?" Rafael swung his legs over the side of his bed.

"The wind," she said. "It's bad, worse than I thought."

He heard the fear in her voice and knew she needed whatever comfort, whatever assurance, he could give her.

He went to her bed and put his arms around her. "It will be all right," he said.

Julie clung to him, arms around his bare shoulders, hanging on as though he alone could save her from the storm.

"I'm here," he said. "I'm here."

He lay down on the bed, taking her with him, and when she protested, he said, "Sh, sh, it's all right, Juliana. I won't let anything happen to you."

He held her as though she were a child, held and soothed her, and at last her body relaxed against his. When she looked up at him, he kissed her forehead and said, "Rest now, *querida*. I'm right here with you."

And at last her eyes closed and she slept.

But Rafael didn't. The heat in his body, though it had lessened, still burned. He ached with wanting her, and though he knew he shouldn't have let this happen between them, he could not be sorry that he had kissed her or touched her.

He felt the brush of her hair against his face and kissed the top of her head. Lord, but she felt good in his arms. So good. The blue bedspread had slipped down and in the faint candlelight he saw the sweet rise of her breasts.

He wanted to touch her again, but he didn't. He only held her, and at last he, too, slept.

CHAPTER SEVEN

It was the silence that woke Julie. She was too warm, bound up in something so tightly she could barely move. She struggled out of it, remembering the storm. And Rafael.

With a start she touched the space next to her on the bed. But he wasn't there. She was alone.

She fumbled for her watch and found instead a note. Sitting up, she pushed the pillows behind her and read.

> The storm has passed. It's six-thirty. I'll wait for you in the dining room between eight and eight-thirty. There's broken glass in the room. Put on your shoes before you get up.

She closed her eyes and tried to assimilate her thoughts. God knows she needed time to sort them out. Still in that state of being half asleep and half awake, she remembered the feel of his hands on her shoulders, his kiss and the way she responded to him. If the window hadn't shattered she knew they would have made love. She also knew that the consequences would have been devastating.

He'd wanted her, yet because he'd sensed how frightened she had been of the storm, he had lain beside her all through the night. He had held her and soothed her; he had made no attempt to make love to her.

What manner of man was he? One moment so cold, so remote. The next, loving and tender.

Still, in the clear light of day it seemed impossible that she had behaved the way she had, that she'd been all too ready to make love with him. The thought of it, of how it might have been, weakened her insides and made her heart beat faster.

With a smothered sigh, she tried to turn on the bedside light, but the electricity was still out. Her watch read seven forty-five. She got up and hurried into the shower. The water was cold, and though she hated cold showers, it helped wake her up and clear her mind so that she felt better when she came out and toweled herself dry.

She dressed in the clothes she had worn yesterday and put the blouse and skirt in the bag they'd come in. Then she ran a comb through her hair and picked up the mascara. When she did she looked at herself in the bathroom mirror, as though expecting that she had somehow changed. She looked the same, but she knew that in some inexplicable way she was not the same. She touched the lips Rafael had kissed and felt them tremble under her fingertips.

She whispered into the mirror, "Rafael," and her body warmed with remembered passion.

What had she done? What was she doing? She knew so little about him; she wasn't even sure she liked him. Yet when he touched her last night she had been ready for his kiss. His kiss.

With a sigh, Julie turned away from the mirror.

* * *

He sat at a table by the now unshuttered windows. The sky looked gray and heavy with threatening rain, but the wind had stopped.

Juliana came to the door of the dining room and stood for a moment as though reluctant to enter, slender and lovely in an apple green summery dress. Her hair, as always, had that tousled, flyaway look. His body tightened with remembered need. If it hadn't been for the shattered window they would have made love last night. It would have been a mistake.

As she came toward him he saw the rise of color in her cheeks, and he felt an unexpected tenderness because she looked so young, so unsure of herself. And because he knew she, too, remembered.

He stood. "Good morning," he said, and went around the table to pull a chair out for her.

"Good morning." The color in her cheeks deepened. A tentative smile curved her lips. "I...I guess the storm has passed. Where is it now?"

"Losing strength as it moves overland. We're going to have rain though so I'd like to get back to the island as soon as we can." He motioned to the waiter. "Coffee for the *señorita, por favor.*"

"How's your hand?" She indicated the bandage across his palm.

"It's all right."

They ordered. She wondered what time he'd left her room but was too embarrassed to ask. Her coffee came. She stirred and stirred and looked out of the window. Everywhere except at him.

They had eggs over tortillas with *frijoles,* all of it covered with hot salsa. Her embarrassment forgotten, she ate with an enthusiasm that made him smile. She might look delicate, but she had an appetite like a field hand.

Margarita had never come down for breakfast. She preferred to have it served in her room, dry toast, black tea.

They weren't at all alike. Margarita had been a cool beauty, a beauty he could touch only by invitation.

It hadn't been like that at first. He had thought her the most sensual woman he'd ever seen. His artist's eye had been attracted to her from the moment they met at a banquet given for him by the president of Mexico at the Casino Militar. He had been commissioned by the government to do a bust of Benito Juarez. Upon its completion and unveiling in Alameda Park, the president had awarded him a gold medal.

"In recognition and appreciation of your art," the president declared as he pinned the beribboned medal on Rafael's chest that night at the banquet.

Margarita had come up to him later to offer her congratulations. He'd known she was an actress of course, and he'd been flattered by her attention. When the orchestra played he asked her to dance. And later he asked her to have dinner with him the following night.

They saw each other every night and at the end of two weeks he asked her to marry him.

"Marriage?" She'd laughed. "Darling, that's so old-fashioned."

He persisted until she said yes. And though he had wanted her so badly his teeth ached, he had not attempted to make love to her. This was the woman he had waited all his life for. There was something sacred in his love for her, and though he wanted her, he also wanted their relationship to be more than just sexual.

She'd laughed when he told her how he felt, and with very little finesse she seduced him.

A month later they were married and he brought her home to Janitzio.

Margarita hated the island, and as the months passed he had a feeling she hated him for taking her there. She began to punish him, in small ways at first.

"That's an absurd sculpture of Franco," she said of the bust the Spanish government had asked him to do. "His nose is too big and his eyes are too small." She'd scraped a long fingernail down the center of the clay, then turned and laughed at him over her shoulder. "Really, Rafael, it's quite inferior."

Six months after their marriage she moved into a different bedroom. "I hate sleeping with anyone," she'd said. "Your body's too warm. I hate it when you're all over me."

She began leaving the island at regular intervals. He didn't suspect anything at first because he knew she had friends in Mexico City, movie people she'd worked with before, directors, producers, actors. He didn't particularly like them, nor did he like her spending so much time with them. But he told himself the island was confining, she would settle down when they had a child.

When she returned from one of the trips he said, "It's time we started thinking about having a family."

"A family?" She'd looked at him incredulously. "Surely you're not serious, Rafael."

When he assured her that he was, she all but laughed in his face. "I'm thinking about making another film," she said. "I don't want to lose my figure."

Nevertheless, two years later Kico was born.

Without conscious thought, Rafael picked up the unused fork beside his plate and jabbed his thumb against the tines, hard, hurting, again and again, pressing it into the ball of his thumb so that his pain would make him forget the other pain.

Julie stared at him. His expression was remote, tortured. He seemed to be in another place, another time. In a moment the tines of the fork would pierce his skin. She reached across the table, pried his thumb away and with her other hand took the fork from him.

He looked at her, his face twisted by anger, his eyes dark with a rage she didn't understand. She pulled back, suddenly afraid. "What...what is it?" she whispered.

He didn't answer; it was almost as though he didn't recognize her. She saw the muscles of his shoulders bunch. His body tightened, coiled as though ready to spring.

"Rafael?" She said his name softly. "Rafael?"

A sigh shuddered through him. "Sorry," he said, and turned his face to the window.

Julie waited. "What is it?" she said at last. "Can I help?"

"Not you, not anybody." He motioned to the waiter for more coffee, and when it had been poured he took a swallow. "I was thinking about Margarita. I'm sorry." He hesitated. "I told you she drowned?"

"Yes, you told me. That must have been terrible for you. You must have loved her very much."

He looked at her with the cold, bitter eyes of a stranger. "No," he said. "I think I hated her." He shoved his chair back from the table. "Are you ready? Do you need anything from the room?"

Julie felt frozen, unable to move, shocked by the coldness in his voice, yet filled with sympathy for him. What had made him look the way he did? Did he feel that in some way he had been responsible for Margarita's death? But he'd said he had dived overboard after her, that he'd tried to find her.

"Well?"

Julie stared up at him.

"Do you have everything?" he asked again. "Or do you have to go up to your room?"

"No, I . . . I have everything."

He took her arm. She flinched but did not step away.

"One of the men in the parking lot will drive us to the dock. I keep my car here at the hotel so whenever I have to leave it's available."

They went out to the patio. It had started to rain. Smashed flowerpots, ruined plants and broken branches were strewn all about. One of the orange trees had been felled, the tin barbecue braziers had been overturned and the patio floor was awash with water.

Rafael hurried Julie out to the parking lot and led her to an overhang of roof. He spoke to one of the men. When the man nodded, Rafael said, "Agustín will drive us."

They got into the car. It was big and sleek and black. Of course.

Agustín said, "I am not sure the boats will be running today, Señor Vega."

"Then I'll hire someone to take us."

"The water will still be rough from the storm and the rain is getting worse. It is better you wait another day."

"No, that's impossible. We have to get back to Janitzio."

They drove to the pier. All of the launches were tied to the dock. "Wait here," Rafael told Julie and the driver.

He walked out onto the pier, unmindful of the rain, and down to where the launches waited. Several men were there, bailing out their boats, trying to repair torn canvas.

"We want to go to Janitzio," Rafael said to one of them.

"No boats today, *señor.*"

"I'll pay whatever you ask."

"It would not be enough," another man said.

Rafael swore. "Look," he went on. "This is important."

A different man came out from under the canvas cover of one of the boats. "A little while ago I saw Pedro working on that old tub of his. He's just crazy enough to take you."

"Where is he?"

One of the men pointed down the pier. "There, you see? The motorboat?" He laughed. "It's older than Pedro. If I were you I wouldn't think about going out in it."

Rafael thanked the men and hurried down the pier to where the boat they had indicated bobbed up and down on the water. It was a small craft and looked as if it had seen better days. So did the man on it.

"*Buenos días,*" Rafael said. "I see your boat survived the storm."

"Just barely, *señor.* The mast is broken, but the motor still runs."

"Well enough to get me to Janitzio?"

The old man peered up at Rafael through the rain. He shook his head. "I would not venture out onto the lake today if the most beautiful woman in Mexico was waiting for me in Janitzio.''

"Then will you rent me the boat?"

Old Pedro scratched his whiskered chin. "You know how to run her?"

"Of course. And I'll see that she's safely tied up once I get to Janitzio."

"She is very valuable to me, *señor.*"

"Two hundred pesos," Rafael said.

"Three."

"*Hecho,* done." Rafael counted out the bills. "Wait here, I'll be right back."

He ran back through the rain to the car. "I've arranged for a boat," he told Julie.

"One of the launches?" Agustín asked.

"No, a private boat." He took Julie's arm. "I'm afraid you're going to get wet again."

"Once more won't hurt."

"Take care of the car," he told Agustín. Then together he and Julie ran down the pier and he helped her down the steps to the boat.

"This is it?" It was small, not more than fifteen feet, weather-beaten, with an inch of water on the bottom. It didn't look as though it would stay afloat in a fish pond, let alone the turbulent waters of the lake.

She turned to Rafael. "The wind has started up again," she said doubtfully.

"The trip is short. We'll be all right."

The man Pedro held his hand up to her. "She's a worthy craft, *señorita.* Weathered storms worse than old Jezebel. You and the gentleman will be in Janitzio in no time at all."

Julie stepped into the boat and felt the muddy water squoosh into her sandals. Rafael came down beside her. The old man said, "Don't give her too much throttle. Ride her easy into the waves."

Julie stared at him. "You're not going with us?"

"No, *señorita*. I wouldn't go out on the lake today for all the money in Texas." He hoisted himself out of the boat and scrambled onto the dock. "I'll have somebody take me over when the weather clears. There's a tarp under the seat you can cover her up with."

Julie looked at Rafael. "Maybe we should wait," she said. But he had already turned to start the motor.

It coughed, sputtered. At last it caught and they lumbered out onto the lake. The waves picked the little boat up and tossed it back and forth as though it were a toy.

The board that served as a seat was wet and dirty, so Julie stood, hanging on to the broken mast. By now she was drenched from the rain and from the waves that washed over the boat. Her hands were cold, the mast was slippery. She wanted to get back to Kico as quickly as Rafael did, but this was insane. They should never have tried to cross.

The boat hit a high wave, crested it and hung as though suspended before crashing down on the other side.

"Hang on," Rafael said. "It's going to be rougher than I imagined."

Julie looked out at the threatening waves and the words of Alicia's warning, "Be careful or you'll end up at the bottom of the lake," echoed in her ears. She tightened her hand around the mast and looked down under the seat. There was the tarp, but that was all. There were no life preservers.

The wind blew Rafael's hair back from his broad forehead. His eyes were narrowed against the wind and there was an expression on his face she had never seen before. Was he remembering another boat, another storm?

Suddenly Julie was afraid, not just of the storm but of him. Margarita had died on a day like this. She'd gone over the side, down into the roiling water. And she had drowned.

A wave smashed into the boat and the small craft tilted hard to the right. Julie lost her grip on the broken mast, staggered, tried to regain her balance and reached for something, anything, to hang on to. She screamed out in fear. Rafael turned and started toward her, hand open, fingers spread. Rain slashed across his face, but she saw his eyes, dark, dark as the roiling water.

She backed away. He reached for her. The boat lurched. She felt herself slipping. And screamed just before she fell backward over the side.

She went down, down into water so deep and dark it was difficult for her to see. She fought her way to the surface, kicking hard, lungs struggling for air. When she broke through she saw Rafael only a few feet away. He swam hard, but before he could reach her another wave crashed over her head and carried her down into the murky depths of the lake.

This was how Margarita had drowned. Dear God...

She kicked hard and fought her way to the surface. Rafael grabbed her.

"No!" she cried, and struggled to break free.

He tightened his hold. "Don't fight me," he shouted over the roar of wind and rain.

But Julie was past hearing, past reason. She fought to get away from him, freed one hand and struck out at him. He dodged her blow but kept hold of her. "What in the hell are you..." he began. Another wave crashed over their heads and they went under together.

She felt his body against hers and the hard strength of his legs wrapped around her. She opened her eyes and through the murky darkness saw his face close to hers. Saw the look of horror, of desperation, in his eyes.

They came back to the surface. He had one arm over her shoulders, holding her. With the last bit of her strength she tried to break free and he hit her. Everything went dark. The thought, Like Margarita, Like Margarita, screamed inside her head.

Julie lay stretched, belly down, on the board seat of the boat. Something pushed against her back. Lifted her arms then pushed. Lifted then pushed. She coughed and vomited water.

Rafael picked her up, bent her over double and smacked her back with the palm of his hand. More water came up.

"You're all right," he said. "We're almost there."

He shoved her down to the bottom of the boat, then started the motor. "Hang on," he shouted above the cry of the wind.

She knelt in the inch-deep dirty water, shivering so hard her teeth chattered. Ten minutes went by. Fifteen. At last the boat bumped the dock.

He lifted her out. Someone ran out onto the pier. "Cover the boat with the tarp," Rafael said, then turned and, with Julie in his arms, raced up the pier to one of the open-air restaurants.

"Whiskey," he said to the woman there. "Do you have whiskey?"

"Nada más que tequila, señor."

"Bring it."

She ran behind the counter. "Ay, *señor,* what happened? The lady is wet. Did she fall into the water?"

He took the bottle of tequila without answering and held it to Julie's lips. "Drink," he said.

She couldn't stop shivering. She tried to drink the tequila but the bottle jarred against her teeth and the fiery liquid ran down her chin.

"I've got to get her out of these wet clothes," he told the woman. "Do you have something she can wear?"

"Sí, Señor Vega. Come with me into the back."

He carried Julie through the store into a small bedroom and put her on the bed.

"Undress the lady while I find something," the woman said.

"No," Julie whispered. But Rafael didn't listen. He lifted her arms and pulled the green summer dress over her head. He reached around and unfastened her bra, made her lie down while he took off her sandals, then her panties.

The woman handed him a towel. "I will call the doctor," she said.

"Tell him to meet me at the Vega hacienda."

He dried Julie, rubbing so hard to bring the circulation back into her arms and legs that she winced.

"Here is a dress, *señor.* It is not a good one, but it will cover her."

Everything became a blur. Rafael carried her outside. The rain had stopped. People stared. It didn't matter. She felt ill, weak. Her head bobbed on his shoulder. He breathed hard from the effort of climbing with her in his arms. She felt the thump of his heart against her cheek and faded in and out of consciousness.

Into the house and up the stairs. A glimpse of Kico's frightened face. The narrowed eyes and knowing look of Alicia Fernandez.

Eloisa undressed her. A man she had never seen before put a stethoscope against her chest and felt her arms and legs.

"A nasty scrape on her leg," he said. "Probably hit the side of the boat when she fell overboard. She's suffering from shock. Needs to rest and keep warm. I'll give her something to relax her."

The prick of a needle in her arm. Drifting. Silence. She thought she was alone, but he was there in the shadows of the room. He leaned over her. He said her name, "Juliana."

And she was lost in the darkness of his eyes.

CHAPTER EIGHT

The next two days passed in a surreal haze of semi-consciousness. Once Julie opened her eyes and saw Rafael standing beside her bed. She whispered his name, then everything faded, everything except for the dark eyes that seemed to look into her very soul.

Alicia came in and stood at the foot of her bed. Arms folded over her narrow chest, she said, "What a terrible experience." But there was no hint of sympathy or compassion in her voice, only malice.

"You almost drowned, didn't you?" Her head swayed from side to side like the flat head of a cobra. "Just like Margarita," she whispered.

Julie woke only when Eloisa brought her meals and helped her bathe. She slept and dreamed terrible dreams, reliving again and again that terrible moment when the dark water had closed over her head. In her dreams Margarita whispered to her, "Come deeper, Juliana. Follow me. Follow me."

Each time she woke her body was as cold as the waters of the lake had been.

Rafael had saved her life. She had to thank him and tell him she was sorry that when they had gone beneath the surface of that dark and swirling water and he'd wound his legs around hers she had panicked. She'd struck out at him, fighting, she thought, for her life.

In the clear light of day she told herself it was fear of drowning that had made her imagine such a terrible thing, but when the dark and lonely night came, she remembered Margarita. Margarita had been alone in a boat with Rafael, as she, Julie, had been. Margarita, too, had gone over the side. It had taken three days to find her body.

Fear gripped her then because she knew and felt what Margarita must have known and felt when the water closed over her head. What had her thoughts been in those last few moments of her life? Had she struggled? When the dark roiling water filled her nose and her mouth, had she tried to scream for help? For him?

There in the midnight shadows the terror came. She told herself there was nothing to fear. She was safe in bed in Rafael's home. Nothing could harm her here.

She slept to dream again, a dream that in its own way was just as disturbing as the other had been. She was in the water, but this time the water wasn't cold, it was as warm and as soft as liquid velvet against her skin. Rafael was with her, holding her. He drew her close and touched her breasts with slick-wet hands. She whispered his name into his mouth. She said, "Make love with me. Make love with me."

And awoke, her body heated and trembling.

How could she fear him, yet be attracted to him? She didn't understand, she only knew that it was true. She was beginning to fall in love with Rafael Vega.

She longed to see him, yet was afraid to see him.

She need not have worried; he made no attempt to see her.

On the fourth day after the accident, Julie felt well enough to get out of bed and take a shower. When

Eloisa brought her breakfast, Julie said, "Put the tray here on the table by the windows."

"But do you feel well enough to be up, *señorita?*"

"Yes, thank you, Eloisa. After breakfast I thought I might take a walk outside. It's a beautiful day."

"It has been like this since the hurricane passed. One would never know a storm had come our way." She took the plate of fruit, the cheese omelet and the warm croissants and put them on the table in front of Julie. "Kico has been longing to see you," she said. "Perhaps if you feel well enough he could come in later."

"Of course. Tell him I'd love to see him."

"He's just outside the door." Eloise smiled and motioned for Kiko to enter, but he stood for a moment as though afraid. "Go on," Eloise said, and motioning him into the room, she left.

"Hi, Kico." Julie held out her arms. "How about *un abrazo,* a hug?"

He came toward her. "Are you all right?"

"Yes, sweetie, I'm fine." She put her arms around him. "I missed you so much," she said.

Small arms came up to encircle her neck. He leaned his face against hers and she kissed his cheek.

When she let him go, he said, "You fell in the lake, didn't you?"

"Yes, I'm afraid I did."

"Like Mama. Only you didn't drown." He looked down at his shoes. "Is it dark down there?" he asked in a voice hushed with fear. "Did you see my mama?"

For a moment Julie was too stunned to speak, then she said, "Your mother isn't in the lake, Kico."

"Yes, she is." A shiver ran through his body. "Is it cold down there?"

Julie put her arms around him again and drew him close. "Yes," she said, trying to speak matter-of-factly, "the water was pretty cold. But your father pulled me out, and as soon as I got dry I was warm again." She tilted his chin up. "Your father's a very brave man, Kico. And a good swimmer, too. He towed me back to the boat as though I didn't weigh anything at all."

She let him go. "How about having breakfast with me?" She spread some strawberry jam on one of the croissants and handed it to him.

His face brightened. He took a bite and the moment passed.

But she couldn't forget the way he had looked, how his small face had pinched with remembered fear because he thought his mother was still in the lake. Hadn't there been a funeral? Hadn't he seen his mother's grave? She had to tell Rafael that Kico needed help to get over the trauma of his mother's death. More help than she could give him.

Rafael wasn't at breakfast the following morning, nor did he appear when she and Kico were having lunch. But that night when she went into the dining room he was seated in his chair at the head of the table.

He stood when she entered. "Good evening," he said. "I hope you're feeling better."

"Yes, much better, thank you," she replied, although her face was still pale and she looked thinner.

She smiled a hello to Kico. "We had our lessons today," she said. "Kico is doing awfully well. I'm very proud of him."

"The lessons can wait. There's no need to tax yourself. Take a few more days off."

"No, I'm all right, really." She looked at Rafael, then away. "There are only a few weeks left before Kico goes away to school," she said in a quiet voice. "Before I leave to return to Guadalajara."

It was the last week of July. The boy would leave for school in the States in another three weeks. And Juliana... He took a deep breath. She, too, would be gone. That, though he didn't want to admit it, gave him pause. He'd grown accustomed to her. In some ways it was as if she'd always been here, a part of his household. A part of his life.

But she wasn't a part of his life and she never could be. It was just as well she was leaving, both she and the boy. With the house to himself he could concentrate on his work.

He'd started on something new, and to his surprise it seemed to be going exceptionally well, better than he had expected. For the first time in a long time he felt the power coming back into his hands, the power to create, to make something come alive from a piece of clay.

It had been a long time, more than two years, since he'd had that feeling. It was like being given a second chance. He didn't know why the power had come back to him, he only knew that it had and that he was obsessed with it. It was all he thought about, all he wanted to do.

It had been a little like that in the beginning, back in his Paris days when all of the creative juices had flowed strong and sure and he'd known with an absolute certainty how good he was.

But even in his Paris days he had never been as passionate about a piece of work as he was about this. He couldn't leave it alone. Though his eyes burned and his body ached with fatigue he could not stay away from it. He wanted to work twenty-four hours a day and he almost did. He had no need for sleep or sustenance. He lived on coffee and an occasional sandwich, and for the past four days he'd worked through the night, falling asleep at dawn and sleeping for an hour or two on the sofa in the studio.

The work possessed him, it was all he thought about. When he had to leave it to sleep or to eat his fingers itched to be back with the clay. The work became an extension of himself. It consumed his waking hours, he dreamed of it when he slept. If he never did a worthwhile thing again, this piece alone would have satisfied him.

He hadn't gone near Juliana, but she was here now and he could get his fill of looking at her. Juliana, so pale, so beautiful.

He remembered the night of the hurricane. How small and unbelievably delicate she had felt in his arms, how warm and sweetly passionate. Her breasts had fit so perfectly in his hands, and she had gasped with pleasure when he touched them.

In another few weeks she would leave and it was better that she did. But he knew, as surely as he knew his name, that he would always remember the way it had been in those few brief moments while the hurricane raged all around them.

As soon as they finished dinner, Kico asked to be excused. "Eloisa and I play dominoes," he said. "Last night I beat her."

"All right," Rafael said, dismissing him. "You can play until it's time for bed."

"Let me know when you're ready," Julie said. "It's been a while since I've tucked you in."

When the boy went into the kitchen, Rafael stood and said, "Come outside with me for a few minutes. I'd like to talk to you."

He helped her up from her chair and led her out to the patio and over to a promontory where they could look down to the lights of the harbor.

A half-moon shone overhead. She could see the harbor below and a launch that had just pulled away from the dock.

"Everything looks so quiet after the storm," she mused. "It's as if the hurricane never happened." She lifted her shoulders and with a smile said, "Jezebel, a wicked, wicked woman." Then the smile faded and her expression grew serious. "I haven't thanked you, Rafael. You risked your life to save me and I'll never forget it. Thank you is such a small word, but I do thank you. If it hadn't been for you..." She shivered and when she did he clasped her upper arms.

"It's over," he said. "Don't think about it."

"I can't help it. Sometimes at night..." She shook her head. "I was so afraid," she said.

"Of me." The hands on her arms tightened. "I saw your face when you started to fall, Juliana. I saw the fear in your eyes."

"No!" she protested. "No, I—"

"That's why you backed away from me when I reached for you. That's why you fought me when I tried to bring you in. You didn't think I meant to save you, you thought I wanted to drown you." His eyes darkened. "Margarita drowned in a storm like that, and you thought..."

"Let me go," she cried, suddenly afraid.

"You still believe it," he said. "You actually believe I wanted to harm you."

She struggled to break free. "It was the fear of the water, the storm . . ."

"Liar!" He glared down at her and she recoiled, terrified of the harsh anger she saw in his eyes, of the hands that held her and would not let her go.

"Damn you," he said and covered her mouth with his.

There was no gentleness in him now. His kiss was overpoweringly masculine, rough and powerful. He took her mouth as if he had every right to, as if she belonged to him and he could do whatever he wanted with her.

She pushed hard against his chest, but he wouldn't let her go. With a muttered curse he clamped his teeth on her lower lip and when she cried out he slipped his tongue into her mouth. She fought against him, fought even when her lips parted. With a strangled sigh she raised her arms around his shoulders and her body swayed against his.

He pressed his hands against the small of her back to force her closer. She came, willingly, eagerly, her mouth soft against his.

He told himself he didn't want her softness. Even as his tongue dueled with hers, even as he pressed her nearer and felt heat surge through his body, he told himself he didn't need this, didn't need her. But God help him, he did need her, needed her with a desperation that shook him to the very depths of his being.

She whispered his name, "Rafael," and he thought he would die from wanting her. But he couldn't, it wouldn't be fair to her. He had to stop. Had to . . .

With every ounce of his willpower he held her away from him. "No." His voice choked with emotion. "No."

Julie stepped back. "What is it?" she whispered.

"Leave me," he said.

"I...I don't understand. What is it? Please tell me."

He turned his back on her. "This was a mistake," he said. "Before in Patzcuaro. And now. A mistake."

Julie held out her hand, as though to touch him, then with a strangled cry she turned and and ran back into the house.

He stared down at the lights below. "Juliana," he whispered into the night. "Juliana."

He gave instructions to Alicia Fernández that he was not to be disturbed. "I'm working on a new project," he said. "I want no phone calls, no interruptions."

He worked almost without stopping. When his eyes became so blurry he could barely see, he slept for an hour or two. He showered when he thought of it but did not shave. When hunger came, he picked up the phone and called the kitchen to ask for more coffee.

This was the best work he'd ever done. He could feel the life flowing from his hands into the work. It controlled him, obsessed him. It was all he thought about. His whole being, everything he was, everything he hoped to be, became filled with it. The clay became life, and he the life-giver.

A week went by. Ten days. He did not see the boy or her. This, his work, was all that mattered. He would not stop until it was done.

Julie asked Alicia about Rafael. "Kico misses him," she said. "Can't he at least have dinner with us?"

"Señor Vega is not to be disturbed." She smiled her thin, tight smile. "You don't understand how important his work is to him, do you? It's his life. It's all that matters."

"And his son?" Julie asked indignantly. "What about Kico? Surely he can spare him an hour or two."

"Not now," Alicia said firmly. "When the work is done he will have time for the boy."

The boy. What was the matter with these people? The boy had a name. Why couldn't Alicia or his father call him by his name?

She didn't understand Rafael. He could be gentle and kind, as he had been that night during the storm. She thought, as she had so many times before, of the way it had been that night when Rafael had kissed her. And later, here in his home, in the moonlight.

There was such passion in him, a passion that he held in check as he held all of his other emotions in check, as though afraid that if he let go, something terrible would happen. She didn't understand him or the feelings she experienced when she was with him.

She did her best to keep Kico occupied. They worked hard on his English, and when the lessons were over they went on long walks together. One day they climbed to the top of the hill to see the statue of Morelos. They even climbed up inside the statue, up the winding stairway, where they could look out over the lake.

On other days they wandered down into the village to have lunch at one of the open-air restaurants. It was on one of the excursions that Kico caught a cold. They'd just finished eating when the first spatter of rain caught them. By the time they reached the hacienda the rain had turned into a thunderstorm.

Kico sneezed several times that night at dinner, and by the next morning he had a temperature of almost a hundred and three.

Rafael had left instructions that he was not to be disturbed, but Kico was ill. That had to be Julie's first consideration.

She left Kico's room with the promise that she would be right back and hurried down the open corridor toward the other wing, where Rafael had his studio.

"Where do you think you're going?" Alicia stepped into the corridor from the patio just as Julie rounded the corner.

"Kico is ill. I'm going to get Señor Vega."

"He's not to be disturbed." Alicia moved in front of Julie as though to physically stop her from going any farther. "I'll call the doctor," she said. "It isn't necessary to bother Señor Vega."

"Bother him?" Julie stared at the other woman. "Kico is his son. Of course he'll want to know the boy is ill."

"I'll take care of it," Alicia insisted. "There's no need to interrupt Señor Vega when he's working."

Julie, hands on her hips, glared at the other woman. "Lady," she said in English. "If you don't get out of my way right now I'm going to punch you in the nose."

Though Alicia spoke no English, her eyes widened and she stepped back a pace.

"Call the doctor," Julie snapped. With that she stepped around Alicia and headed for Rafael's studio.

She hurried past what might have been a sewing room, a bedroom, a small library lined with floor-to-ceiling bookshelves filled with leather-bound books. When she reached the end of the corridor she saw a tall wooden door and stopped. Rafael wouldn't like being disturbed, but surely when he knew the reason it would be all right.

She lifted her hand and knocked. When there was no answer she knocked again, harder this time. But still he did not answer. She hesitated a moment, then turned the knob and went in.

He stood before the clay figure of a woman, studying it with an intensity of expression that silenced her as she was about to call his name. His jeans were spattered with clay and red clay water. So was his bare chest. He was barefoot. He needed a shave.

The figure, perhaps four feet tall, was beautiful in its nudity, its breathtaking symmetry and cleanness of line. As she watched, Rafael reached out and touched the statue's face. As gently as if with a lover's caress, he traced her forehead and her cheeks and ran the tips of his fingers over her mouth.

Julie took a step closer, mesmerized, unable to look away as he encircled the delicate throat and lingered over the shoulders, molding them with his hands. He stroked down over the breasts, as if by his touch he could make them warm and soft, flesh and blood.

The breath caught in Julie's throat, for this was more than a sculptor molding clay, this was a man giving life and love to a woman. His dark eye were filled with desire as he touched her, tenderly, sensuously.

Silently, scarcely daring to breathe, Julie moved closer.

Clay-wet hands caressed the rounded breasts, the small nipples. Julie's mouth went dry, for now it was as though it were her breasts Rafael caressed. A flame kindled and curled deep in her belly. It was all she could do not to cry out.

His hand moved over the curve of the figure's waist, and her skin burned because it was as if his hands were on *her* waist.

When he moved lower to caress the hips, the curve of buttock, she felt herself grow dizzy with longing.

As though drawn by an invisible force, she went closer. He shifted a little to the side and she could see the figure clearly. Clearly...

The breath stopped in her throat. She couldn't breathe or move, she could only stand there, staring at her face, her body. This was a statue of her.

An involuntary cry escaped her lips. Rafael whirled and saw her standing there.

They stared at each other. The color drained from his face. "What are you doing here?" he cried. "How dare you invade my privacy this way?"

"The statue... ?"

As if to protect it, he encircled the slender neck with his fingers.

Julie gasped and her hand went to her throat.

"Get out!" he shouted.

She fought for control. "It's... it's Kico," she managed to say. "He's ill. I thought you should know."

"Kico? Kico is ill?" Rafael shook his head as though trying to clear it. "Very well. Yes, I'll come. You've called the doctor?"

"Alicia..." Julie tried to speak normally. Tried not to look at the nude figure that stood only a few feet away. "Alicia... Alicia is calling the doctor."

He picked up a cloth. "I have to..." He indicated the statue. "I have to cover this. Keep it damp. I'll be along."

Julie wet her lips. "It's very beautiful," she said.

"Yes." But he wasn't looking at the statue, he was looking at her. "Beautiful," he murmured. And turned away.

CHAPTER NINE

He wasn't sure what had prompted him to do the sculpture of Juliana. He only knew that he had to do it, and once he had started he had become totally absorbed.

It was the best work he had done in a very long time, as good as what he had done before Margarita had come into his life.

He put everything he had into it, his talent, his art, his passion, all that he had been before, the artist his soul cried out for him to be. The clay came alive in his hands as he molded Juliana. He captured every plane of her face, every curve and hollow of her delicate body. He had seen her naked only for a few moments the day he had carried her into the restaurant by the dock. But it had been enough, for even in his fear and distress he had been sensitive to the pure beauty of her form.

The statue became a work of love, for with the clay he could express all of the emotion he had begun to feel for Juliana. He gave life to the figure, and in turn the figure gave him back his life. When he molded Juliana with his clay, his whole being, everything that he was, artist and man, became free again. He could express himself through the clay as he could never express himself to her.

Yet when he had seen her standing here in his studio, as still as the statue itself, a terrible confusion had come upon him. It was as if he could not distinguish between the clay figure or the flesh-and-blood woman. He had rested his hand on the throat of the statue, and as though she felt his touch, Juliana gasped and touched her throat.

Was he mad? Was he obsessed? And if this was an obsession, who was the object of it, the clay image he had created or the woman he wanted so badly? Had the statue come alive because he had put all that he had begun to feel for the real woman, his desire and his need, into a piece of clay?

Was it enough? Could he mold Juliana as he had molded the clay? Could he make of her a woman as perfect as the clay figure?

Those were the thoughts that tortured Rafael as he covered the clay with a wet cloth. And went to see what he could do about the boy.

Kico spent three days in bed. Julie took care of him while he was ill. She made sure he took his medicine on time, and she spent long hours sitting by his bed reading to him. By the fourth day he felt well enough to get up for breakfast.

The only time Rafael saw her was when he stopped into the boy's room to see if anything was needed. When that happened the two of them spoke to the boy, not to each other.

Rafael looked tired. There were dark patches of fatigue under his eyes, lines in his face that hadn't been there before. Whenever she saw him, his jeans were splattered with red clay, and she knew he continued his work on the statue. But she didn't know why.

He had caressed the clay figure as though he were caressing her. She had felt his touch and it had excited her, even as it frightened her. The figure, the body and the face, were so completely her. But it was more than that. It was as if he knew everything about her, that he had delved into the secret heart of her, not just her physical being but everything that made her the woman she was, spiritually, emotionally.

Why? Why had he put so much time, so much of himself into the clay figure? She knew now, as she had known that night in Patzcuaro, that she had fallen in love with Rafael. It wasn't a love that pleased or calmed her. She was confused. One moment she wanted to pack her things and get as far away from him as she could. But the next moment she longed to be with him, longed to have him hold her as he had that night in Patzcuaro.

She felt an attraction for him she had never felt for a man before. But that attraction was all mixed up with a chilling fear. She had seen his dark side and it frightened her. He could be as warmly passionate as he had been the night of the storm, or cold and harsh as he often was with Kico.

She didn't understand him, nor did she know how to break through that cold exterior to the man who had held her so gently while the hurricane raged all around them.

He had made no attempt to see her alone since the incident in his studio. And so it was three days later that Julie decided to go to him.

That night she tucked Kico into bed. She read to him until he fell asleep, then tiptoed out of the room. She didn't know what she would say to Rafael, she only knew she wanted to see him.

Because the weather had turned warm during the days she had been taking care of Kico, she'd worn shorts most of the time. But she didn't want to wear shorts tonight, so she went back to her room to change and put on a bit of makeup. After she took off her shorts and shirt she dabbed a little mascara to her eyelashes and a touch of lipstick to her lips, then brushed her short blond hair.

Humming to herself, she went to the closet and looked through her somewhat meager wardrobe before she picked out the pale green summer dress that almost matched her eyes. She reached to take it off the hanger, then stopped. The dress was wet. She frowned. What in the world . . . ? Then she saw the algae and the sopping lake reeds dripping down the front of it.

A knot of fear tightened Julie's stomach and she stepped back, a look of horror on her face. Someone had come into her room. Someone or something had done this to her dress. But who?

With a look of revulsion she yanked the dress off the hanger. Then she rolled it in up and threw it in the wastebasket, just as she had with the doll. The doll who had worn a dress the same color as her now ruined dress. Had Alicia done this? And if she had, should she confront her? Or should she tell Rafael about the doll and about the dress?

Julie stood for a moment, undecided, then she took a different dress from the closet and put it on.

She went through the dark and silent corridors, and as she had that first time, Julie wondered why they were so cold, so cheerless. There was nothing basically wrong with the hacienda itself. It was beautiful from the outside, but there were no flowers on the patio, nothing to give warmth or color to the fine old place.

It was the same inside. The rooms were dark and cheerless, the corridors with their dim lights and portraits of long-dead martyrs were frightening. Rafael was an artist. Couldn't he, with his artist's eye, see how barren and devoid of cheer his home was?

There should be flowers, out on the patio as well as here in the house. Beautiful, sweet-scented flowers to add color and life to the place. Windows should be thrown open to let the sunlight in. The heavy dark drapes should be replaced by more vibrant colors of deep red or forest green. And the saints that seemed to look so disapprovingly as she hurried through the corridors should be relegated to a storeroom.

If this were her home... But it wasn't. It belonged to Rafael. He had lived here with the beautiful Margarita... Margarita, whom he had said he no longer loved.

Soon his son would leave and Rafael would be alone. Alone with the dark shadows and the long-dead martyrs.

Julie shivered as she drew closer to the end of the corridor that led to his studio. How could she help him? What could she do? Could she convince him to keep Kico here at least for another year? The little boy needed him, and though Rafael didn't know it, she thought he needed Kico.

Julie hesitated. Had she heard a rustle in the shadows, the scrape of a heel? "Is someone there?" she whispered.

The light was so dim it was difficult to see. She turned and when she did she saw the dark figure of a woman loom up behind her. "What are you doing here?" Alicia asked. She stepped around in front of

Julie, barring her way. "Señor Vega is working. I won't let you disturb him."

"*You* won't let me?" Hands on her hips, Julie stared at the other woman. Dressed all in black, with that white wing of hair that creased the coal black hair, she looked like the wicked witch in the *Wizard of Oz*. All she needed was a pointed hat.

Julie squared her shoulders. "Let me pass."

"No."

"This isn't any of your business."

"Not my business?" Alicia's face became a mask of hate. She took a step toward Julie. "I've been here a long time. I've taken care of Señor Vega's every need. I've seen the torment he went through when he was married to Margarita. I know what he suffered and I won't let him make the same mistake again."

"The same mistake? What in the world are you talking about?"

"Don't act as though you don't know. I know what you're up to. I know what you want."

"Do you?" Julie frowned. "Is that why you're try-ing to scare me away?" Hands on her hips, she faced the other woman. "It was you who put the doll at the door of my room, wasn't it, Alicia? You who put lake reeds all over my dress."

"What...what are you talking about?"

"Don't play games. I know it was you."

"It wasn't me. I swear..." A look of cunning and of something akin to fear crossed Alicia's face. "It was her," she whispered.

"Her who?" Julie asked, feeling her anger grow.

"Margarita." Hands clasped as though in prayer, she breathed her name again. "Margarita."

Julia's eyes widened. She took a deep breath to steady herself and in a firm voice said, "Get out of my way, Alicia."

It was as though the other woman didn't hear her. "I've done everything for him," she said. "I've taken care of his house, I've looked after the boy. I stood by him when Margarita drowned, and I've waited because I knew that some day he would turn to me."

Julie's eyes went wide. My God, she thought, the woman's in love with Rafael! That's why she's acting this way. That's why she's so possessive of him. Did Rafael know? Did he have any idea how Alicia felt about him?

"The boy will be gone soon," the woman went on. "And so will you. Then it will be only the two of us. I'll take care of him. He'll turn to me then, just as I've always known he would. He—"

"You're crazy!" The word popped out before Julie could stop it and she knew the minute she said it that she'd made a mistake.

Alicia's face went as white as the underbelly of a dead fish. Her black eyes burned like hot coals of fire.

"Crazy?" She grabbed a brass candlestick from the wall niche and took a step toward Julie. "Rafael belongs to me," she shouted. "He's mine."

Julie froze. Her mouth went dry. "Alicia," she tried to say. "Don't do this. Don't . . ."

Alicia raised her arm to strike. Julie lunged for the candlestick, but Alicia was bigger, stronger. They grappled. Alicia hit her with the back of her other hand. Julie screamed and reeled against the stone wall.

Candlestick raised to strike, Alicia advanced on Julie. "You can't have him," she cried. "I'm going to—"

"Stop!" Rafael stood in the doorway of his studio as if unable to believe the scene before him. Then with a cry he ran forward and wrenched the candlestick out of Alicia's hand.

"What in the hell do you think you're doing?" he roared.

Wild with anger, her face distorted with hate, Alicia twisted away from him. "She doesn't belong here," she cried. "Get rid of her. I *demand* that you get rid of her."

Rafael faced her. "Get out of my house," he said. "Pack your things and get out."

Her face paled. "But I...I belong here. Not her. You can't do this to me." She turned her coal black eyes on Julie. "It's because of her, isn't it? I've seen the way she looks at you. I know what she wants. I knew the night I saw her in the hall that she was trying to seduce you. You've been sleeping with her, haven't you? A common *puta*. A—"

"Enough! Pack your things, Alicia. I want you out of here tonight."

She backed away from him. "I know about you, Rafael Vega. I know what you did." She shot Julie a look of pure venom. "You'll see," she said. "He'll do the same thing to you. He almost did the other day in the storm."

"Get out!" Rafael clenched his hand around the candlestick he'd taken from her. "If you're not out of my house in thirty minutes I'll have the police take you away."

Alicia looked at him, then at the candlestick. With a cry of fear she turned and ran back down the corridor.

Rafael reached for Julie's hand. "Are you all right?"

"Yes." She took a steadying breath. "She...she's crazy. Did you know that she's in love with you?"

"Alicia? In love with me?" He swore under his breath. Then suddenly he became aware of the candlestick he was still holding. "She was going to hit you with this," he said. "My God! She could have killed you." He thrust the object back into the wall niche. "If she had hurt you..."

"She didn't."

"You're shaking." He put an arm around her shoulders. "She'll be gone in a little while and I'll make sure she never bothers you again." He paused as though a new thought had suddenly occurred to him. "What were you doing here?"

"I wanted to see you."

"Why?" He frowned, then took her hand and led her into his studio and eased her down on the sofa. "What is it?" he asked. "Why did you want to see me?"

"I'm not sure. I just..."

She shivered again and he said, "Wait." He went to a wall cabinet and took out a bottle of brandy. He poured a splash into a glass and hurried back to her. "Drink this."

She took the glass in both of her hands. The brandy was smooth and fiery hot. She gasped and tried to hand it back to him. "Another sip," he said. And when she had taken it he took the glass from her. "Now, tell me why you wanted to see me," he said.

Julie took a deep breath. "I saw the statue."

"I know."

"Why are you doing it?"

His dark eyebrows drew together, but his voice when he spoke showed no hint of anger. "I don't know," he said. "I'm not sure."

"It's very beautiful."

"It's you."

She wet her lips with her tongue and saw a sudden flame of heat in his dark eyes.

"Rafael..." She shook her head and in a whisper said, "I don't know who you are. You can be as you were in Patzcuaro the night of the hurricane. You kissed me then. You—"

"It was a mistake."

"Was it?" Julie looked into his eyes. "Was it, Rafael?"

His nostrils flared, but he didn't speak.

"You've barely spoken to me since that night. It's as if it never happened. As if...as if you had never touched me." Julie looked down at her hands. In a voice so low he could barely hear, she said, "You shut yourself away, from Kico and from me."

"It's because of my work," he said roughly.

"Is it?" She took a deep breath to steady herself. "I'll be leaving Janitzio in less than two weeks, Rafael."

"No." He clasped her hands. "No."

"I have to," Julie said. "I have a job."

"I don't give a damn about your job."

His dark eyes held hers and wouldn't let go. "I don't want you to go. I won't let you go. Damn it, Juliana..." He gripped her shoulders and pulled her closer. "Stay with me, be with me. I don't want you to go away."

She couldn't speak. The fear came again because there was so much about him she didn't understand, a dark side she had only glimpsed. He was so strong, so overpoweringly masculine that she felt almost helpless when she was with him. And yet . . .

As though drawn by an invisible force, her gaze slid away from his and she looked at the statue, which was so beautiful it made her want to weep. How could he have created anything so beautiful if there was in him not only the genius to create but the heart and the feeling that made him capable of great emotion? The man who could create with such sensitivity was the man she had fallen in love with.

"What are you saying?" she asked. "Are you asking me to live with you? Is that it, Rafael?"

The grip on her shoulders became painful. His eyes burned into hers and for a moment she was afraid again.

"No, Juliana," he said. "I'm asking you to marry me."

"Marry . . . ?"

"You've given me back the talent I thought was gone forever," he said. "I need you, Juliana. I want you."

No word of love. Only of want and need.

He loosened his grip on her shoulders and began to stroke her face. "I'll send the boy away," he said. "It will be just the two of us here on the island."

"No, don't sent Kico away. It's wrong to send him away. He's too young to go away to school. Maybe in a few years, but not now."

She saw the anger begin to build, then it was as though a light flickered behind the darkness of his eyes and he said, "Are you saying that you'll stay? That you'll marry me?"

"I'm saying . . ." She took a deep breath. "I'm saying that I'll think about it."

IT'S FUN! IT'S FREE!
AND IT COULD MAKE YOU A

MILLIONAIRE

If you've ever played scratch-off lottery tickets, you should be familiar with how our games work. On each of the first four tickets (numbered 1 to 4 in the upper right) there are Pink Strips to scratch off.

Using a coin, do just that—carefully scratch the PINK strips to reveal how much each ticket could be worth if it is a winning ticket. Tickets could be worth from $100.00 to $1,000,000.00 in lifetime money ($33,333.33 each year for 30 years).

Note, also, that each of your 4 tickets has a unique sweepstakes Lucky Number . . . and that's 4 chances for a **BIG WIN!**

FREE BOOKS!

At the same time you play your tickets to qualify for big prizes, you are invited to play ticket #5 to get brand-new Silhouette Shadows™ novels. These books have a cover price of $3.50 each, but they are yours to keep absolutely free.

There's no catch. You're under no obligation to buy anything. We charge nothing—ZERO—for your first shipment. And you don't have to make any minimum number of purchases—not even one!

The fact is thousands of readers enjoy receiving books by mail from the Silhouette Reader Service™. They like the convenience of home delivery . . . they like getting the best new novels months before they're available in bookstores . . . and they love our discount prices!

We hope that after receiving your free books you'll want to remain a subscriber. But the choice is yours—to continue or cancel, anytime at all! So why not take us up on our invitation, with no risk of any kind. You'll be glad you did!

PLUS A FREE GIFT!

One more thing, when you accept the free books on ticket #5, you are also entitled to play ticket #6, which is GOOD FOR A GREAT GIFT! Like the books, this gift is totally free and yours to keep as thanks for giving our Reader Service a try!

So scratch off the PINK STRIPS on all your BIG WIN tickets and send for everything today! You've got nothing to lose and everything to gain!

Here are your BIG WIN Game Tickets potentially worth from $100.00 to $1,000,000.00 each. Scratch off the PINK STRIP on each of your Sweepstakes tickets to see what you could win and mail your entry right away. (SEE BACK OF BOOK FOR DETAILS!)

This could be your lucky day - GOOD LUCK!

FOLD AND DETACH ALONG THIS DOTTED LINE—RETURN ALL GAME TICKETS INTACT.

TICKET 1
Scratch PINK STRIP to reveal potential value of cash prize if the sweepstakes number on this ticket is a winning number. Return all game tickets intact.

LUCKY NUMBER $1,000.00

4H 346280

TICKET 2
Scratch PINK STRIP to reveal potential value of cash prize if the sweepstakes number on this ticket is a winning number. Return all game tickets intact.

LUCKY NUMBER $50,000.00

2R 237598

TICKET 3
Scratch PINK STRIP to reveal potential value of cash prize if the sweepstakes number on this ticket is a winning number. Return all game tickets intact.

LUCKY NUMBER $100.00

9Q 361654

TICKET 4
Scratch PINK STRIP to reveal potential value of cash prize if the sweepstakes number on this ticket is a winning number. Return all game tickets intact.

LUCKY NUMBER $1,000,000.00

7K 221603

TICKET 5
FREE BOOKS
Scratch PINK STRIP to reveal number of books you will receive. These books, part of a sampling program to introduce romance readers to the benefits of the Reader Service, are free.

AUTHORIZATION CODE 4

130107-742

TICKET 6
FREE GIFT
All gifts are free. No purchase required. Scratch PINK STRIP to reveal free gift, our thanks to readers for trying our books.

AUTHORIZATION CODE MYSTERY GIFT

130107-742

YES! Enter my Lucky Numbers in The Million Dollar Sweepstakes (III) and when winners are selected, tell me if I've won any prize. If the PINK STRIP is scratched off on ticket #5, I will also receive four FREE Silhouette Shadows™ novels along with the FREE GIFT on ticket #6, as explained on the back and on the opposite page. 200 CIS AQYE (U-SIL-SH-11/94)

NAME _____

ADDRESS _____ APT. _____

CITY _____ STATE _____ ZIP CODE _____

Book offer limited to one per household and not valid to current Silhouette Shadows™ subscribers. All orders subject to approval.

© 1991 HARLEQUIN ENTERPRISES LIMITED.

PRINTED IN U.S.A.

THE SILHOUETTE READER SERVICE™: HERE'S HOW IT WORKS

Accepting free books places you under no obligation to buy anything. You may keep the books and gift and return the shipping statement marked "cancel". If you do not cancel, about a month later we will send you 4 additional novels, and bill you just $2.96 each plus applicable sales tax, if any.* That's the complete price, and–compared to cover prices of $3.50 each–quite a bargain! You may cancel at any time, but if you choose to continue, every other month we'll send you 4 more books, which you may either purchase at the discount price...or return at our expense and cancel your subscription.

*Terms and prices subject to change without notice. Sales tax applicable in N.Y.

"I see." He picked up the rest of her brandy and drank it down. "I realize this has been sudden," he said in a matter-of-fact voice. "Of course you need time to think about it."

"Yes." Without his hands to warm her she felt chilled.

"You'd have everything you want, you know," he went on in the same voice. "I'm a relatively rich man. You'd never lack anything. I'd see to it that you had your own money, your own account, I mean. I'd make sure the hacienda was in your name as well as mine, and that you were always provided for."

"I don't want your money," Julie said. "If I agree to this . . . this arrangement, it won't be because of the money, it will be because I . . ." She bit her bottom lip. No, she wouldn't say the words, wouldn't say, "because I've fallen in love with you."

He hadn't mentioned love. Rafael had said he needed her and wanted her. But love . . . ?

Julie stood. "I have to think about what you've said. About everything."

"Of course." He, too, rose. "I'll take you back to your room. I'm sure Alicia has gone by now, but I don't want you to be alone until I'm sure she's out of the house."

They left the studio, and when they started into the corridor, Julie said, "Do you really *like* all of these paintings?"

He looked startled. "I've never given them much thought. They've always been here. This was my grandfather's house, then my father's and now mine." He looked at the paintings as though for the first time. "You don't like religious art?"

"Some of it," Julie said. "But no, I don't like these."

"Then we'll get rid of them. I'll do anything you want to the house, Juliana. However you want it, that's the way it will be."

"And Kico?" She held her breath.

"I don't know," he said.

She started to turn away, but he took her hand and kissed it. She felt his breath hot against her skin and the touch of his tongue, warm and moist. Before she could pull away, he put his arms around her and covered her mouth with his.

For a moment she stiffened, then her lips softened and parted. She felt his tongue, soft and silky hot against hers, and she clung to him, melding her body to his, lost again in the thrill of his embrace.

He cupped the back of her head and she felt the hard splay of his fingers against her scalp. He ground his mouth against hers, and she answered him with softness.

He pressed one hand against the small of her back and brought her up against him.

She didn't move away. She took his face between her hands and kissed him as he had kissed her. She lingered over the corners of his mouth, she ran her tongue over his lips and searched the moistness of his mouth. And felt him harden and grow as he pressed against her.

"Come back to the studio with me," he whispered.

She held him there and looked deeply into his eyes as though she could see behind them into the man. Who was he really? What lay behind the brusqueness, the coldness, the passion?

She wanted to take his hand and go with him back into his studio. She wanted to lie with him there, make love with him there. Yet she held back, unsure of herself, unsure of that disturbing unknown of him. For if she made love with him now she would be lost. Once she lay in his arms it would be too late to ever turn away from him.

Her hands slid to his shoulders and she held him as though reluctant to let him go. "I need time," she said. "I'm sorry."

She felt the tension in his body, the flex of shoulder muscles beneath her fingers. She saw the heated desire in his face, in the suddenly hooded eyes. If he picked her up and carried her into the studio. If he...

"I understand." His voice was harsh and cold. He stepped away from her.

"I'm sorry," she said again.

"It's late. Come along."

They went back down the dimly lit corridor without speaking. At the door of her room he stopped. "I'll see you tomorrow," he said.

He started to turn away, but when Julie put a detaining hand on his arm he looked at her without moving.

"Good night, Rafael." She rested the palm of her hand against the side of his face. "Good night."

Then she went inside and closed the door behind her.

It was only later she remembered she hadn't told him about the doll or her ruined dress.

CHAPTER TEN

Every time Julie closed her eyes she thought of Rafael and what it would mean to her if she married him. She had loved living in Mexico these past two years. Guadalajara was a big, beautiful city with wonderful shopping, concerts, theater and great restaurants. She had friends there and men whose company she enjoyed. One more year of teaching and she'd have saved enough money for the backpacking trip to Spain she'd been planning.

Janitzio, though charming in its own way, simply wasn't Guadalajara. It was a village, an island that could be reached only by boat from Patzcuaro. And Patzcuaro, while certainly picturesque, was nothing at all like Guadalajara. Could she be happy living in a place so different from anything she had ever known?

Could she, because she loved Rafael, marry him on his terms? He had offered her security, but if she married him, and it was a pretty big *if,* it wouldn't be because of that. Financial security had never been high on her list of priorities. As long as she had enough money for a decent apartment, good food, a new blouse or a skirt now and then, she was happy.

Her friends in college had called her a hopeless romantic.

"Julie'll turn down chateaubriand and champagne at the Doral in Miami Beach for a hamburger with somebody she likes," her friend Raye had often said.

It was true. She'd much rather have a hamburger or a hot dog with somebody whose company she enjoyed than a fancy dinner with somebody who bored her.

Rafael didn't bore her. He intrigued her and, yes, sometimes he frightened her. But when he put his arms around her she forgot to be afraid. She experienced feelings with him she'd never known before. He'd haunted her dreams from the first moment she'd seen him. His kisses thrilled her as no other man's ever had. When she was in his arms she could forget her fears.

He had not told her that he loved her, but surely he must. Why else would he have asked her to marry him?

Those were the questions that troubled Julie all through that long and sleepless night. It was dawn before she fell asleep and almost nine when she awoke the next morning. And though the hour was late, she lay in bed for a little while looking at the sunlight on the purple bougainvillea that grew outside her window. From the patio came the trill of a bird, with notes as sweet and clear as the finest musical instrument.

It's lovely here, she thought as she lay in bed. Or it could be. If I lived here I would bring light and color into the hacienda. I'd plant roses and all kinds of flowers in the garden. I'd fill the spooky corridors with greening plants.

If I lived here.

Finally she got up. Moving quickly, she showered and dressed and hurried from her room.

Rafael was alone in the dining room when she entered, and she stood for a moment watching him. Even in blue jeans and a white cotton shirt with rolled-up sleeves he was very much lord of the manor. There was something about him, a certain haughtiness, an almost old-world presence that made him stand out from other men. If he had lived in Spain two hundred years ago he would have been a grandee. Or a high priest of the Inquisition who sentenced his enemies to the rack. If he had lived here in Mexico . . . A chill ran down her spine because she knew he would have been an Aztec king. The king who ordered the sacrifices, or the priest who held the knife that cut the beating heart out of the still-living victims.

He put sugar into his *café con leche* and absent-mindedly stirred it. His expression was thoughtful. Dark smudges underlined his eyes. He, too, looked as though he hadn't slept.

"Good morning, Rafael," she said.

He raised his head and for a moment there was in his eyes a vulnerability she had never seen before. Then the look faded and his expression became stiffly formal.

"Good morning," he said. "It's late. Are you all right?"

"Yes, thank you. I'm sorry I overslept. I didn't sleep very well last night."

He rose and pulled her chair back. "That's my fault. I'm afraid I upset you."

She smiled. "May I have a cup of coffee?"

"Certainly." He poured it for her. "The eggs are cold. I'll tell the cook to prepare something else."

He reached for the silver bell beside his plate, but before he could ring it, Julie put her hand over his to stop him. "That can wait," she said.

His shoulders stiffened. His face went still, and though he didn't move, it was as if he were braced for a blow. For the first time since she had met him, he seemed unsure of himself.

"About last night..." Julie began.

He tightened his other hand around the handle of his coffee cup and carefully set it down.

"Yes," she said.

"Yes?"

"Yes, Rafael, I'll marry you."

He didn't smile. He scarcely breathed. A moment passed before he said, "I'm very glad to hear that, Juliana."

She waited for a kiss, an embrace, a look that told her he cared about her and that he was happy she had accepted his proposal. But all he said was, "I'd like to have the wedding as soon as possible."

"How...how soon?"

"We should be able to get all of the paperwork done by next week. There'll have to be a civil ceremony of course, that's required by law, but if you'd like, I suppose we could also be married in the church."

"I'd like that, to be married in the church, I mean." She took a sip of her coffee, proud of herself because her hand did not shake. She had expected something from him, some small show of emotion to tell her that he was pleased. But there'd been nothing, only that cool, matter-of-fact voice.

"Perhaps you'd like to invite your family."

"It's awfully short notice. My sister Pam is expecting a baby sometime soon. My mother might want to be with her. But I'll call of course." Julie hesitated. "There's something else we need to talk about, Rafael."

He raised a questioning eyebrow.

"It's about Kico. I'd like to keep him here with us. I don't want you to send him away to school."

"I really don't think..." He was about to say that whether or not Kico went away to school was no affair of hers. But something in her eyes stopped him. She might look delicate as a flower and fragile as a dove, but he'd already discovered she had strong opinions on how things should or should not be done. If he refused to keep the boy here she might very well change her mind about marrying him. He couldn't let that happen; he couldn't lose her.

"He'll take up too much of your time," he said.

"No, he won't."

"I want you to spend time with me."

"I'll spend all the time you want with you. I'll give you all..." She almost said love, all the love you want and there will still be love to spare. But because she couldn't, she said, "You have your studio, Rafael. When you're working I'll enjoy being with Kico."

He tapped his long fingers against the white tablecloth. "Very well," he said at last. "If that's what you want. It means we'll have to hire another housekeeper right away so that someone is in charge while we're away."

"We're going away?"

The tight smile did nothing to soften his features. "Our *luna de miel*," he said. "Our honeymoon."

She blushed. "Oh."

"Have you ever been to Paris?"

Paris? They were going to Paris?

"And Madrid if you'd like to."

She thought about the money she'd stashed away for backpacking through Spain. The trip she'd planned would have meant eating at stand-up counters in railway stations and sleeping in youth hostels. She didn't think that was the kind of trip Rafael had in mind.

"Yes." She cleared her throat. "I...I'd love to go to Madrid. And...and Paris."

"I'll arrange it. We can probably be married by the end of next week. We'll spend the night in Mexico City and fly to Paris the following morning."

Next week? She had to call her mother, buy a gown, write to her friends. Paris! Good heavens, she was going to Paris!

Her head was in a whirl and her stomach fluttered with the nervous tizzies.

Rafael shoved his chair back from the table. "I'm going in to Patzcuaro to get things started," he said. "Is there anything you need?"

"No...no, I don't think so."

"I'll be back in time for dinner. We can tell Kico about the marriage then if you like."

"Yes, that would be..." She swallowed hard, trying to keep back the tears because she wanted, needed, some word of kindness, a touch that showed he cared. "That...that would be nice," she said. "I mean our telling him together."

He rested a hand on her shoulder. "It's going to be all right," he said. "When we're married, I mean. It's going to be fine."

She couldn't answer him, she could only nod and think, What have I done? Dear Lord, what have I done?

She phoned her mother. "I hope you're sitting down," she said. "I have something to tell you."

"My God!" her mother said. "You're pregnant!"

Julie laughed and some of her tension eased. "First things first. I'm getting married."

"To who? Whom? When? Where? You're kidding!"

"Nope." Julie settled back in her chair, more at ease now that she'd heard her mother's voice. "To Rafael Vega," she said. "The man whose little boy I've been teaching."

"This is awfully sudden, isn't it, Julie? You haven't known him for very long."

"A little over two months."

"Darling..." She heard the hesitation in her mother's voice. "Are you sure, Julie? Do you love him?"

Julie tightened her hand around the phone. "Yes, I love him."

"When's the wedding?"

"Next week, Mom. That's why I'm calling. I was hoping you and Dad could come."

"Next week? Darling, I can't. Pam's baby is due and I promised her I'd be there. Dad's going to drive me to Jacksonville this weekend and we'll stay there till the baby arrives. Couldn't you postpone the wedding?"

"No, I...I don't think so." Julie's throat closed with disappointment and her eyes stung. She didn't want to cry, mustn't cry, because it would upset her mother.

"I'll bet Susie'll want to go," her mother said. "If she can possibly arrange it, I know she will."

"Okay." Tears were too near the surface to say more than that.

"I know you probably already have a wedding dress picked out, Julie, but if you don't, I was wondering if you'd like to wear mine. Susie could bring it..."

The tears came then, tears because it was dear of her mother to offer the wedding dress and because she was sick with disappointment that her mother and father couldn't come to her wedding. And because suddenly she wasn't sure she could go through with this without some moral support.

"Julie?"

"Yes." She squeezed hard on the bridge of her nose. "Yes, of course, Mom. I'd love to wear your wedding dress."

"Then Susie will bring it if she comes. If she doesn't, I'll express it to you."

"Fine, Mom. That will be fine."

"Darling? Is everything all right?"

"Wedding jitters," Julie said. And wanting to cheer her mother, she added, "Guess what, Mom? We're going to Paris on our honeymoon."

They talked for a few more minutes. Her mother said, "Take lots of pictures, dear. I'm so anxious to see what your Rafael looks like."

Her Rafael. Julie put the phone down. Would he ever be her Rafael?

There were lit candles on the table that night, along with a bouquet of summer flowers Julie had found in the market. She had asked Juanita to prepare the *sopa Tarasco* that she and Rafael had had at the hotel in Patzcuaro, along with a green salad, broiled white fish and fresh asparagus. And a chocolate soufflé for dessert.

She wore the long skirt she had bought in Patzcuaro, but instead of the off-the-shoulder blouse, she chose a white silk blouse with a ruffled collar and long sleeves.

She was in the dining room when Kico came in. He looked at the candles. "Is it a party?" he asked.

"Not a party," Julie said. "But it is a special occasion."

Rafael arrived a few minutes later. He, too, looked at the candles, the flowers and the wineglasses. But all he said was, "Good evening."

"The table looks pretty," Kico said. "Doesn't it, Papa?"

"Yes, very nice."

"We never had candles before, did we?"

"That's because I like to see what I'm eating."

"I can see." Kico pointed to his salad. "That's a tomato and that's a black olive and that's—"

"Enough." Rafael took a sip of his wine. "I have something to tell you," he said. "Miss Fleming . . . Juliana and I are going to be married."

"Married?" The boy's eyes widened. He looked from his father to Julie. "You're going to live here all the time?"

"Yes, Kico. I hope that's all right with you."

"All right!" He grinned, then the grin faded and he said, "But I won't be here. I'm going away to that school."

"I don't think so." She looked at Rafael and waited for him to tell Kico the news.

"We've decided that you're to stay here with us. When you're older you'll go, but until then you'll attend school in Janitzio."

"Here? I can stay here with you and Señorita Julie?"

"I think we'd better forget the *señorita*," Julie said with a smile. "Why don't you just call me Julie? And yes, your father wants you to stay with us so that . . ." She hesitated. "So that we can be a family. The three of us together."

"Will you be my new mother?"

"I'll be anything you want me to be, honey. I know I can never replace your real mother, but I'm going to do my very best."

Rafael frowned. He'd acceded to Juliana's wishes because he'd been afraid that if he didn't he would lose her. Perhaps it had been a mistake. He should have insisted the boy be sent away because he didn't want or need any reminders of the past. But if he went against Juliana's wishes she might refuse to marry him. He couldn't take that chance.

She'd taken a liking to the boy and obviously Kico was crazy about her. He'd go along with her wishes, at least for this year. But next year it would be a different matter.

"I'd like to discuss the wedding plans," he said. "I've applied for the marriage license. Tomorrow we'll both have to go into Patzcuaro for blood tests and to fill out certain forms. You said you've never been married before, correct?"

"Right."

"That will make things easier. We won't have to wait for papers to be sent from the States. I've spoken to a judge. We can have the civil service next Friday morning. I also spoke to the priest. Are you Catholic?"

Julie shook her head. "Does it matter?"

"No, but I'll have to tell the priest. He'll want to be sure that if there are issue they'll be raised in the church."

Issue? Their children would be issue?

She said, "Rafael . . . ?" just as the telephone extension in the kitchen rang.

A moment later Eloisa opened the dining room door and said, "It is for you, Señorita Julie."

She pushed her chair back. "Excuse me," she murmured, and hurried into the kitchen.

When she picked up the phone, Susie said, "Julie! I can't believe it! You're getting married! What's he like? Tall, dark and spectacular?"

"Of course. Can you come, Susie? When will you be here?"

"When's the wedding?"

"Next Friday."

For a moment there was silence on the other end. Then Susie said, "I'm sorry, Julie. I can't. I have to be in Atlanta for a meeting next Thursday and Friday. There isn't any way I can get out of it."

"I . . . I see."

"Can't you put it off until the following week?"

"I don't think so, Sooze."

"God, I'm so sorry."

"I know."

There was another silence, then Susie said, "Look, sis, I know you're disappointed. So am I. Why don't you and Rafael and his little boy plan on coming to Florida for Christmas? The whole family will be there then. We'll have a reception at the club and invite all your friends. It'll be a sort of delayed wedding reception."

Christmas. If Rafael agreed. She thought about the family all gathered around the table for Christmas dinner, of her brothers and sisters and her nieces and nephews all chattering at the same time. How would Rafael, so quiet and serious and coldly polite, react to her gregarious, outgoing family?

"We'll certainly try," she said carefully.

"Try? Try? You're coming and that's it. Uh, Julie? Is everything okay? You sound a little...I don't know, maybe a little down."

"No, no, I'm fine. A few wedding jitters, that's all."

"I'll send the wedding dress express first thing in the morning."

"Okay. Tell everybody hello for me."

"I will. Take care, Julie. Love you."

When she hung up, Julie stood for a moment, her hand still on the receiver.

"Is everything all right?" Juanita asked.

"Yes," Julie said. "That was my sister." She looked at the older woman. "Señor Vega and I are getting married next week. My family won't be here."

"Ay, *muchacha,* I'm sorry." Juanita put an arm around Julie's shoulders. "But I'm happy for you and Señor Vega and for the little boy, too. You will bring joy back into the house. Perhaps you will even make the señor smile again."

Julie went back into the dining room. "That was my sister," she said when she sat down. "She won't be able to come to the wedding, either."

"I'm sorry."

"She suggested...well, actually she insisted that the three of us go to Florida for Christmas."

"Florida!" Kico's eyes widened. "*Qué fantástico!* Can we see the Seminole Indians? Can we go to Disney World? Can we—"

"It hasn't been decided," Rafael said stiffly. "It depends on my work."

"But you can work anytime."

"That's enough, Kico. Eat your dinner. We'll talk about this another time."

Another time? Julie and Kico looked at each other.
Then silently they finished their dinner.

The rest of the week passed in a whirlwind of activity. Julie and Rafael had their blood tests. Julie filled
out forms and had her fingerprints taken. She visited
the small church of San Jeronimo and, because she
didn't think Rafael would do it, spoke to a woman
from the altar society and ordered flowers for the altar.

The civil ceremony at the house would take place at
noon; the wedding in the church would be at five.

Three women came to apply for the position of
housekeeper. "It's up to you," Rafael said when he'd
set up the interviews. "Select whoever suits you."

The first two were acceptable, but the third applicant was perfect. Eufrasia Ponce lived in Janitzio. In
her early fifties, she had warm brown eyes and cocoa
brown skin that looked as though she had scrubbed it
smooth. She arrived for the interview wearing an embroidered blue skirt and a bright red Tarascan Indian
blouse.

She had worked for a family in Morelia for the last
five years, she said, but now her elderly father was ill
and she needed to be closer to him.

She said hello to Eloisa and Juanita when Julie took
her into the kitchen, and beamed a happy smile at Kico.
Julie left the four of them chatting while she went into
the study to call Eufrasia's last employer.

"She's a jewel," Señora Sanchez said. "We'll never
find anyone like her again. We offered her more
money, but we understand that because of her father
she wanted to be in Janitzio."

Next Julie went to Rafael's studio.

"I told you it was your decision," he said, a little annoyed at having been disturbed.

"I know you did, but I thought you ought to meet her. Just in case you have any objections."

He followed her back to the kitchen. He spoke to Eufrasia, said a few words, then to Julie said in English, "May I speak to you for a moment?"

When they went into the other room, he said, "Good Lord, she's wearing red!"

"Yes, she is. Isn't that a welcome change?"

He raised an eyebrow. "Did you check her references?"

"Of course."

"And you like her?"

"Yes, I do."

Rafael shrugged. "All right then, hire her."

And it was settled. Eufrasia would begin the following day.

Three days later the wedding dress arrived. Eufrasia brought it to Julie's room. When she left, Julie opened the box and folded back the white tissue it had been wrapped in. She touched the delicate lace with her fingers and lifted it out of the box.

She thought of her parents, of their wedding picture on the piano in the living room. How young and beautiful her mother looked, how handsome her father was.

Suddenly, unbidden, the tears came. She tried to choke them back, and when she couldn't, she lay down on the bed, holding her mother's wedding dress to her, as though seeking comfort from this loving touch from home.

CHAPTER ELEVEN

Judge Tomás Vicente Alemán, accompanied by his secretary, a fussy little man with a fringe of suspiciously black hair around his otherwise bald pate, arrived at the hacienda promptly at noon on Friday to conduct the civil ceremony in Rafael's study.

Julie put her hand in Rafael's and it began. She repeated the Spanish words that legally joined them as husband and wife, but none of it seemed real. She listened, she answered *"Sí."* She tried to smile, but when she did her lips trembled.

She looked at Rafael, hoping he might offer an encouraging smile, a softening of expression to reassure her that, after all, he did love her. But he didn't look at her, nor did he give her hand an encouraging squeeze to let her know he was happy that she had consented to be his wife.

Judge Alemán pronounced them man and wife. She and Rafael, along with the witnesses, Eloisa and Juanita, signed their names in the book of registry the secretary had brought with him. When that was done, Kico tugged at her hand. "Are you my mother now?" he whispered.

Julie leaned down and put her arms around him. She kissed his cheek and she said, "Yes, sweetheart, I'm your mother now."

They went into the dining room for lunch. Rafael poured champagne. The judge offered a toast. Rafael looked at her over the rim of his glass, his expression guarded, distant. She tried to smile, but the smile faltered. When she raised her glass her hand trembled.

The salmon soufflé Juanita had prepared was light and tasty, but Julie could manage only a few bites, so overwhelmed was she by a terrible sense of unreality. A what-am-I-doing-here feeling.

This wasn't how she had envisioned her wedding day. All through her growing-up years she had planned exactly what it would be like. She would be married in the Congregational Church in Key Largo. All of her friends, as well as her parents' friends, would be there. Her father would give her away; her two sisters would be her bridesmaids. Her three brothers, John and Ross and Wade, would smile at her from the front pew next to her mother.

Afterward there would be a reception at the club. Toasts and laughter and dancing...

But this wasn't Key Largo, this was Janitzio, Mexico. And she had never felt more alone.

The luncheon over, the judge and his secretary rose to leave. Julie shook hands with them. They wished her well. Rafael took them to the door and when he returned he said to her, "Why don't you rest until it's time to go to the church? It's going to be a long day. We have an eight o'clock flight to Mexico City so we'll have to leave for Morelia right after the church ceremony. Have you finished packing?"

"Almost."

"I'll send Eloisa to help you. As soon as you've finished I'll take the luggage to Patzcuaro." He hesitated. "I'm sorry your parents or your sister couldn't come, Juliana. I know how disappointed you must be.''

''Yes, I . . . I am.'' She forced a smile. ''But it's all right. You'll meet them when we go to Florida for Christmas. We . . . we are going then, aren't we?''

A slight frown creased his forehead. ''We don't need to talk about it now.'' And before Julie could answer he called for Eloisa and said, ''Please help Señorita Juliana . . .'' He stopped and a strange look came over his face. ''But you're not Señorita Juliana anymore, are you? You're Señora Juliana Fleming de Vega.''

He saw the uncertainty in her eyes and wanted to say something to reassure her, something to tell her that it was going to be all right between them. But he couldn't because he didn't think it would be. This marriage was a mistake. It would have been better for both of them if they'd had an affair, if he'd simply bedded her and gotten her out of his system.

After Margarita, he had vowed that never again would he fall in love or tell a woman he loved her. His attraction, his purely sexual attraction, for Juliana had come as a surprise. She wasn't like any woman he had ever known, and younger than the women he'd known before Margarita.

Margarita had been his age, worldly, sophisticated. She could walk into a room of movie and theater people, of artists and writers, of the rich and infamous, with noble names and family fortunes, and in ten minutes completely take over the room. He couldn't imagine Juliana ever doing that. Margarita, for all her faults, had been like a beautifully plumed bird, vivacious, sparkling, forever fluffing her feathers. Next to her Juliana seemed as plain as a sparrow.

And yet, sparrow or not, Rafael knew he wanted her. Wanted her to warm his bed, to hold when the demons of the night descended, and yes, to ease his physical ache for a woman. Perhaps that was cold-blooded. If it was he couldn't help it. He would be a faithful husband; he would give her security. Surely that would be enough.

It had to be. He had nothing more to give.

At three that afternoon Julie bathed and dressed in a pale pink suit.

Eloisa wrapped Julie's mother's wedding gown in white tissue and put it in the box it had come in so that she could carry it to the church.

"It's so beautiful," she exclaimed when she ran her hand over the delicate silk. *"Qué lástima* that your mother is not here to see how pretty you will look when you wear it."

"Yes," Julie said. And bit her lip to keep from crying.

Rafael and Kico were waiting for her in the living room.

"Ready?" Rafael glanced at his watch. He wore a dark suit, a white shirt and a conservative tie. "We'd better leave," he said. "You didn't forget anything?"

"No, I don't think so."

"Then come along." He took her arm and together, with Eloisa and Kico, they left the hacienda and made their way down the hill to the church below.

As far as he was concerned, all of this fuss of being married in the church was unnecessary. He saw no need for another ceremony and wished now he had told her so right from the beginning. He and Margarita hadn't had a church wedding.

When they reached the church, anxious to have this over with, he said, "Go along and change, Juliana. We have to be at the airport in Morelia at least an hour before flight time."

She wanted a word of reassurance, of kindness. She wanted him to say, "I'm glad you're my wife because I care about you, because I want to spend the rest of my life with you. I'm glad we're marrying in the church so that our marriage will be sanctified in the eyes of God."

But he said nothing.

A woman from the altar society showed Julie and Eloisa to a small room off the church entrance. "You can change in here," she said. "I've arranged for the flowers you requested and I've taken the liberty of asking the organist to play. I hope that's all right."

"That was kind of you," Julie said. "I appreciate it."

"I'll be here for the ceremony, so if you need anything, don't hesitate to let me know. Very likely a few of the local people will slip into the church to watch the wedding. I hope you don't mind."

When the woman left, Julie took off the suit and Eloisa opened the box that held the wedding gown. Carefully then Julie folded back the layers of white tissue. She wished her parents were here to see her in the gown, that Susie had been able to come, and... She gasped.

Before she could pull back, a black spider, its body as big around as a silver dollar, scurried across her hand. She screamed and dropped the box.

"What is it?" Eloisa saw the spider. *"Dios mío!"* she cried, and yanking off her shoe smacked at it. She missed, hit it again, and this time it didn't move.

Julie scrubbed at her hand and fought the nausea that rose in her throat. She'd closed her eyes when Eloisa went after the spider, and now she said, "Is it . . . is it dead?"

"*Sí, señora.* But *Dios mío,* how did it get into the box with your dress? I myself packed it and I'm sure I put the lid on." Her face wrinkled in concern. "I have seen no spiders in the house. It's very strange." She crossed herself and in a hushed voice asked, "Is it a bad omen, Señora Julie? Do you think . . . ?"

"No, of course not," Julie said, more sharply than she had intended. "Now hurry and help me dress."

But when she slipped the white lace gown over her head her hands shook. How had the spider gotten into the box? Was it indeed an omen?

She turned so that Eloisa could fasten the pearl buttons down the back of the gown, then stepped into her white pumps and put pearl earrings in her ears. That done, she lifted the small coronet of white lace covered with seed pearls and placed it on her head.

Eloisa handed her the veil and helped her adjust it. "*Qué bonita,*" she exclaimed. "How beautiful." And Julie saw that Eloisa's hands were trembling, too.

Trying to get control of her nerves, Julie looked at herself in the mirror that hung behind the door. The gown really was beautiful. But had she made a mistake in wanting to wear it and in wanting a church wedding? Neither her family nor her friends were here, only strangers. And the stranger who was her husband.

How was it that she had come here to this village so far from home, to this small church of San Jeronimo to marry a man she barely knew?

"The organ is playing, Señora Julie," Eloisa said.

Someone tapped at the door. Eloisa opened it and the lady from the altar society handed Julie a beribboned bouquet of white roses. "From Señor Vega," she whispered.

Julie took them, and with a murmured "Thank you," touched the delicate petals with her fingertips. This was a small gesture, but it warmed her heart, and when Eloisa said, "It is time, Señora," she was able to smile. Clasping the flowers to her, she stepped out into the church.

The music swelled with the first clear notes of Grieg's "Morning." A white-robed priest waited at the altar. Rafael stood at one side, his expression serious, unsmiling.

She came slowly down the center aisle. She saw the woman from the altar society. A few village women. Kico in the front pew beside Juanita and Eufrasia. Calla lilies at the altar, their scent mingling with the heavy aroma of incense. The flickering light of the tall white candles. Paintings of martyred saints.

She reached the altar. Rafael stepped forward and took her hand.

"Estamos aquí en la presencia del Dios... We are here in the presence of God..."

"Do you, Rafael, take this woman?"

Rafael caught the scent of the roses. He felt the tremble of her hand in his. "Yes," he said. "I take this woman."

"To love, to honor, to be faithful unto her?"

Faithful. Yes, he would be faithful.

"Do you, Juliana, take this man?"

Her voice was so low he barely heard her say, "Yes, I do."

"To love, to honor, to obey."

"Yes."

Rafael took her left hand. "With this ring," he said, and placed a plain gold band on the third finger of her left hand.

"I now pronounce you man and wife. In the name of the Father, the Son and the Holy Ghost." The priest smiled. "You may kiss the bride," he said.

Rafael lifted her veil. There was in his eyes an expression Julie had never seen before. He kissed her and his lips were cool on hers.

The bellman took their luggage into the bedroom of their suite at the Airport Fiesta Americana. Rafael tipped him. He left and they were alone.

"Would you like to go downstairs to dinner?" Rafael asked. "Or would you rather eat here in the room?"

"Downstairs," Julie said too quickly. "If...if that's all right with you."

"Of course."

"I'll just unpack a few things. My suit. The one I'm going to wear tomorrow."

"There's no hurry." Rafael crossed the room and snapped on the television.

It came on too loud and the sound made her flinch. She went into the bedroom, nervous as a cat and ready to bolt. She looked at the king-size bed in the middle of the room. Panic choked her. She sucked in a breath, then resolutely went to her suitcase and took out the gray suit she would travel in tomorrow. Paris, she told herself. Think about Paris.

They took the elevator down to the lobby. A group of mariachis were playing in the lobby bar. Rafael didn't ask her if she wanted a drink. Taking her arm, he led her to the restaurant.

"Would you like wine?" he asked when they were seated.

Julie nodded.

He ordered. The waiter handed her a menu. "I'm not very hungry," she said. "I'll just have a salad."

"Nonsense. It's been a long day. You need something substantial."

Julie closed the menu and laid it on the table. The waiter returned with the wine. Rafael ordered two hearts-of-palm salads and steaks, medium rare. She took a sip of her wine.

"I'd like to call Kico when we go back to the room," she said.

"Of course."

"Do you think he'll be all right? I know Juanita and Eloisa are reliable. He likes them and he likes Eufrasia, but he'll miss you."

"You're the one he'll miss. Not me."

"But you're his father," Julie protested. "He loves you."

Rafael shrugged. "School starts in another week," he said. "That will keep him busy."

"How long—" Julie took another sip of her wine. "How long will we be in Europe?"

"I'm not sure. I'll need to see some people in Paris and an art dealer in Madrid. Two weeks, possibly three." Rafael picked up his glass and studied her over the rim. "We'll need to buy you some new clothes," he said.

New feathers for the sparrow.

Her suit was a subdued pink; Margarita would have chosen red. The ivory blouse fastened at the throat;

Margarita's would have plunged low enough to show the rise of her breasts.

He picked up the glass of wine and downed it. Don't think about Margarita, he told himself. Not now. But he couldn't help it. Margarita had been a woman you gave your all to, a woman to die for, to lose your soul to. As he had lost his.

It would not be like that with Juliana. Never again would he go through the hell of loving someone the way he had once loved Margarita.

Juliana was... He supposed *nice* was the word. And attractive enough in her own way. He was physically attracted to her and he knew from the way she had responded to his advances that she was to him. The strangeness would pass. She'd enjoy Paris and Madrid, and once they returned to Janitzio life would return to normal. He could devote himself to his work. She would oversee the running of his home and make sure that he was not disturbed. It would be a pleasant enough life, which was all he wanted or expected. He'd had enough of both passion and excitement to last him a lifetime.

They finished their dinner. He asked, "Would you care for a drink at the bar?" and when she shook her head, he took her arm and led her to the elevator.

Once in their suite, he said, "Why don't you go and change into something more comfortable. I'm going to watch television for a while."

She went into the bedroom. She called Kico, promised she would bring him back a special present when she returned, and when she undressed ran hot water for a tub. There was a small bottle of bubble bath among all of the things on the complimentary tray and she poured it into the steaming water.

With a sigh she closed her eyes. She wished she was here alone, wished that when she got out of the tub she could get into the big bed by herself. And that tomorrow she was catching a plane to Florida instead of Paris.

Soon she would lie in the king-size bed with Rafael. He would want to make love. She didn't think it would matter to him whether she did or not. She was his wife, it was expected.

She wished she had more experience. Perhaps if she had, if she could please him in bed, he wouldn't be sorry he had married her.

Don't think about it, Julie told herself. Think about Paris and what it will be like to walk down the Champs-Elysées. She tried to hum a few lines of "The Last Time I Saw Paris," but the words stuck in her throat.

He was watching a rerun of last week's bullfight in Mexico City when she came out of the bedroom. He looked up when he heard her come in and his face went suddenly still. In the white, off-the-shoulder ruffled nightgown that cupped her breasts and fell in a swirl of softness to her ankles, she looked very young, very innocent.

"I'm...I'm sorry I took so long," she said. "I mean, if you wanted the bathroom."

He stared at her for a long moment. He snapped off the television, then rising from the sofa, he held out his hand and said, "Come here, Juliana."

She came toward him slowly, reluctantly. He took her hands and said, "I like your gown."

"Thank you." She looked at his tie, not at him.

He put his hands on her shoulders and drew her closer. "A kiss for the groom."

His kiss was gentle, his lips were warm. He touched his tongue to hers and she felt a tingle of response. But still she held back, her body stiff, unyielding in his arms, even when she felt the heat of his breath as his tongue slipped past her lips to seek her tongue.

With one hand he clasped the back of her head so she couldn't move away while he ravished her mouth. He pressed her against the sofa, and when her knees bent, he pushed her down against the cushions. He held her close and whispered her name against her lips.

"Rafael?" Her voice was as tentatively sweet as a caress. "Darling..."

He stopped her words with his mouth because he didn't want her tenderness. He only wanted her...soft body, sweet scents, the tangle of her hair brushing against his face.

He ran a line of kisses down to her throat. He kissed her ears, and when she shivered he took one tender lobe between his teeth to nip and to soothe. He kissed her mouth and cupped her breast through the silky fabric of her gown. When she moaned he knew a moment of triumph, for soon he would possess her.

He rolled away, and gathering her in his arms, he carried her into the bedroom and placed her on the bed the chambermaid had turned down while they were at dinner. He ripped his tie off, then his shirt. He sat on the bed to untie his shoes, to pull his trousers off.

His shoulders were wide and finely muscled, his stomach flat, his legs long and muscled like his shoulders. He hooked his thumbs under the elastic of his briefs and Julie turned away.

"Turn off the light," she said in a strangled whisper.

"No." His voice sounded harsh in the stillness of the room. He pulled the sheet back and came in beside her. "Sit up," he said. "Take off your gown."

"Rafael . . . ?"

He tugged at her gown and pulled it over her head. Her earlier passion forgotten because of his brusqueness, Julie lay down and covered herself with the sheet.

He lay with her. She felt the whole masculine length of him against her naked body. He pressed his mouth to hers and rubbed one hand across her breasts. The kiss deepened. His mouth was hot, demanding, moist.

He trailed a line of kisses down her throat. He licked at her ears, he lapped at her breasts. He pulled the sheet away and his hot gaze skimmed over her body like an artist studying the subject of his work with a critical eye. He encircled her throat as though measuring it and ran his hands down over her shoulders and her breasts.

"You really are beautiful," he murmured, as though it surprised him to find her so. He cupped her chin and ran his fingertips across her lips. When she shivered and tried to draw away, he said, surprised, "You're afraid of me, aren't you?"

"No." She pulled the sheet up to cover her nakedness. "No, of course not."

Something not quite a smile tugged at his lips. "That's all right," he said. "A little fear is good." He cupped one breast and, watching her, squeezed the nipple between his thumb and first finger. Her eyes widened. Her lips parted. Yes, he thought with a sense of satisfaction. Ah, yes.

With his hands under her shoulders, he took one tender peak between his teeth to lap and to suckle. He teased her with his tongue, back and forth, lapping, swirling, and when she whispered, "Oh, Rafael, Rafael..." a thrill unlike anything he had experienced in a long time shot through him.

Not taking his mouth from her breast, he eased his hand down over her belly and her hips. He reached the apex of her legs, felt the crisp curl of hair there and began to touch the warm, intimate part of her.

She tried to push his hand away, but he wouldn't let her. She was soft as silk there, and though she protested, her body lifted to his hand and he felt her grow hot and moist. And when he scraped his teeth against the nub of her breast, she whimpered with pleasure.

He came up over her. He imprisoned her with his legs. His tumescent manhood pressed against her thigh. He took her mouth. He whispered "I want you" against her lips.

Her body stiffened with fear. "Wait," she said. "Wait, I—"

"You are my *mujer,*" he said. "My woman."

He grasped her hips and with his knee he thrust her legs apart. Then that male part of him, that pulsing, hard part of him, thrust into her and a pain unlike any other tore through her. She cried out.

"What...?" He froze. "Juliana?" He sounded angry. "*Por Dios,* why didn't you tell me?"

"I...I'm sorry." She trembled, hating this. Afraid. Embarrassed.

"*Pero, por Dios...*" His body poised over hers, tense, barely under control.

She felt the terrible strain as he tried to hold back. Then with a groan he began to move against her.

He moaned because it was good. So good. All warmth and velvet softness. He lapped at her breast. He sought her mouth and wanted to cry out with the sheer joy that joining his body to hers had brought.

Juliana was his now, his to have and to hold and to make love to. Forever his.

His movements quickened. He thrust against her and tightened his hands on her shoulders. This was better than he had dreamed it would be and his body shook with the fine, hard pleasure of taking her like this.

He ground his body into hers, unaware that he said her name over and over again, unmindful of her whispers of discomfort. He reveled in the feel of her beneath him, in the warmth that held him. He wanted to make it last, to go on and on like this until he was spent, exhausted.

He had wanted her from the moment she had stepped into his home. Every time he touched her, the need had grown almost beyond bearing. She had refused him the night he had asked her to come back into his studio with him, but she couldn't refuse him now. For she belonged to him. She was his woman.

He gripped her shoulders and moved like a wild man against her. Wild? Yes! Mad? Lord, yes! His breath came in painful gasps. He threw his head back as though in agony. A bright white light exploded in front of his eyes and with a cry he collapsed over her. Spent and at peace. At last.

He hadn't expected her to be a virgin. He thought that by the time they were Juliana's age, all American women... But Juliana wasn't all American women. She was Juliana.

He had been her first, and while there was a side of him that felt a sense of triumph in the knowledge, that took pride in the thought that there had been no other man before him, there was in him a growing doubt, a suspicion that he had somehow wronged her.

He reached out and took her hand in his. What have I done? he asked himself. My God, what have I done?

CHAPTER TWELVE

For a long time neither of them spoke, but at last he said, "Why didn't you tell me you were a virgin?"

"I was embarrassed. I mean, because I'm twenty-seven and I've never..." She felt her cheeks grow hot. "I should have had at least *one* experience by now."

"No." He caressed the back of her hand with his thumb. "I'm glad you didn't. I'm glad I was the first."

She stole a look at him then, but before she could say anything he moved away from her and got up to go into the bathroom. In a few moments he came back with a towel wrapped around his waist, and before Julie knew what he was going to do, he pulled the sheet back and picked her up in his arms.

"What are you doing?" she asked, startled. "Let me get my nightgown."

"You won't need it in the bathtub." He pushed the door open with his foot. The bathroom was steamy. He closed the door and, taking her to the tub, laid her down in the hot, scented water. "This will make you feel better," he said.

She hadn't expected this small kindness, nor had she expected to be starkers in the tub in front of him or anybody else.

He took the towel off and before she could say, "What are you doing?" he'd climbed into the tub behind her.

"Lean on me." He eased her back against his chest, his legs on either side of her.

She tried to relax, but she'd never shared a bathtub with anybody before. Rafael might be her husband, but this was all too new to her. Her body hurt and she was embarrassed. She didn't know what to say or how to act. The hot water soothed her, though, and gradually she felt some of the tension go out of her body. In a little while Rafael began to soap her shoulders and that was nice. But when his soapy hands moved to her breasts she tried to stop him.

"I'm only washing you," he said. "That's all I'm doing. Close your eyes, *querida*. I won't do anything you don't want me to do."

The touch of his hands and the warmth of the water lulled her to a dreamy quietness. Half drowsing, half awake, she sighed and moved closer.

He rubbed her stomach. He made curlicues of her hair. She felt him grow, but she did not move away. Only when he touched her in that most intimate of places did she try to still his hand.

"Shh," he whispered against her ear. "I'm not going to hurt you."

It felt...all right. Well, nice. Mmm, a little more than nice. She sighed and closed her eyes.

He lifted the hair off the back of her neck and kissed her there. In a little while he slipped away from her and moved around to face her. He brought her legs up over his. He put his arms around her to bring her closer so that he could kiss her. And while he kissed her he began to caress her breasts. He drew soap bubbles out to small peaks and flicked them away so that he could touch her nipples. He caressed them ever so gently and that, too, was nice. Very nice.

But when she felt the hardness of him against her inner thigh she tried to move away.

He took her chin with his fingers and made her look at him. "I hurt you before," he said. "I won't hurt you again."

There was something in his voice she had never heard before, a tenderness in his eyes she had never seen.

He kissed her, and with his mouth still covering hers, he slowly, carefully entered her.

Instinctively, remembering the earlier pain, she flinched. "No," he murmured against her lips. "It will be all right, Juliana. I promise you it will be all right."

His voice soothed her. She curled her fingers in the thatch of his chest hair, and because she was embarrassed to look at him, she closed her eyes. Together they moved with the gentle rhythm of the warm water. She sighed. This felt . . . well, good.

He caressed her breasts, and when he squeezed her tender nipples she moaned into his mouth.

Something was happening to her body. A pleasure she had never known before. Her eyes drifted closed. She put her arms around his waist and pressed close to him so that her breasts rubbed against his chest.

The kiss deepened. She whispered his name and he said, "Is this all right, Juliana? Am I hurting you?"

"No," she whispered.

"Is it good for you?"

"I...I don't know. I...I..." But suddenly there were no words to tell him. Only feelings. Tumultuous, never-felt-before feelings. They rocked against each other. She clung to him, lost in his mouth, in the hands that caressed her breasts. She was filled by him, experiencing all kinds of new sensations with him. And yes...oh, yes, carried to spellbinding ecstasy by him. With him.

She cried out and he clasped his arms around her. "Juliana!" he whispered as his body shuddered against hers. "Juliana!" And held her as though he would never let her go.

She lay on her side facing him, one hand curled under her cheek, her hair tousled. Last night after they had made love she had insisted on putting the nightgown on again. Her modesty amused him and he knew he would soon cure her of that, for while he liked seeing her in the gown, he also liked taking it off.

Her body was really quite beautiful, her breasts small but sweetly shaped, her pink-tinged nipples the size of tiny pebbles. He studied the outline of her breast, and when he rubbed the tips of his fingers across one nipple, it hardened with his touch. He rolled it between his thumb and first finger. She sighed and stretched a lazy-cat stretch, sinuous and soft, but did not fully awaken.

He pushed the gown down and kissed the hardened nipple. She roused and, still half-asleep, all slumberous and warm, murmured a small protest at having been disturbed.

He kissed her closed eyes and the tip of her nose. He licked the tender skin behind her ear and ran his tongue around the shell-like curve.

She shivered and moved closer.

He kissed her breasts again, and when her arms crept up around his neck, he took one rigid peak between his teeth and gently tugged.

She murmured in surprise and tightened her arms around him.

He drew her closer, stroking her back, liking the feel of the silky material of her gown under his fingertips. In a minute or two he would take it off, but for now it was enough to touch her like this, to kiss her breast and feel the response in the slight trembling of her body.

He cupped her face between his hands. "Open your eyes, Juliana," he said.

The long lashes fluttered and eyes as green as summer grass looked into his. He pressed his mouth against her rosy lips and it was as if an electric shock went through his body.

"Juliana," he said, and pulled the gown up over her hips.

She tensed, but he could not stop. He said, "Part your lips for me," and when she did he kissed her again, a deep and searching kiss. She whispered a moan into his mouth and he began to stroke her back and her thighs, her sweetly rounded bottom. "So soft," he said. "So smooth."

He eased the gown farther up and raised himself over the whole silky length of her, his woman, his wife. He felt strong, powerful. He took her lips as he would soon take her body. He sensed her shyness and it exhilarated him. When he grasped her hips she uttered a small protest and tried to draw away, but he said, "Yes, now!" and joined his body to hers.

He moaned aloud when her softness closed about him and her body quivered beneath his. Tentatively her hands came up to caress his shoulders, and when they did he thought of all the things that he would teach her of the art of love. What a joy it would be to bring her along slowly, slowly, so that one day she would be everything he had ever dreamed of having in a woman.

He took her mouth again as he began to move against her, relishing every movement, every sensation. *Por Dios,* he'd never known such pleasure. He wanted to get lost in her, lost so that he could forget all that had gone before. He closed his lips over the peak of her breast and she whispered her pleasure. He cupped her bottom to bring her closer, so close that she became a part of him. He held her with his arms and gripped with his legs, and when at last she lifted her body to his, he said, "Yes, Juliana. Like that, my dear."

Soft little moans whispered from her lips. She strained against him, but he said, "Not yet, *querida*. Wait, Juliana. I want more. So much more."

His body on fire, he thrust and withdrew to thrust again. She said, "Oh please, oh please, oh please," and he tightened his arms around her. She moaned with a passion he knew was part agony, part ecstasy. As it was for him. He didn't want this to end. He wanted it to go on and on until there was no strength in his limbs, no breath in his body.

He kissed her, his tongue searching and finding hers. He rubbed the palm of his hand across her breasts, then left her mouth to take one hard-nubbed peak between his teeth to bite and to lap.

She said, "Oh...oh, Rafael," and her body became like a wild thing beneath his. He tightened his mouth on her breast and his tongue went crazy against the tender peak as he thrust deep into her.

Her body rose to meet his and she was shaking now, shaking and whispering his name in a frenzy of passion, and the sound of it, the sound of that strangled cry against his shoulder, sent him spiraling over the edge. He moved frantically against her, out of control, lost in an ecstasy that shook him to the very roots of his being. For nothing, nothing had ever been as good, as pleasurable as this.

He grasped her chin and cried his cry into her mouth. His legs tightened around her, he rocked her closer, so close he could feel the beating of her heart against his breast.

Little by little the terrible tension eased. He stroked her back and she lay with her head against his shoulder.

He knew now that he had been right to marry her. He had only suspected the passion that lay just below the surface of her quiet demeanor and he had been right. She was a warm and loving, a passionate woman. That's why he had married her.

But why, he wondered as he lay there with her in his arms, had she married him?

They flew first-class to Paris. The seats were comfortable and the flight fairly smooth. Rafael seemed perfectly at ease, but Julie wasn't. She liked traveling but hated flying. While Rafael read a newspaper she concentrated on keeping the plane in the air. She clutched the armrests and every few minutes looked out of the window to make sure the motors were still going.

"Juliana?" He lowered the newspaper. "Are you all right?"

"Yes." She cleared her throat and tried again. "Uh, sure."

"You don't like to fly." It sounded like an accusation. "Why didn't you tell me?"

"I didn't want you to think I was silly."

He put the paper down and took her hand. "I don't think you're silly," he said. "Being afraid isn't a crime. Everybody's afraid of something."

"What are you afraid of, Rafael?"

For a moment he didn't answer. His gaze slid from hers and he said, "Of many things, Juliana."

She wanted to press him, to say, "Tell me, Rafael. Because if you do, I may be able to help you." But she said nothing.

"Why don't you try to rest? I promise you the plane isn't going to fall in the ocean, but if it does I'll be sure to wake you."

That brought a smile to her lips.

"Go to sleep," he said. "Everything is all right."

In a little while her eyes drifted closed, but she did not sleep.

What manner of man was this husband of hers? He was so overwhelmingly male, so powerfully sexual that he almost frightened her. Her own response surprised her. She had hoped when she married that she would enjoy sex, but what she had experienced this morning went far beyond simple enjoyment. The hotel could have burned down around her ears and she wouldn't have let Rafael stop all the lovely things he was doing.

Under half-closed lids she stole a glance at him. He frowned at something he was reading and she thought, Yes, that is Rafael, serious, brooding, sometimes withdrawn and often angry. Yet last night and this morning he had been so very tender.

She'd never dreamed lovemaking could be like that or that she could feel such an immensity of passion. Her cheeks burned as she remembered his every touch, her muted whispers and how she had pleaded for release.

Suddenly Rafael lowered the newspaper. His eyes met hers and it was as though he knew exactly what she was thinking. She saw the rise of heat in his eyes, and in a voice so low she could barely hear, he said, distinctly, every word carefully spaced, "When we get to Paris I'm going to make love to you for a very long time. I'm going to do everything to you and with you I have ever dreamed of doing because you're my woman. *Mi mujer.*"

Heat suffused her body. Her pulse raced. Her breasts swelled, her nipples hardened.

He put his arm around her and drew her closer. "Go to sleep," he said, "and think how it will be when we get to Paris."

The late afternoon sun cast shadows of light on the beautiful old buildings. *Les bateaux-mouches* glided by on the river Seine. The leaves of the poplar trees were golden in the fading light of day. It was hard to believe that she was here in this most beautiful of cities, here with Rafael, who was her husband.

Their hotel, the St. Denis, was on a tree-lined street just off the Champs-Elysées. Rafael registered and they were shown to a cagelike elevator that whisked them up to the twentieth floor. The bellman opened the door to their suite, turned on the television, showed them how to control the air-conditioning and opened the doors leading out to their balcony.

Paris lay before them. Behind her Julie heard Rafael speaking to the bellman, then the sound of the door closing. He came up behind her and rested his hands on her shoulders. "It's something special, isn't it?"

Too overcome to answer, Julie could only nod. "How long can we stay?"

"A week or ten days. As long as you want to."

"It's a lovely place to spend a honeymoon."

"Yes, it is." He stepped away from her. "Would you like to have a shower? It's late and you're tired. Shall we have dinner in the room?"

"Yes, I'd like that."

"The bellman put our bags in the bedroom. Why don't you just put a gown and robe on when you've finished your shower."

"All right." She remembered what he had said on the plane, how low and seductive his voice had been, how it had vibrated with sensuality. But there was none of that now. He was pleasant, almost impersonal.

She went into the bedroom, a luxurious ivory-and-gold room. A quilted satin spread covered the bed. Satin drapes hung from the windows. A bouquet of white roses was on the dresser and she wondered if he had arranged to have it here.

She undressed and went into the bathroom, which was as large as her living room had been in Guadalajara. Here, too, the colors were ivory and gold. Deep piled ivory carpet, ivory curtains. Big gold towels. A double sink with ornate gold fixtures. Small bottles of shampoo, scented soaps and lotions.

The tub was large, the shower glassed in. She took a bar of the scented soap and a small bottle of shampoo and stepped into the shower.

The warm water felt good after the long trip from Mexico. She washed her hair, then soaped her skin and held her head back to let the water cascade over her body. It felt wonderful. She felt wonderful. She was in love and in Paris and everything was perfect. It . . .

The glass door slid open and Rafael stepped into the shower. Instinctively she put an arm over her breasts and a hand at the apex of her legs.

He laughed. "I love your modesty," he said. "But you must not be modest with me. With me everything is all right." He took a step closer. "But only with me, Juliana. Remember that."

He took her arm from her breasts, her hand from the apex of her legs, and put his hands on the wall in back of her, holding her there while the water cascaded over their naked bodies. He kissed her and pressed his slick, wet body against her.

"Remember what I said in the plane?" He took the soap from her and began to lather her body. "But we will go slowly, yes? We will touch each other and when we can no longer stand the touching we will make love."

He soaped her breasts. He rubbed his hands around and around, then held her under the water to rinse the soap so that he could kiss her there. He swirled his tongue around and around the sleek mounds, he lapped and suckled, he nipped and teased until her knees weakened and she sagged against him.

Still holding her, he began to soap her belly and her bottom. "So nice," he murmured. "So round and firm. Your skin is like velvet." He touched her between her legs. "As it is here. Like velvet against my fingers."

Her legs were trembling, the excitement building. But still she was shy because this was so new, because he was seeing her like this, naked and vulnerable.

"Rafael," she said, "Rafael, I..." But he stopped her protests with wet kisses, and all the while his soapy fingers caressed her.

Weak with longing, Julie clung to him, her arms around his neck, holding on to him lest she fall.

"Wash me," he said against her lips, and handed her the soap.

She began to lather his chest.

"All of me," he said.

She moved to his waist, his flat stomach, his hips.

"Now touch me as I touch you," he said against her lips, and when she hesitated, he took her hand and guided it to him. "Touch me here," he said. "So you will know how much I want you."

Soapy slick, he throbbed in her hand. "Like that," he whispered against her mouth. Head back, eyes closed. "Oh, yes. Like that."

He began to touch her as she touched him, all the while whispering his passion against her lips, wet mouth against wet mouth, until at last it became too much.

He turned off the shower, and taking one of the big soft towels, he put it on the bathroom floor. Then he picked her up, all wet and dripping in his arms, and laid her down on the towel.

He stood above her, naked, his eyes as dark as the Mexican sky at midnight, his thick wet hair as black as the wings of a crow.

He knelt beside her. "Do you want this as much as I do?"

"Yes." Only a whisper. "Oh, yes I do."

He stroked her cheek and leaned to kiss her. "My sweet *gringa*," he said, and easing his body over hers, he gripped her hips and with a sigh of pleasure joined his body to hers.

She gasped and tightened her hands on his shoulders, holding him as he held her, loving him, loving the feel of him inside her throbbing with life. She lifted her body to his and clasped him with her legs.

He moved against her, almost wild with a passion he could barely hold in check. Their wet bodies thrummed with life and a passion that left them breathless. He kissed her, and when he did he knew he was going over the edge. Knew and cried out, "I can't wait...can't..." just as it happened for her.

He took her mouth. "Give me your cry," he pleaded. "Give me..." And when she did, he tightened his arms around her and rolled with her so that she lay on top of him.

He couldn't stop kissing her or thrusting his body tight to hers. "I'll never stop wanting you," he said against her lips. "You're mine. My Juliana. My wife. *Para siempre mi mujer.*"

He rained kisses over her face, but the words he spoke were words of passion and desire, not of love.

The next morning he began to show her Paris. They had breakfast at a small restaurant near the Arc de Triomphe, then walked along the Seine before they went to the Tuileries and the Louvre.

"We'll come back again," he said when they left the museum. "There's too much to try to see it all in only a day. Right now I think we must look for a present for you."

"A present?"

"I didn't give you an engagement ring. It's time I did." He took Julie's arm and led her into a jewelry shop. "You can select a diamond if that's what you want," he said. "But I'd like to look at the emeralds."

When a man in a tailored pin-striped suit approached, Rafael said, in almost perfect French, "We would like to see a ring for the lady. An emerald, I believe."

The man unlocked a safe at the far end of the room, and when he had removed a velvet tray he placed it on the counter in front of them. *"Alors, monsieur,"* he said.

Julie gasped. She'd never seen anything more beautiful than the glittering green stones.

"Which one do you like?" Rafael asked. "Take your time, try a few on."

They were all so beautiful, and very likely so expensive. "I can't decide," she said.

"Would you like to look at some diamonds?"

"No, no, I love the emeralds." She picked up a gold ring with a small stone and slipped it on her finger. "This is very nice," she said.

"But not quite what I had in mind." He picked out a ring with an emerald as large as her thumbnail and surrounded by diamonds. "Try this."

"But it must be..." Julie lowered her voice. "Rafael, this probably costs a fortune."

He took her hand and slipped it on her finger. "Do you like it?"

"Of course I like it!"

He folded his hand over hers. "We'll take it," he said to the man in the pin-striped suit. "And some matching earrings."

Julie felt dazed. She didn't quite understand the value of the franc to the dollar, but she knew the jewelry must be terribly expensive.

When they left the shop, with the ring on her finger, Rafael asked if she was too tired to walk a bit. And when she said no, he tucked her arm through his.

They crossed the Île de la Cité and strolled along the Seine, looking at the bookstalls, the posters and the prints. They went to Notre-Dame, and when they left the cathedral, Julie insisted on seeing Shakespeare and Company, the bookstore once owned by Sylvia Beach and made famous during the twenties when John Dos Passos, Hemingway and Gertrude Stein had gathered there.

They had a late lunch at a fashionable restaurant on the Left Bank and afterward they took a taxi to a street lined with small boutiques.

"But I really don't need anything," Julie protested when Rafael took her arm and led her into the shop.

"Of course you do. This morning while you were in the shower I spoke to the agent I had when I lived here before, Paul St. Jacques. He's invited us to a party tomorrow night and I want you to wear something special."

They were seated by an elegantly dressed middle-aged woman who introduced herself as Madame Lebeau and offered cocktails or tea.

"Tea, *s'il vous plaît*," Rafael said.

"Oui." The lady clapped her hands and when a maid appeared she quickly ordered. And to Juliana she said, "What can we do for madame today?"

"We're going to a small dinner party tomorrow night and *madame* would like a new gown," Rafael said.

"I think I have just what you want, but of course I will show you other things, as well. You are a size six, *madame?*"

Julie nodded.

"You look well in pale green, yes?" And without waiting for a reply, she said, "Enjoy your tea. I'll return in a moment."

A dinner party. She spoke no French. Did his friends speak English? "How many people do you think will be there?" Julie asked. "Tomorrow night, I mean."

"Twenty or so, I imagine. Paul likes to give big parties."

"I know about three words in French. *Bonjour, bonsoir* and *arrivederchi.*"

"That's Italian."

Julie laughed. "See what I mean?"

"You'll be fine. Most of the people I knew here before speak English." He looked up as Madame Lebeau emerged from behind a curtain.

She said, *"Voilà,"* held the curtain back, and with a flourish a pencil-thin model stepped out wearing the most beautiful gown Julie had ever seen. Pale, pale green, cut low in the front, with a nipped-in waist and ankle-length skirt. Over it the model wore an ivory evening coat embroidered with designs of pale green sequins to match the color of the gown.

"I don't even want to know how much it is," Julie whispered. "But I'm sure it's far too expensive, Rafael."

"Do you like it?"

"Yes, but—"

"We'll take it," he said to Madame Lebeau. "But we must have it by tomorrow afternoon."

"Of course, *monsieur.*"

"Now we would like to see some of your suits."

There were two styles Julie liked, a black with a double-breasted jacket with satin lapels and a narrow skirt, the other a more casual red with brass buttons. Both of them fit as though they had been tailored for her. The gown, though, had to be altered and when that was done she tried on shoes. Plain black pumps for the suits, high-heeled ivory satin to go with the gown and evening coat.

"Maybe I should get my hair done tomorrow," Julie said when they left the shop with their packages. "I have to look really elegant to wear a gown like that."

Rafael shook his head. "I like your unruly hair." He brushed a curly strand of it back from her face. "I like to get my hands in it. I like to feel it against my skin."

It started again for him, the curl of heat, the slight quickening of his pulse. She knew it. Her eyes widened, her tongue darted out to lick her upper lip.

"Don't do that," he said. "Don't..." A taxi passed. He signaled it to a stop. "Hotel St. Denis," he told the driver, even as he told himself that this was absurd. He wasn't a lovesick boy, he was a thirty-five-year-old man. It was ridiculous to behave this way, to let himself be ruled by a purely physical drive. *Por Dios,* he thought almost angrily, why does she affect me this way? Why can't I get enough of her?

It would pass. He would satiate himself, and when he had he would settle down. He had married Juliana because she suited him and because he desired her. But he mustn't let his desire take over. This was for him a convenient arrangement, not a love match.

He had to touch her. There was no window separating them from the driver, so because he could not kiss her, he took her hand and brought it to his lips. He kissed her fingertips, parting his lips just enough so that he could take one finger between his teeth. He bit down, and when she didn't try to pull away, he rubbed his tongue across the ball of her finger. And heard her gasp.

The taxi stopped. Without counting them, Rafael shoved a few francs into the driver's hand. They went into the lobby. He gripped Juliana's arm. The elevator came. An older woman and a little girl got on. He stood next to Juliana and looked straight ahead.

When they got off at their floor he hurried her down the hall to their room. He shoved the key in the lock, got her inside and pulled her to him.

"This is madness," he said against her lips, and went a little crazy when she answered his kiss, lips parted, eagerly searching for his tongue.

He tore open the buttons of her blouse and reached around her back to unfasten her bra so he could touch her breasts. He squeezed her nipples and when she cried out he said, "Tell me if I hurt you. I don't want to hurt you."

"You don't," she whispered, and her breath was hot on his throat.

He sank to the floor in front of the door, taking her with him. He pulled her skirt down, her panties. Then his trousers. No time for finesse, he burned for her, had to have her.

With a terrible gasp of need he thrust into her. Thrust and thrust again. She cried out, not in pain but in a sudden wrenching release. It's the same for her, he thought. Madness, sheer madness. Then he, too, cried out. And took her mouth and held her to his beating heart.

CHAPTER THIRTEEN

That night they took the *bateaux-mouches* up the river Seine. Because the night was warm they sat at an outside table. Rafael ordered champagne. They ate stuffed artichokes and a casserole of roast chicken. They ordered raspberry crepes, and when the orchestra began to play a medley of old French songs, Rafael took Julie's hand and led her to the space on deck where people were dancing.

She had worn the new red suit tonight. A breeze off the river ruffled her hair and the lacy collar of her white blouse.

Rafael touched the collar. "I tore your other blouse," he said.

"It doesn't matter."

"I'll buy you another." He touched her cheek. "This . . . this little madness between us, this insatiability, it will pass, Juliana."

She raised an eyebrow.

"I can't seem to keep my hands off you. I've never been like this before. Not with . . ." He stopped. "It isn't like me. I'm sorry if I've been too demanding."

A smile tugged at the corners of her mouth, but she didn't say anything. Moonlight touched her hair. He brushed his lips across the top of her head and drew her closer into his arms. She was small and delicate. He felt the fragile bones of her back against his fingertips and vowed that he would treat her more gently.

This afternoon he had taken her too quickly, half-dressed, his pants down around his ankles. My God! What had he been thinking of? What in the hell had gotten into him?

He would be more temperate in the future. They wouldn't make love tonight. Two or three times a week should be enough for any man.

Then Juliana sighed and he felt her breath against his throat. Without conscious thought he tightened his arms around her.

"*C'est l'amour,*" the chanteuse sang. "This is love."

They went back to their table. The crepes arrived as the boat glided past Notre-Dame.

"It's all so beautiful." She reached across the table and took his hand. "Thank you for bringing me to Paris, Rafael."

Her eyes were luminous in the candlelight. He stroked the back of her hand. And knew that in spite of what he had told himself only a few moments before, tonight they would make love again.

Paul St. Jacques's penthouse apartment on the Rue de Rivoli overlooked the Tuileries. Most of the guests were already there by the time Julie and Rafael arrived. Though she loved the gown and evening coat Rafael had insisted she have for the dinner party, they were so elegant she'd been afraid she might be overdressed. She wasn't. All of the women there were dressed to the nines, and the men, like Rafael, were in evening clothes.

A uniformed maid took her wrap, then led them into the salon, where a group of more than twenty were gathered. Immediately one of the men broke away and hurried toward them.

"Rafael," he said. "How good it is to see you. And this is your new wife." He kissed Julie's hand and gave her an admiring up-and-down look. "You've done very well for yourself, *mon ami,*" he said to Rafael. "She is as lovely and as delicate as an orchid." And still holding Julie's hand, said, "Come along, *ma chère.* I want you to meet my other guests."

Introductions followed. The French names were difficult for Julie to remember; Henri d'Autriche, Monique, Claudette, Gaston Allais, Françoise somebody. Other names she couldn't quite catch. She offered her hand, she smiled and said, *"Enchantée."*

The men shook hands with Rafael, the women kiss-kissed his cheeks. Someone handed her a glass of champagne and an attractive redhead said, "Ooh la la, look at that ring. It must have cost a fortune, yes? But Rafael has always been *très* extravagant with his women."

"Madeline, *ma chère,*" the man next to her said, "do be careful of your claws. They tend to scratch."

Julie edged away. When she did, Paul St. Jacques took her arm and said, "Don't mind Madeline. She and Rafael used to be—shall we say friends?—when he lived here in Paris. But that was years ago, of course. I doubt he even remembers her." He smiled. "Come and let me show you the view from the terrace."

In his mid-forties, Paul St. Jacques was tall and elegantly thin. His salt-and-pepper hair was carefully styled, his mustache trimmed. He was handsome and he was smooth and he made Julie feel uncomfortable.

But the view from his balcony was breathtaking. From here she could see the Eiffel Tower, the Invalides and the lights along the Champs-Elysées.

"Is this your first trip to Paris?" he asked.

Julie nodded. "My first time in Europe."

"What a thrill it must be to see it all for the first time. I'm glad you came to Paris first. It is the most beautiful of cities, yes?"

"Yes, it is."

He stepped closer. She could smell his cologne, too strong, too sweet. "I wish I were the one showing it to you," he murmured. "Perhaps when Rafael is busy with his appointments you and I can see a bit of Paris together."

Surprised and a little embarrassed, Julie pointed to one of the lit boats moving slowly down the Seine. "We had dinner on one of those last night," she said.

"*Très romantique,* yes?" He put an arm around her waist.

"Monsieur St. Jacques . . ."

"Paul," he whispered in her ear. "You must call me Paul, *ma chère* Julie."

"Please," she said, and tried to step away from him.

He drew her closer. "Please what, *ma petit?* I would be happy to do anything that pleases you. Whatever—"

"Juliana?" Rafael stood in the open doorway. "There are some people I want you to meet, but if you're occupied . . ."

She stepped away from St. Jacques.

"I was showing your lovely wife the view from the balcony." He gave Julie a lingering look. "It is beautiful, *n'est-ce pas?*"

Rafael took a step forward, but before he could say anything, Julie hurried to him. "You were talking to someone when I came out," she said nervously. "Monsieur St. Jacques offered to show me the view."

"And what else?" He took her arm in a grip that was almost painful.

They went inside. He introduced her to a Monsieur and Madame Berdonneau. Monsieur Berdonneau owned a gallery on the Boulevard St. Germain, Rafael explained.

"I could sell as many pieces of your sculpture as I could get," he said to Rafael in English. "At least once a month someone asks for one of your pieces and I must tell them I do not have any. *Pourquoi?*" He shook his head. "I can see why your husband prefers to spend time with you, *madame,* but can you not persuade him to also work in his studio?"

A waiter passed. Monsieur Berdonneau took two glasses of champagne, gave one to Julie and one to Madame Berdonneau. "You are here for your honeymoon, yes? But a little business, too, Rafael. Will you come to my gallery sometime in the morning? Eleven perhaps?"

"Of course, Andre."

"And bring Madame Vega with you. I'm sure she would be interested in seeing the gallery."

"I'm afraid my wife has other plans."

Julie looked at him but said nothing. She couldn't believe that he was angry because she had gone out onto the balcony with Paul St. Jacques, but something had upset him.

In a little while Paul appeared to usher everyone in to dinner. The dining room table, set with fine china, crystal and silver, glowed with candlelight.

Paul fussed with the seating. "Monique, you're next to Gaston. Claudette, you sit at Pierre's right, will you, dear? Rafael there at the end of the table next to Madeline, yes? Then Monsieur and Madame Berdonneau. And you, *ma chère* Julie, will sit next to me."

She looked quickly at Rafael. His dark eyebrows drew together in a frown, but he said nothing. Paul St. Jacques held her chair. He filled her wineglass when the champagne pâté was served. He moved his chair closer during the fish course and took her hand over the raspberry sorbet. He touched her knee while she tried to eat her *boeuf bourguignonne.*

"For dessert we have *la mousse au chocolat,*" he whispered in her ear when one of the white-jacketed waiters served them. "I hope you like it."

She tried to edge away as she took a bite. "It's very good," she said.

"As sweet as you, *ma petite* Julie."

She'd had just about enough of Paul St. Jacques. If he hadn't been Rafael's agent she would have dumped the chocolate mousse right into his elegant lap. But because he was Rafael's agent and presumably his friend, she simply tried to shift her chair a bit to the left and looked down the length of the table, hoping to catch Rafael's eye to let him know how uncomfortable she was.

But Madeline Duvalier had captured his attention. Full breasts at half-mast, all but spilling out of her low-cut gown, she leaned toward him and covered his hand with hers while she whispered something into his ear.

Julie looked down at her chocolate mousse. She didn't understand this kind of sophistication, if indeed that's what it was. She wanted to scratch Made-

line Duvalier's eyes out and tell Monsieur St. Jacques
to go take a flying leap off his balcony.

"Permit me," he said. "A bit of chocolate here..."
And before she could stop him he ran his finger across
her lower lip.

She froze. From the end of the table she heard a
chair scrape back. Rafael strode around the table to the
back of her seat. "It's late," he said in English. "I'm
afraid we have to leave."

"But, my dear Rafael..." Duvalier, too, rose. "You
cannot think to leave now. We will have a few after-
dinner drinks, yes? Then Claudette will play the piano
and we will dance until dawn and watch the sun come
up over Paris." He took Julie's hand. "Your lovely
Julie doesn't want to go, do you, my dear?"

"We have to," Rafael said before she could answer.

"But I need to talk to you, *mon ami*. I've been approached by the government about a sculpture and I
have told them that you are the one to do it."

"I'll call your office tomorrow and we'll set up an
appointment." Rafael took Julie's arm, and when Paul
stepped forward as though to embrace her, Rafael put
his arm around her waist. *"Bonsoir,"* he said to the
table in general. "My wife isn't feeling well. I'm afraid
we must go."

He steered her to the foyer and they collected her
evening coat from the maid. He didn't speak in the elevator that took them to the lobby, or in the taxi on the
way to their hotel.

When they entered the hotel and went through the
lobby, she said, "I'm glad we left when we did."

He looked straight ahead. "Are you?"

"Yes. My French is almost nonexistent. I'm..." She
wanted to word it delicately, but there really wasn't any

delicate way to tell him she didn't like his friends. "I'm afraid I don't have much in common with your friends," she said.

"That's strange." He opened the elevator door once they reached their floor and motioned for her to precede him. "I thought you had a great deal in common with Paul." He stopped in front of the door to their room and unlocked it. Once they were inside, he said, "When you were out on the balcony he had his arms around you. At the dinner table he couldn't keep his hands off you."

"Oh, for heaven's sake," Julie said, "the man's a twerp."

"I beg your pardon?"

"He's silly and pretentious. You'd have realized how uncomfortable I was if you hadn't been so entranced with Madeline's *chichis*."

"Don't be vulgar." He glared at her, then turned and snapped on the television. A woman who looked like Madeline was demonstrating a lacy bra. He switched channels.

Julie went into the bedroom and closed the door behind her. She couldn't believe that Rafael was angry because of Paul St. Jacques. And though she hadn't enjoyed the party, she didn't like being hauled away as if she were a naughty child.

She undressed, took a quick shower and got into bed. From the other room she could hear the blare of the television. She turned off the light on her side of the bed and closed her eyes. When Rafael came in she pretended to be asleep.

He undressed and got into bed. He made no attempt to touch her, but lay with his back to her.

Her earlier anger faded. She didn't want it to be like this between them. "Rafael?" she whispered, and touched his shoulder.

He didn't respond, but she knew he wasn't asleep. She hesitated, then with a sigh moved to her side of the bed. But it was a long time that night before she fell asleep.

He'd thought she was different, but he should have known better. She flaunted her beauty just as Margarita had. When he'd seen her on the balcony with Paul he'd felt a blinding, almost uncontrollable rage. He'd wanted to wipe that lascivious look off Paul's face and hurl him off the balcony. And he'd wanted to shake Juliana until her teeth rattled.

He'd been a fool to think she was different.

She turned and murmured in her sleep. Her leg brushed his and he felt himself grow hard. Damn her! Damn her for making him want her this way.

He looked up at the ceiling and tried to think about something else, anything to stop the terrible hunger in his gut and in his groin. I don't need her, he told himself. I don't need anyone. And hated himself because he felt so empty, so bereft.

He was gone when Julie awoke the next morning. She got up and dressed, and hoping he might phone, she had breakfast in the suite. When eleven o'clock came and she still hadn't heard from him, she went down to the concierge and arranged for a city tour.

The double-deck tour bus stopped at the Eiffel Tower, the Palais de l'Elysée, Palais de Luxembourg, the Palais Royal and the Louvre. She enjoyed the tour and it was after five before she returned.

Rafael was waiting for her. "Where in the hell have you been?" he asked.

"I took a tour."

"With Paul?"

"Of course not!" Hands on her hips, Julie glared at him. "How can you even think that?" She threw her purse down on the sofa. "You weren't here. You didn't even leave a note. What was I supposed to do, sit here in the suite like a good wife and wait until you decided to come back?"

"A good wife? You might try acting like one."

"Dammit, Rafael..." She shook her head. "I don't understand you. *I* didn't come on to your friend last night, he came on to me. I didn't like it, but I didn't know what to do about it."

"Didn't you?" He turned away from her. "If you'll excuse me, I have to change. I'm having dinner with Monsieur Berdonneau tonight. You can eat downstairs or have your dinner sent up, whichever you choose."

Julie stared at him. This was the man she loved, the man she had married. She couldn't believe that he could be so warm and loving one day, so coolly remote the next. This was their honeymoon. How could he behave this way?

When he came out of the bedroom an hour later she was sitting on the sofa watching television. "I may be late," he said. "Don't wait up."

"I don't intend to."

At the door he hesitated as though there were something more he wanted to say. But he didn't. He simply went out and closed the door behind him.

* * *

Julie kept looking at the bedside clock. Twelve o'clock came, one. Finally, a little after two, she heard the door of their suite open. In a moment or two the light in the front room was shut off and he came into the bedroom. She lay very still, turned away from the light on his side of the bed, pretending to sleep.

With hooded eyelids she watched him throw his clothes carelessly over a chair. That wasn't like him. He headed for the bathroom and she saw him stagger. When he came back he got heavily into the bed, but he didn't turn off his light. She lay very still, waiting. Was he asleep? Should she reach over him and turn the light off?

When after a few minutes he didn't move, she sat up and leaned across to switch off the light. When she did, he pulled her down over him.

For a moment Julie didn't move. "Let me go," she said.

"No." He kissed her and she could smell the brandy on his breath. "Take off your gown." The words were slurred.

He rolled her onto her side and tried to pull the gown down over her arms. The straps broke. He shoved the gown down around her waist. And paid no attention when she said, "Stop it, Rafael."

But when she tried to get away from him, he clasped her hands with one of his and raised them over her head.

He kissed her. His breath was hot, his mouth was hungry.

"Let me go," she tried to say, but he stopped her words with an angry kiss and ground his mouth against hers.

He cupped her breast, and when she tried to twist away, he leaned to kiss her there. He took one peak between his teeth and ran his tongue back and forth across it. He suckled, he teased, he scraped and he licked.

And though her body heated, she cried, "No, Rafael. Let me go."

"You want this," he said. "You like it." He ran his fingers across her other breast and scraped the nipple with his nails. And when she shuddered, he said, "Yes, little *gringa,* you like this and you want it as much as I do."

She shook her head from side to side. "No, no, I don't."

He rubbed the palm of his hand across both breasts. He squeezed each nipple, and when she cried out he took her with his hungry mouth.

She didn't want to be made love to, not like this, not in anger. But when he touched her, when he kissed her... She moaned into his mouth and he whispered, "*Tu eres mi mujer,* Juliana. You are my woman."

He trailed a line of kisses across her ribs and down to her belly. He pulled the nightgown down over her hips and heard the fabric tear. He kissed her thighs, and held her when he nipped the tender skin there. Then suddenly before she could move, his mouth was on her.

"No!" she cried out. "Don't! Oh, don't!" And fought to free herself.

He wouldn't let her go, wouldn't stop though she pleaded, begged...

She writhed under the hands that held her. She moaned, she whimpered, "Please, please, please, please," because she had never known such a scalding, all-invading heat. It permeated every part of her body, every pore and every cell. It was heaven, it was hell.

She struggled to free herself, even as her body lifted to his. Then she was like a wild thing, trying to break free, even as her body soared and crumbled and broke into a million shards of an ecstasy that left her breathless, dizzy and trembling with reaction.

He came up over her and grasped her hips. He joined his body to hers and plunged like a wild stallion against her, head thrown back, the cords of his neck taut with strain.

"Again!" he cried. "Again for me. With me..."

She had no control, she was caught in a whirlwind, powerless against him, carried with him higher and higher on the crest of blinding passion.

"Now!" he cried.

And with a sob, crying his name in frenzied anguish, she tumbled with him over the edge of foreverness.

He collapsed over her, breathing hard, holding on to her as though he were afraid to let her go. In a little while her breathing slowed. She put her arms around him. She kissed his shoulder, and with his body still joined to hers, she slept.

And didn't feel the tears that flooded his eyes fall upon her breast.

What have I done? he asked himself. Dear God, what have I done? Only an evening ago he had told himself he would treat her more gently. Yet tonight, in unreasoning anger, he had taken her like a drunken fool. If he had hurt her, if he had bruised her, he would never forgive himself.

He kissed the top of Julie's head. "Forgive me," he whispered. "Forgive me."

Julie awoke to the smell of coffee, and when she opened her eyes she saw Rafael, dressed in pajamas and a robe, sitting beside her on the bed.

"I thought you could use this," he said.

She pushed her hair back from her face and sat up against the pillows. When she realized she was naked she pulled the sheet up over her breasts.

He handed her the coffee. "I owe you an apology," he said.

She didn't say anything.

"I had too much to drink last night. I'm sorry. I forced myself on you. It won't happen again."

Julie put the coffee cup down on the nightstand. "We've been angry with each other," she said. "I don't want us to be like that." She reached for his hand. "There was no reason for you to be jealous, Rafael."

"I know. I'm sorry."

"I love you, Rafael."

He sat very still. "You don't have to say that."

"Yes, I do, because it's true. I've loved you since that night in Patzcuaro when you lay on the bed with me and held me against the fury of the storm."

Emotion choked him. He wanted to tell her that he loved her, too. If only he could say the words. If only... But he could not. It wasn't in him to say them, and so he said, "My dearest girl," and gently kissed her.

When he let her go he lowered the sheet from her breasts. "Did I hurt you last night?" he asked.

"Of course not." She tried to cover herself, but he wouldn't let her.

He pulled the sheet down over her waist, and when he saw, against the paleness of her skin, two marks where his fingers had bruised her, he said, "That's what I did to you."

His face twisted with pain. He leaned down and kissed the faint blue marks and said, "Forgive me."

And when he felt her hands caress the top of his head, he took his robe off and his pajamas and lay down beside her. "I'm sorry," he said when he put his arms around her. "So sorry."

"Darling..."

The word made him go hollow inside. He cradled her in his arms. He kissed her, and when he felt her sweet response, he began to make love to her, slowly, gently. And in that final moment he said, "My dearest, my precious Juliana."

But he would not, because he could not, say that he loved her.

Paul St. Jacques called to invite them for dinner. Rafael refused, but agreed to meet Paul during the day to discuss a new commission. It was arranged, a contract was signed, and he hoped he would never have to see Paul again.

He was very careful of Juliana now, always gentle, always polite, but somehow curiously remote. And though they made love, it was not with the wild abandon of the first few days of their honeymoon. He held a part of himself back, afraid of hurting her again and fearful of offering more than he was capable of.

Juliana had changed during these first weeks of their marriage. She had blossomed, she had come into her own as a woman. Her warmth comforted him, her passion thrilled him. But still he held back, afraid that if he gave his heart he would be hurt, as he had been hurt before.

At the end of their second week in Paris they flew to Madrid. It pleased him to see her pleasure at being there. He laughed when she told him she'd saved three thousand dollars for a six-month trip to Spain. He spent that much the first week they were there.

They stayed in a five-star hotel. They had lunch at Botin's, because she said that was where Hemingway had always eaten; and late dinners at Madrid's fanciest restaurants. He bought her a dark green suede coat, black leather pants and a matching jacket, silk blouses, shoes and bags. Because he wanted to please her.

They had lunch with two friends of his, the man in charge of buying works of art for the government of ▁pain and an old friend who owned a gallery.

Juan Ortiz, the old friend, sat across the table from Juliana. "Your Spanish is perfect," he said. "But your accent is Mexican, not Spanish. If you were to stay here for a while you would speak our way."

With a smile, Juliana said, "Rafael and I are flying back to Mexico next week."

"But Rafael has much work to do now. You will stay and I myself will teach you to speak as we do."

"I'm afraid that's impossible, Señor Ortiz. You see, Rafael and I haven't been married very long. I love him far too much to be away from him even for a day." She held up her wineglass. "May I have a little more wine, darling?"

The muscles that had tightened relaxed. She'd handled Ortiz's mild flirtation well. Because he was here. If he hadn't been would she have done the same thing? Or would she have . . . ?

Por Dios, he must be losing his mind. Juliana had done nothing wrong. Yet when they left the restaurant and Juan Ortiz kissed the back of her hand, he wanted to snatch her away and say, "This is *my* wife. My Juliana. My love."

But he said nothing. Because he did not believe in love; he never would.

CHAPTER FOURTEEN

They returned to Janitzio on a crisp autumn day. They had called Kico from Mexico City to tell him when they might arrive, and when they climbed the hill to the hacienda, followed by two men who carried their luggage, he was on the promontory waiting for them.

"Here I am!" he called out. "Up here! Up here!" He turned and started down the path toward them, and when he reached them, Julie scooped him up in her arms and gave him a hug. "I missed you so much," she said, kissing both his cheeks. "We both did, didn't we, Rafael?"

"Yes, of course." He patted Kico's shoulder. "Have you been a good boy?"

"*Sí,* Papa." Kico picked up the small bag Julie had put down. "I can carry this," he declared.

"Good!" Julie ruffled his hair. "Because that's the suitcase with all of your gifts."

"You brought me something?"

She'd bought him a whole lot of somethings; Nintendo games, a backpack, a French cap, a woolen jacket and T-shirts from every city they'd visited. "I do believe I did," she said with a laugh. And turning to Rafael, she added, "It's good to be home, isn't it?"

He looked at her strangely because he remembered Margarita's reaction when she'd first seen Janitzio. "But, darling," she'd said. "Surely you don't live here *all* the time. I assumed you kept a home in Mexico City or Acapulco. You don't really expect me to live here. It's so. . ." She shuddered. "So isolated."

Which was exactly why he'd chosen to live in Janitzio rather than Mexico City. He didn't want a lot of interruptions or people stopping in for drinks every afternoon. He'd thought she understood that when they married.

"I live in Janitzio because I work better here," he had told her. "We won't be hermits, Margarita. We'll go to Mexico City occasionally." And even though he loathed the place, he added, "Or Acapulco every six months or so."

"Every six months!" A look of pure horror had crossed her face and her dark eyes had grown cold and angry.

"We're on our honeymoon," he said, trying to be patient. "We don't need anybody else."

"Speak for yourself, darling." Her voice had been harsh and there had been an expression on her face he'd never seen before.

A week later she'd flown to Mexico City, "to consult with her agent," she said. She'd been gone for three weeks and when she returned she brought some of her friends with her; Graciela Torres, who made a career out of marrying and divorcing very rich men, Juan Montes, Alfredo Zavala, the leading man in her last film, and Felipe Gonzáles, his agent.

They'd stayed for a week, and when they went back to Mexico City, Margarita went with them. "Just for a day or two," she'd said.

That had been the pattern of their eight-year marriage. The longest period of time she'd stayed on the island had been during the last five months of her pregnancy.

Juliana wasn't like Margarita, but how long before she, too, would become bored with the island? And with him? Europe had been exciting for her, but Janitzio was a far cry from either Paris or Madrid or the Costa del Sol, where they'd spent the last ten days of their honeymoon.

He hadn't meant to stay away so long. Two weeks, he'd thought before they left, three at the most. But after Madrid he had suggested they spend a few days in Torremolinos. The few days had become a week, then ten days of what he would always remember as the happiest time of his life.

They had a suite of rooms on the twentieth floor of a hotel that overlooked the Mediterranean. They sunned and swam every day and Juliana's skin tanned to a rich cocoa brown, except for the narrow stripes of fair skin her bathing suit covered.

"I could do like the European women," she'd said one morning when they were getting ready to go to the beach. "I could go topless."

"Over my dead body," he'd growled at her.

"You don't like my breasts?" She'd tried to look innocent, but the twitch of a smile betrayed her. "Maybe I could show just one at a time," she went on. "That'd be different."

He'd come up behind her and covered her bare breasts with his hands. "These are mine," he'd said. "And don't you forget it."

They made love then, as they had every day and night and midafternoon since they'd been married. He couldn't help himself. She was a fever in his blood, softness and sweet scents, warm and eager as soon as he touched her. And though he told himself that this insatiability would soon wear off, it hadn't. Juliana had only to look at him a certain way, or say his name in a slightly breathless manner, and his body caught fire. Would that change now that they were back in Janitzio?

He watched her going up the path with Kico and wished he hadn't agreed to let the boy stay, that he'd insisted he be sent away. He wanted to be alone with Juliana without the interference of a child, without any reminders of the past.

Her affection for Kico was real. She'd spoken of him often while they'd been away and she'd insisted on calling him every few days to make sure he was all right. She's playing mother, he'd told himself. That worried him. They hadn't discussed having children. He didn't want to, at least not for a long time. Perhaps in five or six years, but not now. Now he wanted Juliana all to himself.

The three servants were waiting for them when they reached the house. Juliana embraced them, as happy to see them as they were to see her. She'd bought presents for them, of course, even though he'd insisted it wasn't necessary.

Once in the living room she hugged Kico again and, clasping his hands, whirled around the room with him. Both of them were laughing, and as Rafael watched he felt a pang of jealousy, not because she was giving attention to the boy, but because he suddenly felt like an outsider, like an orphan with his nose pressed against the glass of a home where there was love and laughter.

He wished they were still in Torremolinos, making love out on their balcony in the darkness of the night

while the waves crashed against the shore below and the
moon turned Juliana's skin to gold.

But they weren't in Spain, they were here in Janitzio. He had work to do, commissions for new sculptures he had received while they were abroad. Perhaps
if he lost himself in his work his need for Juliana would
diminish. Perhaps.

They had lunch, at Juliana's suggestion, out on the
terrace. Juanita had prepared a typical Mexican *co-
mida; chiles rellenos,* chicken in mole sauce, rice and
beans and a salsa hot enough to convince Julie she really was back in Mexico.

She was glad to be home, for that was how she
thought of the hacienda or anywhere else where Rafael was. While they had been in Europe she would say,
when they were shopping or at the opera or sightsee-
ing, "I'm tired, Rafael. I want to go home."

He'd smiled, correcting her. "You mean back to our
hotel."

"Yes, of course."

"But you said 'home.'"

"That's what it is," she'd said. "As long as you are
there, wherever we are is home to me."

She loved him so much more than she had thought
it possible to love. Loved going to sleep with her head
on his shoulder and waking with him beside her each
morning. He had only to look at her or touch her and
her body caught fire.

On their last night in Torremolinos they'd gone to a
garden restaurant overlooking the Mediterranean.
There had been candlelight and good red wine and a
chateaubriand that melted in their mouths. But halfway through the meal Rafael's leg had brushed against

hers. She'd turned to smile at him, and when she did he began to caress her thigh. They looked at each other and it began, that slow rise of heat. The hand on her thigh tightened, she'd heard the rasp of breath in his throat. "Don't look at me like that," he said.

She pretended an innocence she didn't feel, pretended she didn't understand. She ran her tongue across her lower lip and watched the flare of his nostrils, the narrowing of his eyes.

He'd thrown a sheaf of bills down on the table, and once outside the restaurant, in the shadow of the garden, he'd pulled her into his arms and covered her mouth with his. "You've bewitched me," he said against her lips. "I don't even know what I'm doing half the time. All I want to do is make love to you."

"And I want you, too," she'd said. "Now. Tonight. Always."

But they were home now, back in Janitzio. Would that change?

When twilight came they went back into the house. She gave Eloise, Juanita and Eufrasia their presents, and when it was bedtime for Kico she went to tuck him in. The presents she'd brought him were piled on his bed and he had on an I Love Paris T-shirt.

"The Nintendo games are really neat," he said. "Do you think Father will let me play them on the television in his office?"

"I'm not sure." Julie thought for a moment. "It might be better if you had your own television and VCR, Kico."

"My own..." He stared at her, eyes wide. "Really?"

She ruffled his hair. "I'll see what I can do," she said.

Rafael had disappeared when she went back to the living room. "He said he would be in his studio for a little while," Eufrasia told her. "Meantime, *señora*, I have unpacked your things." She hesitated. "You will be in Señor Vega's bedroom, *sí?*"

"*Sí,*" Julie answered with a smile, imagining Rafael's reaction if she told him she'd prefer her own room. She *wanted* to be with him. She couldn't even imagine how she had survived all these years without him.

His bedroom was, to be kind about it, austere. All dark wood, with drapes as heavy as the brown spread that covered the king-size bed. The two armchairs on either side of the fireplace were brown, too. It was a man's room, a somber, cheerless room. But his room.

The only touch of cheer was the bouquet of white roses on the dresser.

As she had the day of their wedding, Julie touched the delicate petals. This was the side of Rafael she loved the most, this touch of unexpected sweetness.

With a smile she went into the bathroom. Here there were thick black towels, a sink big enough to splash in and a black marble tub that looked large enough for two people to bathe in comfortably. Had he bathed in it with Margarita? The thought of it, of his having lain in the bed with Margarita, of his making love in this big sunken tub with Margarita, as he had with her in Paris, tightened Julie's stomach.

She hadn't thought all that much about his previous wife, but here in the room he had shared with her she did. He and Margarita had been married for a long time; they'd had a son together. Surely there had been good times, loving times.

But that was the past, she was the present. She loved Rafael, she would be a good wife and in time he would forget the awfulness of Margarita's death.

Julie bathed then, and by the time Rafael came in she had changed into one of the new nightgowns he had bought for her in Madrid. It was an old-fashioned gown, white, with a high neck and long sleeves. "You look prim and proper in it," he'd said the first time she'd worn it. "Now raise your arms and let me take it off you."

"Why are you smiling?" he asked now.

"I'm remembering the first time I wore this."

"Ah, yes." He, too, smiled. "Give me a few minutes to bathe and we'll see what we can do about getting it off." He hesitated. "Does this room suit you?"

"It's a bit somber."

"Somber?" He looked around. "Yes, I suppose it is." He shrugged. "Change it any way you want to. But no pink ruffles, all right?"

She put her arms around him. "No ruffles of any kind." He kissed her, and when he felt her warmth and softness under the fabric of the gown, he said, "Maybe I can bathe later."

She placed her hands against the small of his back and brought him closer. "Splendid idea, Señor Vega," she said, and with a laugh stepped away from him to turn back the spread and the linen sheet beneath it.

Something black scurried across the sheet. She screamed. "Oh, no! No!"

"What is it?" Rafael ran to her side. "Juliana, what is it?"

"The spider!" She looked at it, horrified as it scurried down toward the bottom of the bed.

Rafael swept it off with his hand and stomped on it. *"Por Dios!"* he exclaimed. "How in the hell did it get in there?"

Her eyes were wide, her face was white. "It happened at the church, too," she whispered. "A spider just like that one."

"The church? What are you talking about?"

"When I was dressing. There was a spider in the box with my wedding dress."

"Why didn't you tell me?"

"I...I don't know. So much was happening. The wedding. The drive to Morelia to catch the plane to Mexico City. The flight to Paris. I forgot about it, Rafael." Clasping her hands together, she looked at the bed. "How did it get here?" she whispered. "Do you think somebody—"

"No," he said. "Of course not."

"But two spiders?" A shiver of fear ran through her. Was this, as she had thought on her wedding day, an evil omen? Or had somebody deliberately put the spider in the box that held her gown and now here in the bed that she and Rafael would share for the first time?

He put his arms around her, and when she had quieted he took the sheets off the bed, examined them carefully, shook them out and remade the bed.

"It's all right," he said while he undressed. "No more spiders. The only strange creature that will be in the bed tonight is me."

Julie tried to smile. She let him lead her to bed. They made love, they bathed together, and afterward she snuggled close to him. But it was a long time that night before she slept, because no matter what Rafael had said, she knew that an evil presence had been in this room tonight.

* * *

For the next few days Julie busied herself in the house. She opened windows to let the light in. She brought plants and flowers from the market and filled the house with them. Two afternoons while Rafael worked in his studio, she drove into Morelia with Eufrasia to select material for new drapes for the living room and dining room, as well as for both bedrooms. She chose a bright blue for Kico's bedroom, a soft beige and white and gold for her and Rafael's room.

Each night when she and Rafael went through the corridors to their room she looked up at the martyred saints, and finally one night she said, "Do you mind if we get rid of them?"

"I told you before you could do anything you wanted with the house. If you can't stand the paintings, then by all means get rid of them. We can donate them to the church if you like."

The following evening while Rafael went to work in his studio, Julie, armed with a ladder, began taking the paintings down. She lifted two of them off the wall, then stared up at a seventeenth-century martyr who looked, she thought, more like a Spanish inquisitor than a saint and said, "Sorry, old boy, but you're coming down."

She reached for the painting and lifted it off the hook that held it to the wall, just as the lights went out.

Darkness surrounded her and she gasped, teetering on the ladder, trying not to drop the heavy painting. She grasped it in one hand and the top of the ladder with the other and cautiously started down. She stopped. She thought she'd heard something. But what?

"Is someone there?" she asked.

There was no answer and she told herself she was being foolish, that the suffering saints had spooked her. But no, she sensed something, heard something. A whisper of cloth, a hushed breath.

"Eufrasia? Eloisa? Is that you?"

There was no answer. "Listen," she said. "This isn't funny. It..."

Something rushed at her through the darkness. She felt the ladder start to topple. She let go of the painting, heard it crash before she fell, down into darkness.

Dazed and dizzy, Julie managed to make it into the living room. She called out to Eloisa, who took one look at her and ran to get Rafael.

She'd hit her head when she fell. It hurt. So did her wrist. She slumped on the sofa and tried to calm her queasy stomach. Someone had pushed her; someone had tried to hurt her. But who?

Rafael ran in. "Juliana!" he cried. "What happened?"

"I was up on the ladder," she said. "I... I fell."

"Call the doctor," he told Eloisa.

"No," Julie protested. When she leaned forward and put pressure on her hand she winced. "I think I sprained my wrist," she said.

Rafael eased her back and gently felt her wrist. It was red and swollen. He hoped it wasn't broken. "What happened?" he asked.

"I'd just taken one of the paintings off the wall when the lights in the corridor went off. I heard something. Then..." She put a hand to her head. "Somebody... somebody was there. I heard him. He pushed the ladder over."

"Somebody pushed you? That's impossible, Juliana." His dark eyebrows came together in a worried frown. "Are you sure?"

"Damn right I'm sure."

"Call the police," he said to Eloisa. "Tell the sergeant in charge what's happened and that I want him to send a man to check every inch of the house. When the man comes, you go with him."

"Me, *señor?*"

"Along with Juanita, if that'll make you feel better."

"Muy bien, señor." She looked worriedly down at Julie and in a whisper said, "It was a *fantasma* who pushed you, Señora Juliana. A ghost who walks through the house at night and—"

"That's enough, Eloisa. I won't have that kind of talk. Now go and do as I said, and never say anything like that again."

A ghost who walks at night. Julie shivered. And though Rafael said, "The girl is speaking nonsense," she couldn't help but wonder if perhaps there was a ghost. A something or somebody who really did walk in the night.

They were asleep when they heard Kico scream. Julie was out of bed, reaching for her gown and robe by the time Rafael swung his legs over the side of the bed.

"Another nightmare," he said as he pulled his briefs on.

Whatever it was, there was sheer terror in the little boy's voice.

Together she and Rafael ran down the hall to his room. Rafael snapped on the light. The little boy sat straight up in bed, his eyes wide with fright, screaming, "She's here! Mama's here!"

Julie reached him before Rafael did and gathered him in her arms. "It's all right, Kico. We're here, love. Your papa and I are here. Nothing's going to hurt you, Kico."

She rocked him back and forth until, little by little, his sobs subsided. When they did she brushed the damp hair back from his forehead, and Rafael said, "Another nightmare, boy?"

Kico shook his head. "It wasn't a nightmare, Papa. I saw her. I saw Mama."

Rafael sat down on the bed. "No you didn't. Mama's dead. She's with the *angelitos*."

"No! No! No!" Kico shrieked. "She came up out of the lake." He tightened his arms around Julie's neck. "I saw her. I saw her."

"Kico, baby, your mother wasn't in the lake and she wasn't here." She looked over his head at Rafael. "Didn't he go to her funeral?"

"I thought he was too young."

"Has he ever been to the cemetery?"

"Of course not. That's no place for a child." Rafael shook his head. "Kico will get over this, Juliana. The nightmares will pass and he'll be perfectly all right." He patted Kico's shoulder. "Won't you, boy?"

Kico sniffed. "I . . . I guess so."

"Lie down and go back to sleep," Rafael said.

But Kico clung to Julie. "Don't leave me," he pleaded. "If you do she'll come back."

"I won't leave you, sweetheart." She looked up at Rafael, and when she saw him frown, she whispered, "I'll just stay until he goes to sleep."

"Very well, but don't be too long." He looked down at Kico. "It was only a nightmare," he said again.

Julie got up when Rafael left. She turned on the bedside light and crossed the room to turn off the overhead light.

That's when she saw the wet footprints.

She stared down at them. Footprints. Made by wet bare feet. She started to call out to Rafael, but stopped, because if she did, if she told him in front of Kico, Kico would be terrified. But God in heaven, how had the wet footprints gotten there? Had Margarita risen from the lake? Had her ghost come here to haunt them?

Stop it! she told herself. Stop it!

She remembered the doll with the blond hair she had found at the door of her room, the green dress that had hung dripping with algae in her closet. Fear choked her and she started to tremble.

"Julie?"

She looked at Kico. She fought for calmness, fought for sanity. Maybe Kico had gotten up in the night. Maybe somehow his feet had gotten wet. But these weren't a child's footprints. An adult had made them. But who?

"Julie?" he said. "Is anything wrong, Julie?"

"No, Kico. Nothing's wrong." She forced what she hoped was a cheerful smile. "Suppose you snuggle down," she said, "and I'll stay right here with you until you fall asleep." She lay down and put her arms around him. "How's this? Better?"

"Nice," he said, and snuggled against her.

Julie kissed the top of his head. "Go to sleep now, sweetie, I'm right here with you."

And though her voice was calm she wasn't. She could feel the frantic beating of her heart, and a chill that not even the little boy's warmth could dispell shivered through her. For evil was afoot in this house. And she was afraid.

CHAPTER FIFTEEN

"That's impossible!" Rafael said the next morning when Julie told him about the footprints. "You're imagining things."

"I saw them," she insisted.

"Then there's a reasonable explanation. Kico probably got up to go to the bathroom and somehow got his feet wet."

"They weren't a child's footprints, Rafael. They were an adult's."

"Look," he said with a shake of his head, "you've been upset ever since we returned from our trip. First there was the spider in the bed and then you fell off the ladder." He picked up her hand and kissed her still-bandaged wrist. "Still hurt?" he asked.

Julie pulled her hand away. "I saw the footprints, Rafael." She hesitated. "There've been other things, too. Before we were married, I mean."

He raised an eyebrow.

"I found a doll outside my bedroom one morning." Remembering her fear and revulsion, she took a deep breath before she went on. "It had blond hair and it was wearing a green dress like mine. It . . ." she looked up at him. "It was dripping wet, as though it had been drowned."

"My God, Juliana."

"That's not all. A few days later when I opened my closet the green dress there was wet and dripping with algae."

His face went white. "Why didn't you tell me?"

"So much was happening. I knew you weren't happy about my being here. I was afraid that you'd think I was imagining things. Then when . . . when things began to happen between us I forgot about both incidents. But last night when I saw the footprints..." She shivered. "It all came back, Rafael, and I knew I had to tell you."

"The footprints were the boy's," he said. "Or yours or mine. We were both barefoot when we ran into the room."

"But our feet weren't wet."

Rafael drew her into his arms. "I'm sorry about the things that happened to you before, Juliana. I know how frightened you must have been, but I honestly believe there was a reasonable explanation for what happened. Perhaps one of the maids—"

"No," she said. "It wasn't one of the maids."

"You're going through a period of adjustment, my dear," he said, trying to calm her. "Settling into the role of *ama de casa,* of being a housewife and a mother. Coming back here must seem pretty tame after France and Spain."

"It doesn't seem tame." She didn't want him to change the subject. "And I did see the wet footprints."

"All right," he said gently.

Frustrated because she knew Rafael didn't believe her, Julie stepped out of his arms. "I don't need a period of adjustment," she said. "I love being here with you and Kico."

"But maybe that's part of the problem."

Julie stepped a little away from him. "What do you mean?"

"Kico. You should have let me send him away."

"I don't understand you," she said, reaching for her robe. "I've seen how you treat him. It's as though he were a stranger. Most of the time you call him 'boy,' as though you can't bear to say his name. You never show him any affection, you barely seem aware of his existence." She faced him. "He's a little boy and he needs you. Can't you see that? He's your son and he—"

"He's not my son."

Her eyes went wide with shock. "My God," she said. "What a terrible thing to say."

"Terrible, but true." His nostrils pinched, his mouth drew tight. He walked over to one of the chairs next to the fireplace and slumped down into it. "I've known from the beginning he wasn't mine."

"I don't believe it." She put her hand to her head as though to steady herself. "If... if that's true..." Julie stared at him. "Who— My God, Rafael, what are you saying?"

"That he isn't mine." He looked at her, his face haunted, his eyes dark. "It started right after our marriage," he said in a toneless voice. "The first was Alfredo Zavala, her leading man in the last picture she made. When I found out about it I wanted to kill him. And her."

Julie stared at him, then slowly walked across the room and eased herself into the other chair.

"I beat the hell out of Zavala," he said. "It took two weeks before he'd go out in public again. As for Margarita..." He shook his head. "She begged me to forgive her. She said she couldn't help it, that's what happened sometimes on a movie set. The film she made with Alfredo had been a sensuous one. There'd been bedroom scenes, they'd both been half-naked. She said she couldn't help herself and that it would never happen again.''

"And you believed her?''

"Yes, I believed her." He ran a hand through his hair. "There were other men after that. Some of them I knew about, some I didn't. She moved out of our bedroom . . ." He looked at Julie. "This wasn't our room, Juliana. I never slept with Margarita here.''

A sigh trembled through her, but before she could say anything, Rafael went on.

"She spent more and more time in Mexico City. I told myself I didn't care, the marriage was a farce anyway. What did it matter? But there were times . . ." He clenched his fist. "Times when she came to me in the night, all silk and lace and perfumed body, and God help me, I still wanted her.''

He looked at Julie and his eyes were haunted. "What kind of a man does that make me?" he asked. "A cuckold husband who still desired his wife. A buffoon, grateful for a few favors.''

He got up and went to stand in front of the fireplace. "There were other men after Zavala. I don't know how many before Felipe.''

"Felipe?''

"Felipe Gonzáles, my agent." His expression hardened. "My friend.''

Julie started to rise and go to him, but he held up his hand, stopping her. "No," he said, and she sank back down to the chair. As terrible as this was to hear, it was even more terrible for him to tell her. She had to let him; she couldn't stop him now.

"I'd started to drink too much," Rafael went on. "I couldn't work. I spent a lot of time away from the island. I went to Puerta Vallarta, to Acapulco. I picked women up and tried to make love to them. But I couldn't. I didn't want anybody else, only Margarita. Even then." He gazed down into the fire. "One night in Acapulco I ran into them."

"Them?" Julie asked.

"Margarita and Felipe. I was drunk. I shoved her away and I beat the living hell out of him. The police took me to jail and an ambulance took Felipe to the hospital. There was a photographer in the bar. He took pictures. The next morning when I paid off the police and got out of jail, I saw the newspapers. I'd made the headlines complete with a photograph of me, drunk, disheveled."

He turned away from the fireplace and went back to the chair, his face ravaged, his eyes dull with pain. "That did it for me. I knew it was over. All I felt for Margarita, and for myself, was disgust. I didn't want any part of her."

Julie got up from her chair and went to kneel beside him. When he made as though to stop her, she said, "I need to be close to you."

Rafael leaned his head back against the chair. "Two months went by and I didn't hear from her, then suddenly she was here. I told her I didn't want her and she said...she told me she was four months pregnant. She said the baby was mine."

Julie took his hand, but she didn't say anything.

"She had the baby. Kico. And she continued to live here until . . . until the accident."

For a long time neither of them spoke. He looked exhausted, depleted by what he had told her. Julie could find no words of comfort, she could only hold his hand to let him know she was there for him.

"He isn't mine."

"Of course he is."

"No. I knew from the beginning he wasn't. I thought about sending him away after Margarita's death, of taking him to Felipe and saying, 'Take the brat, he's yours.' But I couldn't. The boy had been through enough." His voice hardened. "I'll feed and clothe him and see that he has a proper education. But that's all I can do. I don't have anything else to give."

She leaned her face against his knee and he began to stroke her hair. For a long time she didn't say anything, then raising her head she said, "You told me that..." This was very hard for her to say, but she must. "You told me that you and Margarita had slept together, even after she..." Julie looked up at him. "I think you're wrong, Rafael. I think Kico is your child. I see you in him, the way his shoulders go back when he's angry, the way he cocks his head when he's thinking."

"No, you're wrong. He's not mine. He's Felipe's kid."

Julie waited, then, as calmly as she could, said, "You're the only father Kico has ever known, Rafael. He loves you and he needs you. Surely you know that. Can't you accept him? Can't you love him?"

For a moment Rafael didn't speak. He looked at her and almost absentmindedly began to stroke her hair again. "I don't think I can," he said in a voice so low she could barely hear him. "I don't believe I have it in me to love Kico." His hand stilled. "To love anyone."

The only sound in the room was the crackle of the fire. She felt hollow inside. Devoid of feeling. Empty.

Then unexpectedly she felt a surge of anger, not at Rafael but at what he had suffered at the hands of a totally immoral woman. Margarita had gutted him. She'd taken his pride, she'd left him without the will to love again.

But he was capable of love, for though he had never said the words, he had shown his love for her in countless ways; in the white roses he had placed in their room every morning, in a thousand tendernesses, in the fine passion when they made love and his gentleness afterward. Love showed in the touch of his hands when he stroked her to quietness, in the way he gathered her in his arms and told her how much she pleased him, how dear she was.

Perhaps he didn't know, perhaps he was unable to face the idea that he had fallen in love with her. But in time he would. In time, if she loved him enough, he would acknowledge his love. And when he did, when he was able to open his heart to her, then surely he would also open his heart to Kico.

She had only to wait. And to keep on loving him.

October came. The nights were cold, the days were bleak. Rafael spent his days and often part of the night working in his studio. Before he and Juliana had left on their honeymoon he had completed the bust of Cervantes and fired it. But the statue of Juliana was still in clay. He would fire it when he finished a small piece that Paul St. Jacques had asked for before he and Juliana left Paris.

He had four other commissions, and a week ago he had received a call from the personal secretary of Mexico's president asking him to prepare sketches for a large sculpture to be placed in the lobby of the government building. With the request had come an invitation to attend a presidential reception.

Juliana had been pleased when he told her about it. "The president of Mexico," she exclaimed. "What an honor for you, Rafael."

He knew it was expedient that he attend the reception and that very likely Juliana wanted to go. He'd been neglecting her, and though he had told her it was because of his work, they both knew that something had changed for them since the morning he'd told her about Margarita.

But if Rafael was withdrawn, Julie wasn't. If anything, she was even more loving. She pleased him in a thousand different ways, and when in the night he turned to her, she came into his arms with her sweet eagerness. And in her final moments, when he said only, "My dear, my dearest Juliana," she spoke unashamedly of her love.

"I love you," she said as she held him close to her breast. "I love you, Rafael."

But still he could not, he would not, say the words she wanted to hear.

Never in all her life had Julie seen a more beautiful room. Crystal chandeliers sparkled from the mosaic-tiled ceiling. One wall was mirrored, the other painted with a Diego Rivera mural. At one end of the room an orchestra played, while white-jacketed, white-gloved waiters moved through the crowd of elegantly dressed men and women.

The president, his wife and members of his cabinet stood at the entrance, greeting the guests as they came in.

"This is my wife, Juliana, *Señor Presidente,*" Rafael said when he shook hands with Mexico's head of state.

"*Mucho gusto.*" The president bowed over her hand. "We're delighted you could join us, Señora Vega. I have long known what a brilliant artist your husband is, now I can see what a true eye he has for beauty."

"Thank you, your..." She caught herself before she said "Your Excellency," and managed to say, "Mr. President."

He introduced her to his wife then, and with Rafael guiding her, they proceeded down the reception line.

After that there were more introductions. Everyone seemed glad to see Rafael. Men gave him the warm Mexican *abrazo,* women smiled warmly. These people were not like the people she had met in Paris at Paul St. Jacques's party. They seemed honestly pleased to meet her, and several of the women invited her to lunch. A young woman close to her own age said, "Rafael is a wonderful man. That's why it's so nice to see him happy again. My husband is a great friend of his, so I hope you and I can be friends, too."

When she and Rafael moved a little apart from the others, he took two glasses of champagne off the tray of a passing waiter and gave one to her. Touching his glass to hers he said, "You look lovely tonight, Juliana."

She'd worn the green dress and evening coat they'd bought in Paris, and the emerald earrings Rafael had given her. This afternoon she'd wanted to get her hair done, but as he had in Paris, Rafael had said, "No, I like your hair exactly the way you wear it."

"Loose and windblown," she said with a grin.

"That's right." He'd grinned back at her. "I don't want to feel hair spray when I get my hands into it." Then he'd put his hands in it, splayed his fingers along her scalp and pulled her closer. "I don't want to have to worry about messing it up when I make love to you."

She'd pretended an exasperated sigh. "I suppose that's what you're going to do now."

"Damn right," he said.

And so tonight, instead of an elegant hairdo, Julie's blond hair curled softly about her face.

The orchestra played Mexican waltzes and she and Rafael danced. They hadn't danced since that night on the Seine and it was wonderful to be back in his arms again. She was glad they'd come to Mexico City. It was exciting to be here, to meet the president of Mexico and his wife. She loved the elegance of it, the glamour and the excitement. And she loved dancing with Rafael.

The music stopped. Someone made the announcement that dinner was served and the guests began to move toward the banquet room. As they did, a man brushed against Rafael. *"Perdóname,"* he murmured. Then, "Rafael?"

Rafael turned. He froze and started to move past the man.

"Rafael, wait." The man put a detaining hand on Rafael's arm. "I'm glad to see you, old friend."

Rafael jerked his arm away. Surprised, Julie looked from him to the other man. He was almost as tall as Rafael. Handsome in a professorial kind of way, slim, gray-haired, impeccably dressed.

"Please," he said. "Isn't it time to let bygones be bygones? We were friends long before Margarita came into either of our lives."

Rafael's face was white. "Get out of my way," he said.

"But we have to talk," the man insisted. He turned to Julie. "My name is Felipe Gonzáles," he said. "Your husband and I were friends once. I hope you can convince him to at least speak to me."

She was almost too stunned to reply. This was the man who had been Margarita's lover, the agent, the friend who had betrayed Rafael's trust. She didn't know what to say or what to do. She was afraid that if he pushed Rafael too far there would be a scene, and so she said, "I don't interfere in my husband's business, Señor Gonzáles."

"Will you at least try to get him to have lunch with me so we can talk? I'll be in Patzcuaro on business next week. I beg you to convince him to meet with me."

She felt Rafael coil as though ready to spring. Taking his arm to lead him toward the dining room, she said, "You must excuse us, Señor Gonzáles."

"That son of a bitch," Rafael said under his breath.

"Rafael, don't. It's over. Don't let him spoil the evening for you."

But the evening was already spoiled. They barely touched their dinner, and though Julie did little more than sip her wine, Rafael downed glass after glass. Several times she glanced down the table to where Felipe Gonzáles sat. Each time she did he smiled.

He looked to be a decent sort of man, yet he had betrayed Rafael by having an affair with Margarita. Had he fathered Kico? She studied his face, looking for a resemblance. And saw none.

"I suppose you think he's handsome," Rafael said.

"No. No, I was just . . . just looking at him."

"Wondering how he'd be in bed?"

She went still, so angry it took every bit of her will-power not to slap him. In a quietly controlled voice she said, "I'm not Margarita, Rafael." Then she pushed her chair back from the table and walked out of the room.

He came after her and took her arm. "I'm sorry," he said. "I didn't mean it. It was seeing Felipe again. It brought everything back. I didn't mean to hurt you."

"But you did." She took a deep breath and tried to quell her anger. "Maybe you should talk to him," she said. "Maybe if you did you could put the past behind you and—"

"No! You know what the bastard did to me. How can you even suggest such a thing?"

He looked angry again and so she took his arm and said, "Let's get out of here, Rafael. Let's go back to the hotel."

He was silent in the taxi and in the elevator up to their floor. When they went into their suite he said, "You go on to bed. I'm going to watch television for a while. Last week's corrida. Something."

She started to shake her head but stopped. Perhaps he needed this time alone to sort out his thoughts. "All right," she said. "But don't be too long."

She took her clothes off, then changed into a short peach satin nightgown. She picked up a book she had brought with her from Janitzio and settled into bed. But she couldn't concentrate on the book. All she could think about was the look on Rafael's face when he'd first seen Felipe Gonzáles. How painful it must have been for him.

Once again the ghost of Margarita had appeared. Would that ghost ever be laid to rest? Would Rafael ever be able to bury the past and get on with his life?

Was he even now thinking about Margarita, about the way it had been before Felipe Gonzáles or the other men had come into their lives?

She threw the book across the bed. No, dammit, she wasn't going to let him think about Margarita. Muttering to herself, Julie threw back the sheet and went into the other room. A rerun of "Cheers" was playing on the television set. Carla and Cliff, the mailman, were exchanging barbs in Spanish. Rafael had his tie off and his shirt unbuttoned. He stared at the screen with unseeing eyes.

"Rafael?"

He turned to look at her.

"Come to bed." She went over to the set and shut it off. "It's late," she said.

"You're being bossy," he growled. But after a moment's hesitation he got up and followed her into the bedroom. There he yanked off his shirt and threw it over a chair before he sat down to take off his shoes, his socks and his trousers.

When he stood to pull down his briefs, Julie said, "I'll do that."

He looked at her, startled. "I thought you were mad at me."

"You'll know it when I'm mad." She eased the briefs down over his hips, and when he stepped out of them, she said, "Come to bed."

He frowned. "You taking charge?"

"Damn right." She took his hand, led him to the bed and pushed him down. "Now shut up and behave," she said.

"*Por Dios!* I hate a dominating woman." He looked ferocious, but the beginning of a grin betrayed him.

"All right," he said, sounding doubtful. "Have your way with me if you must."

"I intend to." She slipped out of her gown and came into bed beside him. Cradling him in her arms, she kissed him softly, lingeringly.

And felt his tension fade. She touched her tongue, all silky smooth, to his. She explored his mouth and cat-licked her way around his ear.

He reached for her breasts and felt the nipples harden at his touch. He ran his fingers across them and smiled with satisfaction when she gasped. He let her go long enough to clasp his hands around her waist and bring her closer so that he could nuzzle her breasts, and when he did she began to touch him, for though she submitted to his kisses, it was she who was in control and she was letting him know that she was.

She took him in her hand, rubbing, gently squeezing, and when she did he fastened his teeth around one pebbled nipple and gently bit her there. She cried out, not in pain but in passion, and raised herself over him.

"Kiss me," she whispered. "Kiss me hard."

He took her mouth. He plunged his tongue past her teeth and she touched her tongue to his, kissing him as he kissed her. She gripped his shoulders and her body was hot and ready against his.

When he let her go, he said, "I want you, Juliana. Now, *mujer. Por Dios,* now."

She smiled down at him. "Not just yet," she said.

"Juliana—"

She put a finger against his lips. Then she took her finger away and gently kissed his mouth. "I love you," she said. "Let me show you how much I love you."

She trailed a line of kisses down over his chin, his throat. She lingered over the hollow there, then moved to that special place between his neck and shoulder where she loved to rest her head at night. She curled her fingers in his chest hair and lapped at a nipple. When he groaned she moved on down over his belly, nipping at the tender skin there.

His body was on fire. He couldn't wait. But when he told her he couldn't, she said, "Yes, you can."

He threaded his fingers through her hair. "Do you know what you're doing to me?"

"Oh, yes," she answered. "I know."

Hot, biting kisses trailed across his hips, his thighs. She licked at his skin. "Juliana, Juliana..." he said.

She stroked his arousal and his body jerked as though he had been touched by a live wire. She ran her nails over him, and when he groaned, she said, "Shh, Rafael. Shh." And touched him with her lips.

He had never asked her to do this. In time, he had thought, but not yet. She's still too innocent, too inexperienced. That she had done this of her own volition thrilled him beyond anything he had ever known.

Her tongue was silky soft, lightly teasing, gently stroking. He reached to touch her breasts and heard her murmured pleasure.

It became everything. Agony, ecstasy. His body floated on the sharp, keen edge of sensual pleasure. He wanted this to go on forever because it was heaven being caressed this way by her. Her mouth was so soft, her lips, her tongue, so warm. Stroking, stroking him until he thought his body would surely burst. If she didn't stop soon...

He put his hands on her shoulders and drew her away from him. She came up beside him, but when he made as though to cover her, she said, "No, darling. Let me."

She straddled him, and holding his gaze, lowered herself over him. She began to move, slowly at first, rocking back and forth against him.

He reached for her breasts and her movements quickened. He squeezed her nipples and she cried out. He lifted his body to hers with a passion he could barely control, and she leaned back, body taut, as out of control now as he was.

Rafael plunged up against her and grasped her hips to force her closer. She clasped his shoulders, not even aware she dug her nails in.

"Stay with me!" he cried. "Ride with me."

He tightened his hold on her hips as she raised herself over him, again and again until it was past bearing. For him. For her.

He thrust up hard. She screamed a muffled scream and a million skyrockets exploded in his brain. Her name, "Juliana, Juliana, Juliana," poured from his lips in a rush of feeling he'd never known before.

She collapsed over him and he held her to his beating heart. "Sweet love," he whispered. *"Mi preciosa, mi querida mujer."*

Later, in that drifting place of half waking, half sleeping, it came to him that what he felt for Juliana went far beyond the physical. In sharing this most intimate of experiences, this ultimate closeness, their minds, their hearts, their very souls had touched.

He knew now that he loved her. And that frightened him more than anything ever had.

CHAPTER SIXTEEN

In late October a gloom seemed to settle over the island. Julie couldn't explain it. She didn't speak to Rafael about it, but she knew it was there. The scent of evil had invaded their home.

She slept badly and sometimes when she awoke in the middle of the night crept silently out of bed and went to stand by the window to look out at the lake whose waters were as dark and deep as her husband's eyes. Each morning she arose with a sense of impending disaster.

She tried to keep herself busy with the house. New drapes were made for the living room and dining room in a rich burgundy wool, and with the addition of new lamps with Tiffany shades, the heretofore gloomy rooms became warm and colorful.

At her suggestion, Rafael hired a gardener from Patzcuaro, and the man, whose name was Jose Luis, came early each morning to work in restoring the patio into a flower-filled garden.

Little by little the hacienda was transformed into a home where light streamed in through the open windows, where greening plants flourished and love slowly had its way.

But in spite of it all, Julie could not dispel the feeling that something wasn't right. Little things happened, unexplainable things. Another black spider appeared on the rim of the tub one morning as she was about to step into it. Rafael ordered someone to come from Morelia to fumigate the rooms. But even though the man came and sprayed, Julie knew that the black spiders would still reappear.

The day after the fumigator had been there, Juanita found another spider in the flour bin. That night Kico had another nightmare, and the following day, when Julie opened the French doors that led out to the patio, a snake slithered across her path.

Evil. She knew it existed, but she also knew it hadn't come in the form of a ghost. Someone had put the spiders where they would be found, someone had placed the snake across her path. And someone had come in the night to frighten Kico.

"These things aren't just coincidence," she said to Rafael. "Someone is causing them to happen."

"Surely you don't suspect Juanita or Eloisa or Eufrasia."

"Of course not."

"The doors and the windows are locked when we go to bed and we're the only ones who have the keys to the house." He put his arms around her. "You've let a few spiders spook you, *querida*.

Spiders. She thought of the lines, "'Will you walk into my parlour?' said a Spider to a Fly." But who was the spider? Was she the fly? Or was Kico?

The nightmares continued to bother him. There were smudges of fatigue under his eyes. He lost weight, and though Julie had Juanita fix things she thought would please him, he only picked at his food.

One morning, he said, "Did you know that next week is Papa's birthday?"

"My goodness, no, but thank you for telling me. I'm surprised you remember the date."

A rare smile tugged at the corners of his mouth. "I remember because mine is two days later." He hesitated. "And after that comes the Day of the Dead."

November 2, of course. It was a peculiarly Mexican holiday, a combination of Halloween, All Saints' and All Souls' Day. A day to mourn the dead, to remember death and to celebrate it.

The first year Julie had been in Guadalajara she'd seen the stands that sold the white candy skulls, candy coffins and macabre dancing skeletons. *Ofrendas,* offerings set up to honor deceased loved ones, adorned shop windows, hotel lobbies, the parks and the entrance hall of the school.

On altarlike tables there were displays of *pan de muerto,* the bread of the dead, tamales and toys, lit candles, flowers and skeleton puppets, often wearing a jaunty cap to resemble one the deceased had worn.

On November 1, a fellow teacher, Silvia Orozco, had brought Julie a white candy skull. There were bright red eyes in the sunken sockets and her name, Juliana, emblazoned across the forehead.

"This is the way we celebrate death in Mexico," Silvia said. "Tonight I'll go with my family to the cemetery. We'll take an embroidered tablecloth to spread on the graves and we'll serve the things my grandparents loved to eat. And of course we will have a bottle of tequila for my dead Uncle Juventino."

"Bizarre," Julie said. But that night she had gone with Silvia to the cemetery. There was music, tears and laughter when family members told funny stories about the dear ones who were buried there. It was all very strange, all very new, but somehow right. The dead had been honored, mourned and remembered. Now the living could get on with their lives.

The Day of the Dead. She pulled Kico close and kissed him. "What would you like for your birthday?" she asked.

"You said that maybe I could have my own television and VCR."

"Did I say that?" She pretended to think about it. "Well, yes, I believe I did."

She'd mentioned it to Rafael soon after they'd arrived back from their trip. He'd shaken his head. "The boy doesn't need a television set," he'd told her. "Besides, I've definitely decided he'll go away to school next year."

She had her own money, she would buy Kico the TV and the VCR. And hope that Rafael wouldn't be too angry. As far as sending Kico away next year, she'd argue about that when the time came.

Rafael had been preoccupied since their trip to attend the president's reception in Mexico City. There was an edge to him she hadn't seen before. He was tense, often irritable. He spent more and more time in his studio and there were nights when he didn't come to bed until long after midnight. But busy though he was, he always had dinner with her and Kico.

One evening in the middle of dinner, Juanita said, "There is a telephone call for you, *señor*." She brought the phone to the table. Rafael said, *"Bueno?"* and listened for a moment, then shouted, "Never call me again!" He slammed the phone down. "It was that *cabrón*, Felipe Gonzáles," he told Julie. "If he ever calls again and you answer, I want you to hang up immediately.''

Felipe Gonzáles did call again, three nights later, but this time Rafael was in his studio and Julie took the call.

''Please don't hang up,'' he said when she answered. ''I know it's presumptuous of me to ask you to intervene, but Rafael and I were friends for a long time, Señora Vega. I'm desperately sorry about what happened and I want to make amends. Could you talk to him, get him to agree to at least speak to me?''

''I'm sorry, Señor Gonzáles. I can't do that.''

''Just talk to him,'' he pleaded. ''His friendship means a great deal to me. I'll be in Patzcuaro this week. If you could get him to agree to see me I'd be most appreciative. If not, perhaps I could meet with you.''

That night when she and Rafael were alone in their room, Julie told him about the call.

''I told you not to talk to him,'' Rafael said furiously. ''You should have hung up the moment you knew who it was. What did he say? What did he want?''

''He said he was going to be in Patzcuaro this week and that he hoped you would agree to see him.''

''Hijo de—'' Rafael slammed his fist into his hand. ''What else did he say?''

Julie hesitated. She knew Rafael would be even angrier if she told him that Gonzáles had suggested she meet with him, but she didn't want to hold anything back. ''He said that if you wouldn't, perhaps I would.''

''What?'' His face was mottled with rage. ''That son of a bitch! If I ever get my hands on him again . . .'' He gripped Julie's shoulders. "Hang up on him the next time he calls. Do you understand?"

"Yes," she said. And wished she hadn't told him.

The following day Julie took the boat to Patzcuaro and the bus to Morelia. She picked out a television set and a VCR and asked that they be delivered in time for Kico's birthday. In a bookstore she found a beautifully illustrated edition of Rodin sculptures for Rafael and had it gift wrapped.

Back in Patzcuaro she took a taxi down to the dock and caught a launch back to the island.

Rafael was waiting for her in the living room when she arrived home. "Where have you been?" he asked.

"In Patzcuaro."

"Why?"

"Why?" She hesitated, for though she hated to lie she didn't want to tell him that she'd gone to Morelia to buy his and Kico's birthday presents. "I...I just went over to look around."

His face tightened. "To look around?"

"Uh, yes."

"Alone?"

"Of course alone."

He took a step toward her. "You went to meet Felipe, didn't you?"

She stared at him, too shocked for a moment to say anything.

"I want the truth, Juliana. He called you again, didn't he? You went to meet him."

"How can you even suggest such a thing?"

"Because Margarita—"

"I'm not Margarita."

"Aren't you?" He gripped her shoulders. "You're lying to me. Dammit all, I want the truth."

"All right!" Her face white with anger, Julie faced him. "I went into Morelia to buy birthday presents for Kico and for you." She threw the package at him. "Happy birthday, Rafael."

He stared at her for a moment without speaking. Then he said, "Oh, my God. What am I doing?" He tried to put his arms around her, but she pulled away. "I'm sorry," he said. "I thought—"

"You thought wrong."

"It's what Margarita used to do. She'd tell me she had to go shopping so she could get away and meet Felipe. They'd go to the hotel on the plaza. The day... the day it happened, the day she drowned, I knew she was going to meet him. We had a terrible fight. I forbid her to go and she laughed in my face."

He turned away from Julie, shaking his head as though trying to shake away his anger and his pain. "I ran out of the house ahead of her, determined to take the boat out myself so she couldn't use it. Let her take one of the launches, I thought. I'd be damned if I'd let her have the boat.

"There was a storm. I told you that, didn't I?" Before Julie could answer he went on. "I'd already started the motor when she ran out on the dock. Before I could pull away she got in. She said, 'Let me have the boat.'

"I grabbed her arm and tried to shove her back onto the dock. She called me a bastard. She hit me and I said, 'All right! I'll take you to meet your lover. I don't give a damn what you do. I hope to God you drown.'"

He looked at Julie with dark and haunted eyes. "I gunned the motor and sped out on the lake. There was thunder, lightning, a rain so blinding I could barely see. The waves were high, but I didn't care. Margarita wasn't afraid. She laughed whenever we hit a wave broadside, laughed with the wind blowing her dark hair around her face. I wanted to kill her, wanted to wipe the laughter off her face."

His voice was hoarse. His hands were shaking. "I started toward her. She backed away and she...*Dios, perdóname,* she went over the side."

"But it wasn't your fault," Julie said. "It was an accident. You didn't mean—"

"If I hadn't threatened her she wouldn't have backed away," he went on as though he hadn't heard her. "I threw the anchor down and went in after her. I looked, so help me God, Juliana, I looked for her. I dove down again and again, but the water was dark, roiled from the storm and the wind. I couldn't find her and finally I...I gave up. But I shouldn't have. I should have kept looking for her. It's my fault she drowned. My fault."

"No, no, no." The voice was high, piping, frantic. "It was my fault. All mine."

Kico stood in the doorway, his small face white and anguished. "It was me, Papa," he sobbed. "It was my fault. I was afraid of the storm and I said, 'Don't go, Mama. Please don't go.' I took hold of her hands and I hung on hard as I could. But she pushed me away. I said, 'I love you, Mama. Please don't go away.' But she didn't love me back and so she went and it's my fault she did because she would have loved me if I'd been good and I wasn't good so she didn't. She's drowned dead in the lake because I'm bad and because I couldn't hold on to her hands."

What color there had been in Rafael's face drained away. As though someone had hit him a stunning blow, his face crumpled. He said, "Oh, my God," and with a strangled cry he ran to Kico and picked him up in his arms.

"It wasn't your fault," he cried. "You've never been a bad boy. Mama fell out of the boat because of the storm. She loved you, Kico. She loved you more than anything or anybody."

Thin arms encircled Rafael's neck. The small face, wet with tears, rubbed against Rafael's face.

"Don't cry, son," Rafael said. "Please don't cry. I love you and Julie loves you. You're our boy."

Tears filled Julie's eyes as she slowly backed out of the room. This was father and son time, a healing time. They needed to be alone.

Everything seemed better after that. The following week Rafael and Kico celebrated their birthdays together. Juanita prepared a special dinner, complete with two birthday cakes. There were eight candles on Kico's chocolate cake, thirty-six on Rafael's. They opened their presents and afterward Rafael set up the television set and the VCR in Kico's room and together, while Julie watched, they played a Nintendo game. It was the first time since her marriage that she felt they really were a family.

That night when they went together to tuck Kico in, it was Rafael who leaned down to kiss the little boy's forehead. "Good night, son," he said. "Happy birthday."

When they went back to their own room and closed the door, Julie put her arms around Rafael. "I love you," she said. And it didn't matter that he could not tell her that he loved her. He had opened himself up to loving Kico; perhaps someday he would love her, too.

They made love that night. It was slow and sweet and in that final moment she had held his face between her hands and said, over and over again, "I love you, Rafael. I love you."

When she awoke in the morning he was gone. But there was a white rose on the pillow where his head had lain.

And a black spider on the bathroom sink.

It rained almost every day that last week in October. On Friday the rain stopped, and in the afternoon when Kico came home from school, Rafael said, "I need to go into Patzcuaro for a little while. How'd you like to come with me?"

Kico hesitated. "It might storm," he said.

"Oh, I don't think so. But if it does you'll be all right because I'll be with you." Rafael rested his hand on Kico's head and in a conspiratorial whisper said, "I want to buy a present for Juliana. I need you along to help pick it out."

Kico brightened. "I really like her," he whispered back. Then hesitantly he said, "If Mama is in heaven and she's not coming back, do you think it would be all right if I call Julie mama?"

Something clutched at Rafael's insides. He hadn't realized until only these last few days what a nice child Kico was, how sweet his disposition. He hated himself for having missed some very special years with the boy, but he vowed now that he would make up for them. It no longer mattered whether he or Felipe had fathered Kico. Even if Felipe was the biological father, he, Rafael, would from this day forward be his father in every way that counted.

"Well?" Kico looked anxiously up at him. "What do you think? Is it all right if I call Julie mama?"

"Absolutely. Why don't you start just as soon as we come back from Patzcuaro?"

Together then, Rafael with his hand on Kico's shoulder, they went out to the patio to find Julie and tell her they were going to Patzcuaro.

After they left she busied herself with the new plants José Luis had brought for the garden. Two hours passed before she realized the air had grown cooler and the sky had darkened. The slight cooling breeze became a wind, and when she felt the spatter of rain she took off her gardening gloves and straightened. As she did, a feeling of unease came over her. She felt as though someone were watching her, but when she looked around no one was there.

She went quickly back into the house and closed the French doors behind her. She called, "Eufrasia?" before she remembered that Eufrasia's father had taken ill and she'd left early today. And that Eloisa, who'd been suffering with a toothache for almost a week, had finally gone to a dentist in Patzcuaro. Juanita, as always, was busy in the kitchen.

Several times she went to the window and looked out at the lake. A storm was coming; Kico wouldn't like being out on the lake in a storm. And she didn't like being here alone, except for Juanita, who was in the kitchen at the other end of the house.

Feeling chilled, she took a hot shower, then dressed in pants and a light sweater. The rain was coming harder now and she went to check the windows in Kico's room, as well as in the living and dining rooms. She couldn't settle down. She picked up a book and tried to read but couldn't concentrate. She went out to the kitchen to have a cup of tea with Juanita, but Juanita wasn't there. Instead there was a note on the sink that read "I have run to the store in the village."

Julie began to make tea. While the water was boiling she picked up the sugar bowl and took the top off. A black spider ran up her arm. She screamed and dropped the bowl. The spider scurried under the counter.

She grasped the edge of the counter and stared down at the smashed bowl, the spilled sugar. Her hands were shaking when she took the broom and tried to clean the floor.

How had the spider gotten into the sugar bowl? Dear Lord, what was happening here?

The wind grew stronger, battering the house with a violence almost as strong as Hurricane Jezebel. Were Kico and Rafael on the lake now or were they already making their way up the hill to the house? She prayed they were almost home, but knew that was unlikely. If they'd already crossed the lake they would wait in a shop until the rain passed.

She went back to the living room to once more make sure the doors and windows were secure and no rain was coming in. And when she was sure it wasn't, she decided to check Rafael's studio. If a window was open the rain might damage the sculptures.

A gust of wind hit the house. The lights flickered and went out. With a muttered "Damn!" Julie took a candelabra off the desk and lit the three candles. As she started out of the room, thunder crashed and a jagged bolt of lightning streaked across the room.

She went into the corridor. The saints she hadn't yet removed frowned down at her. It was dark here, and as silent as a tomb. But as she drew nearer to the studio she heard something. A pounding sound? Afraid that one of the windows had blown open, she hurried on, reached the door of the studio and threw it open.

She held the candelabra high above her head. Her eyes widened. "Oh, my God!" she whispered, and ran into the room. The bust of Cervantes lay smashed. The recently commissioned statue of de Gaulle was on its side, one arm smashed. Another bust lay broken in pieces.

Julie took another step. Lightning flashed. A figure came toward her.

Alicia, her face twisted, her eyes wide with a maniacal gleam, clutched an iron bar in her hand.

Julie stared at the former housekeeper. "You," she whispered.

"Of course me."

"You put the black spider in the box with my wedding gown. The other spiders, the one just now in the kitchen. The doll. You put it there. And my dress, the algae on my dress. You pushed me off the ladder. You've gone into Kico's room at night. The wet footprints. That was you."

"Of course it was me. This house belongs to me, and Rafael would have belonged to me if it hadn't been for you. I want you gone, you and the boy." Her face twisted with hate. "I'll destroy you—first the image, then you."

She ran to the nude statue Rafael had made of Julie and raised the iron bar above her head. Julie dropped the candelabra and sprinted forward grabbing Alicia's arm. They grappled. The other woman was bigger, stronger, but Julie hung on. She could smell sweat, the dead musty odor of her black clothing.

"I'll kill you!" Alicia broke away and raised the iron bar above her head.

Julie screamed and flung her arm up to protect herself. The iron bar slashed down. With a sickening crunch she felt the bone in her arm go. She staggered back, screaming. Alicia struck again. And the screaming stopped.

He and Kico arrived in Janitzio just ahead of the storm. When all hell broke loose they sought refuge in one of the small restaurants that lined the harbor. Rafael had thought to wait until the rain let up, but a strange feeling he couldn't shake unsettled him. He had to get up to the house as soon as he could.

He bought a rain slicker for Kico, and after he had covered the boy, he took his hand and together they'd started up the hill toward the house. As they drew nearer he saw that the lights were out and that the house looked deserted.

He called out when they went in. "Juliana? Juliana, where are you?" When she didn't answer he shouted, "Eufrasia? Eloisa?"

He went into the kitchen for a flashlight. Juanita wasn't there but he found her note saying that she'd gone down to the market. But where was Juliana?

Back in the living room, he said to Kico, "Let's see if we can find Juliana." They'd just started into the corridor when he heard the scream.

"What's that?" Kico asked.

But Rafael was already running down the corridor in the direction of his studio. The scream came again. Juliana!

He ran into his studio. Clay busts lay smashed on the floor. The figure of de Gaulle was toppled and broken, along with other pieces of work. What in the hell . . . ?

He heard a smothered moan. In a circle of light he saw Alicia. She stood over Juliana, iron bar in her hand, arm raised to strike.

"Stop!"

She turned, her face in the candlelight a ghostly white, her eyes narrowed and black with hate.

He leapt at her. He grabbed the iron bar, wrenched it away. When it fell, he yanked her arm behind her back. She fought him. He grabbed her other arm, then pulled his tie off, tied her hands. Took off his belt, tied her ankles together and thrust her away from him.

He ran to Julie. Her head was bloody and he could tell from the angle of her arm that it was broken.

"Papa!" Kico stood in the doorway, his face ashen, his hand to his mouth so he wouldn't cry. He looked at

Julie's fallen body, at Alicia, who lay bound and raging near one of the broken busts.

"There's a phone on my desk, over there in the corner." Rafael picked up the candelabra and lit the candles. "I want you to call Dr. Solorzano," he said as calmly as he could. "His number is 21-58. Tell him Julie is badly hurt and that we need him. Tell him to call the police."

Kico took a shaking breath and ran to the telephone.

Rafael bent over Julie. "Juliana," he said. "Juliana." He touched the side of her head; blood smeared his fingers. He cradled her in his arms. "I love you," he said, over and over again. "Can you hear me, Juliana? I love you, *mi preciosa, mi amor, mi mujer.*"

Her lids fluttered. She opened her eyes.

"My love," he said. And her eyelids drifted closed.

He held her like that, cradled in his arms, until the police came to take Alicia away. Things moved in a kaleidoscopic blur after that. Dr. Solorzano ran in, his nurse only a few steps behind him.

"Let me see her," the doctor said, and reluctantly Rafael let Julie go.

The doctor pressed his fingers against the wound on Julie's head, then looked at her arm. "Arm's broken. Don't think her head is as bad as it looks, but we'd better get her to the hospital in Morelia. I'll phone for an ambulance to meet us at the dock in Patzcuaro."

The nurse poured alcohol onto a cotton swab and held it under Julie's nose. Her eyelids fluttered again and she opened her eyes. "What...what happened?" she whispered.

"Alicia hit you," Rafael said. "She—"

"Your studio…your work. Oh, Rafael, I'm so sorry. I tried to stop her. I tried—"

"It doesn't matter, Juliana. Nothing matters except that you're going to be all right."

He carried her down the hill to where a high-powered police launch waited. Kico followed, for though at first Rafael had thought to leave the boy behind, he'd decided not to. They were a family now, united by a love too long held back.

And when at the dock, Kico patted Julie's face and said, "You're going to be all right, Mama Julie," Rafael put his other arm around Kico. His wife, his son. His to love, his to care for.

And he prayed, "Please God, let my Juliana be all right."

EPILOGUE

In the dim light of the room she saw his face. The dark eyes were filled with love and he said the words she had longed to hear. "I love you, Juliana. I love you."

She touched his hand and slept, knowing that he was with her.

He hadn't left her side since they had brought her here to the hospital. He sat in a chair close to her bed during the day and at night dozed beside her on a cot the hospital provided.

"If anything had happened to you," he said over and over again. "If you had left me..."

"But I didn't leave you," Julie assured him. "I never will."

He spoke openly of his love now, for it was as if all the floodgates of the emotions he'd held in check for so long had burst open. The words he hadn't been able to say before flowed in a litany of love.

"I think I knew from the very beginning that I was falling in love with you," he said. "That first night at dinner when I tried to silence you and you wouldn't stop talking, I didn't know whether to turn you over my knee or haul you up out of your chair and kiss you. You were defiant and angry and so damned..." He searched for a word to describe her. "Adorable," he said at last. "Maddening, but adorable."

"I was a little afraid of you," Julie admitted with a smile. "But I was determined not to show it."

"I was a beast."

"Never that." She brought his hand to her lips.

"I love you so much, Juliana. I'm sorry it took me so long to tell you."

"But you've told me now, that's all that matters."

She left the hospital in a wheelchair and Rafael lifted her into the car for the drive back to Patzcuaro, where a private launch waited for them at the dock. The day was clear and cool, the sky a deep cerulean blue, as it had been the first time Julie crossed the lake.

It was a quiet but a loving homecoming. Eufrasia, Juanita and Eloisa were there to greet her, along with Kico, who handed her a bouquet of yellow daisies and said, "Welcome home, Mama Julie."

There were white roses everywhere. They filled the rooms, they filled her heart.

The three of them had dinner in the bedroom that night. "You can get up tomorrow," Rafael said, "but you'll have to take it easy for a few days."

Kico buttered her roll. He patted her hand. He poured her tea. And asked, "What happened to the Señorita Alicia?"

"She's in jail," Rafael said. "She'll be there for a very long time."

"That's good." He looked at his father. "She pushed Mama Julie off the ladder, didn't she?"

Rafael nodded. "And she came to your room the night you had the nightmare. You understand that now, don't you, Kico. You know it wasn't your mother?"

"I know," he said in a subdued voice. He was thoughtful for a moment and then he said, "Tomorrow night is Day of the Dead, isn't it?"

"November 2? Yes, I guess it is." Julie reached for his hand and, drawing him close, asked, "Have you ever been to the cemetery here in Janitzio on the Day of the Dead?"

Kico shook his head. "I've seen the candles when the other people go," he said. "They take flowers and food and stuff to the graves."

"I was wondering..." Julie looked past Kico to Rafael, and when he nodded, she said, "I was wondering if maybe you'd like to visit your mother's grave. You could take her favorite flowers and Juanita could bake her favorite cake."

"Will you and Father come with me if I do?"

"Of course we will. But you don't have to if you don't want to, Kico. If you don't, it will be perfectly all right with us."

He thought for a few moments. "No," he said at last. "I think it would be..." He wrinkled his face. "Nice," he said. "I think it would be nice."

So it was on the following night at midnight that the three of them followed the candlelight procession to the big black iron gates of the cemetery. Music came from the village below, where colored lights were strung. Launches were tied up in the harbor, others were crossing the lake. All of the boats were lit and there was in the air a feeling of festivity.

Spanish voices mingled with the Tarascan language. Candlelight shone on the faces of the women who knelt beside the graves. Wrapped in dark rebozos, their faces solemn, they put their *pan de muerto* on the place where their loved ones rested, along with the flowers and other offerings they had brought with them.

Rafael took Kico's hand and led him to a simple gray tombstone. "This is your mother's grave," he said. "Why don't you put the flowers there by the headstone?"

And Julie said, "Can you read the inscription, Kico?"

He leaned closer and, kneeling, read, "Margarita Villareal de Vega. Wife of Rafael, mother of her beloved Enrique." He looked up. "It says I was beloved. That means she loved me, doesn't it?"

Rafael knelt on one side of him, Julie on the other. "She loved you very much," Rafael said. "Never doubt that, son."

Kico nodded. "I hope she likes these flowers," he said. "Do you think it would be all right if we had a piece of her cake?"

Rafael and Julie smiled at each other over his head, a family united in love for the boy who knelt between them, and for each other. Forever.

*   *   *   *   *

Welcome To The
Dark Side Of Love...

AVAILABLE THIS MONTH

COMING NEXT MONTH

Now what's going on in

CONARD COUNTY ?

Guilty! That was what everyone thought of Sandy Keller's client, including Texas Ranger—and American Hero—Garrett Hancock. But as he worked with her to determine the truth, loner Garrett found he was changing his mind about a lot of things—especially falling in love.

Rachel Lee's Conard County series continues in January 1995 with A QUESTION OF JUSTICE, IM #613.

INTIMATE MOMENTS®
Silhouette®

JINGLE BELLS, WEDDING BELLS:
Silhouette's Christmas Collection for 1994

Christmas Wish List

*To beat the crowds at the malls and get the perfect present for *everyone*, even that snoopy Mrs. Smith next door!

*To get through the holiday parties without running my panty hose.

*To bake cookies, decorate the house and serve the perfect Christmas dinner—just like the women in all those magazines.

*To sit down, curl up and read my Silhouette Christmas stories!

Join *New York Times* bestselling author Nora Roberts, along with popular writers Barbara Boswell, Myma Temte and Elizabeth August, as we celebrate the joys of Christmas—and the magic of marriage—with

JINGLE BELLS, WEDDING BELLS

Silhouette's Christmas Collection for 1994.

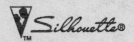

Another wonderful year of romance concludes with

Christmas Memories

Share in the magic and memories of romance during the holiday season with this collection of two full-length contemporary Christmas stories, by two bestselling authors

Diana Palmer
Marilyn Pappano

Available in December at your favorite retail outlet.

Only from Silhouette®

where passion lives.

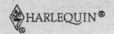 HARLEQUIN®  Silhouette®

The movie event of the season can be the reading event of the year!

Lights… The lights go on in October when CBS presents Harlequin/Silhouette Sunday Matinee Movies. These four movies are based on bestselling Harlequin and Silhouette novels.

Camera… As the cameras roll, be the first to read the original novels the movies are based on!

Action… Through this offer, you can have these books sent directly to you! Just fill in the order form below and you could be reading the books…before the movie!

48288-4	Treacherous Beauties by Cheryl Emerson		
		$3.99 U.S./$4.50 CAN.	☐
83305-9	Fantasy Man by Sharon Green		
		$3.99 U.S./$4.50 CAN.	☐
48289-2	A Change of Place by Tracy Sinclair		
		$3.99 U.S./$4.50CAN.	☐
83306-7	Another Woman by Margot Dalton		
		$3.99 U.S./$4.50 CAN.	☐

TOTAL AMOUNT	$	
POSTAGE & HANDLING	$	
($1.00 for one book, 50¢ for each additional)		
APPLICABLE TAXES*	$ _____	
TOTAL PAYABLE	$ _____	
(check or money order—please do not send cash)		

To order, complete this form and send it, along with a check or money order for the total above, payable to Harlequin Books, to: **In the U.S.:** 3010 Walden Avenue, P.O. Box 9047, Buffalo, NY 14269-9047; **In Canada:** P.O. Box 613, Fort Erie, Ontario, L2A 5X3.

Name: _____

Address: _____ City: _____

State/Prov.: _____ Zip/Postal Code: _____

*New York residents remit applicable sales taxes.
Canadian residents remit applicable GST and provincial taxes.

CBSPR

"HOORAY FOR HOLLYWOOD" SWEEPSTAKES

HERE'S HOW THE SWEEPSTAKES WORKS .

OFFICIAL RULES — NO PURCHASE NECESSARY

To enter, complete an Official Entry Form or hand print on a 3" x 5" card the words "HOORAY FOR HOLLYWOOD", your name and address and mail your entry in the pre-addressed envelope (if provided) or to: "Hooray for Hollywood" Sweepstakes, P.O. Box 9076, Buffalo, NY 14269-9076 or "Hooray for Hollywood" Sweepstakes, P.O. Box 637, Fort Erie, Ontario L2A 5X3. Entries must be sent via First Class Mail and be received no later than 12/31/94. No liability is assumed for lost, late or misdirected mail.

Winners will be selected in random drawings to be conducted no later than January 31, 1995 from all eligible entries received.

Grand Prize: A 7-day/6-night trip for 2 to Los Angeles, CA including round trip air transportation from commercial airport nearest winner's residence, accommodations at the Regent Beverly Wilshire Hotel, free rental car, and $1,000 spending money. (Approximate prize value which will vary dependent upon winner's residence: $5,400.00 U.S.); 500 Second Prizes: A pair of "Hollywood Star" sunglasses (prize value: $9.95 U.S. each). Winner selection is under the supervision of D.L. Blair, Inc., an independent judging organization, whose decisions are final. Grand Prize travelers must sign and return a release of liability prior to traveling. Trip must be taken by 2/1/96 and is subject to airline schedules and accommodations availability.

Sweepstakes offer is open to residents of the U.S. (except Puerto Rico) and Canada who are 18 years of age or older, except employees and immediate family members of Harlequin Enterprises, Ltd., its affiliates, subsidiaries, and all agencies, entities or persons connected with the use, marketing or conduct of this sweepstakes. All federal, state, provincial, municipal and local laws apply. Offer void wherever prohibited by law. Taxes and/or duties are the sole responsibility of the winners. Any litigation within the province of Quebec respecting the conduct and awarding of prizes may be submitted to the Regie des loteries et courses du Quebec. All prizes will be awarded; winners will be notified by mail. No substitution of prizes is permitted. Odds of winning are dependent upon the number of eligible entries received.

Potential grand prize winner must sign and return an Affidavit of Eligibility within 30 days of notification. In the event of non-compliance within this time period, prize may be awarded to an alternate winner. Prize notification returned as undeliverable may result in the awarding of prize to an alternate winner. By acceptance of their prize, winners consent to use of their names, photographs, or likenesses for purpose of advertising, trade and promotion on behalf of Harlequin Enterprises, Ltd., without further compensation unless prohibited by law. A Canadian winner must correctly answer an arithmetical skill-testing question in order to be awarded the prize.

For a list of winners (available after 2/28/95), send a separate stamped, self-addressed envelope to: Hooray for Hollywood Sweepstakes 3252 Winners, P.O. Box 4200, Blair, NE 68009.

CBSRLS

OFFICIAL ENTRY COUPON

"Hooray for Hollywood"
SWEEPSTAKES!

Yes, I'd love to win the Grand Prize — a vacation in Hollywood — or one of 500 pairs of "sunglasses of the stars"! Please enter me in the sweepstakes!

This entry must be received by December 31, 1994.
Winners will be notified by January 31, 1995.

Name _____

Address _____ Apt. _____

City _____

State/Prov. _____ Zip/Postal Code _____

Daytime phone number _____
(area code)

Mail all entries to: Hooray for Hollywood Sweepstakes,
P.O. Box 9076, Buffalo, NY 14269-9076.
In Canada, mail to: Hooray for Hollywood Sweepstakes,
P.O. Box 637, Fort Erie, ON L2A 5X3.

KCH

OFFICIAL ENTRY COUPON

"Hooray for Hollywood"
SWEEPSTAKES!

Yes, I'd love to win the Grand Prize — a vacation in Hollywood — or one of 500 pairs of "sunglasses of the stars"! Please enter me in the sweepstakes!

This entry must be received by December 31, 1994.
Winners will be notified by January 31, 1995.

Name _____

Address _____ Apt. _____

City _____

State/Prov. _____ Zip/Postal Code _____

Daytime phone number _____
(area code)

Mail all entries to: Hooray for Hollywood Sweepstakes,
P.O. Box 9076, Buffalo, NY 14269-9076.
In Canada, mail to: Hooray for Hollywood Sweepstakes,
P.O. Box 637, Fort Erie, ON L2A 5X3.

KCH